Blue Meadow Farm

Book One of the Blue Meadow Farm Series

Lynna Pittman Clark

The Blue Meadow Series:

Dedication

For my beloved David:

You remind me of Jesus every single day.

~~~~~~~

"Thou art coming to a King!

Large petitions with thee bring.

For His grace and power are such

One can never ask too much."

~John Newton

"Now all glory to God Who is able through His mighty power at work within us, to accomplish infinitely more than we ask or think."

~ Ephesians 3:20

Prologue

The weather was warmer than usual for the middle of March. According to the Almanac a scorching hot summer was on tap for Piedmont North Carolina. Rain would be sparse but somehow God willing, she'd survive another year in the landscaping business. As she turned over the soil in her vegetable garden she noticed dogwood trees scattered throughout the woods doing their best to bloom by Easter. They seemed to offer hope. Perhaps this would be a better year.

Her neighbor Jesse told her the legend of the dogwood shortly after her husband died. With its cross shaped blossoms surrounding a crown of thorns, the most intriguing part was the dark bloodstains on the tips of each petal. Every year when they bloomed she could hear the deep voice of her friend.

"God is an Artist and He loves a good illustration darlin'. That's why He made dogwoods. You're an artist too. He made you special that way. Let Him use your brokenness to give others hope. The things you've been through are for a purpose girl."

She didn't feel much like an artist. And she sure didn't feel special. But for some reason she thought about digging up another dogwood to transplant near the house. Or even better, she could plant one at Jesse's. She knew without him she'd be a whole lot worse off or probably even dead. Gently he'd helped her through so many dark days that she'd finally begun to hope again.

As she climbed off the tractor she noticed a small dogwood with a particularly nice shape. Its limbs stretched upward as if surrendering. As she walked through the woods the ground crunched beneath her boots announcing her arrival. Squirrels scurried away and birds grew silent. Pulling a faded red bandana from her pocket she decided it would do. Easily she tore the threadbare cloth into strips then tied them around branches of the chosen tree. If she survived another year she'd come back when the tree was dormant. Though she'd not had much success with transplanting dogwoods she would try again. If for no other reason, Jesse loved them as much as she did. Maybe in her own way she could offer hope to him as well.

Chapter 1   Early June

The reflection staring back at her was hopeless. She tried tipping her chin upward in feign confidence. A little hair gel to tame the light copper curls into a twist might help disguise the fear which caused her stomach to flutter. A successful interview could be the game changer she'd needed for so long. She glanced at her shaking hands. Too bad she couldn't afford a manicure. But perhaps they'd understand. After all she was a Landscape Artist. The title made her laugh relaxing her nerves. It was quite a fancy label for a woman who dug in the dirt for a living. But Jesse had given her the title so she would keep it.

She stood gazing into her closet wondering if she should wear a dress. The blue cotton one still fit though it was a bit faded. But it was soft and comfortable. Perhaps comfort would promote confidence. Lydia had heard that somewhere. Plus a friend had passed down some casual heels which would work nicely. But what if she tripped as she approached the meeting? An image of her lanky frame sprawled face down on the ground started her stomach to fluttering again. She reprimanded herself.

You are such a bumpkin! What made you think you could be considered for such a high profile project?

In her blue cotton dress she practiced walking in the chunky heels outdoors as she knew the interview tent would be set up on site. Finally she kicked them off and stepped into the old cowboy boots which stood guard at her back door. Retrieving a towel from the clothesline she wiped the dust from them and decided to just get it over with.

As she headed toward her truck she realized she was looking down as though searching for lost change.

Good grief girl. Hold your head up and act like you've got some sense. And don't forget to smile… but not too much. Those boys from up North will think you're a goober if you go in grinning like a possum. Not too many teeth, just a pleasant, confident, I know stuff, smile.

She had never used a portfolio before. Hopefully the pictures on her phone would suffice. All her clients had been secured by word of mouth. Just the other day some lady in the grocery store had said loud enough for God and everybody to hear, "Ride by Norma's house and look at what that Miller girl did to her yard. It looks like a park!"

Lydia wasn't sure if the lady knew she was on the next aisle and had said it for her benefit or if she had actually overheard a true compliment. Either way it spurred her on to pursue the interview. She tossed her phone into the truck and straightened the old beach towel over the cracked and worn seat. She smoothed her dress as best she could. The humidity would surely steam the wrinkles out of the fabric anyway. Glancing in the mirror she sighed that it was already wreaking havoc on her hair. Plus she'd have to ride with the windows down since the heat of a North Carolina June was already bearing down. Maybe she would roll the passenger side up to shield some of the wind. But then she might sweat through her dress and have armpit circles.

She sighed aloud and thought again,

Good Lord woman. Just get it over with.

Her old truck started the first time. But it should've since she'd just had to buy a new motor. She'd joked with the mechanic that she was getting a new truck, one part at a time. The truth was that her daddy had taught her to drive on that truck; a three speed on the column. She couldn't afford to part with it even if she wanted to.

Roaring up to the job sight she was amazed at the crowd. The interview tent was surrounded by neatly dressed men she had never seen around town. She should've realized the competition would come for miles. As she reached for her phone which held her makeshift portfolio she noticed her hands were still shaking. They looked even rougher in the sunlight. The one redeeming quality was the wedding band from her beloved high school sweetheart. Though she had been a widow for seven long hard years, she couldn't bear to remove it. Like her daddy's truck, she couldn't let go of it even if she wanted to, which of course she didn't.

The whole area was filled with trucks; big shiny new pick-ups with fancy company emblems on the sides. She made her way to the end of the road where she squeezed her truck into a small opening. The old beach towel followed as she exited. Retrieving it from the road she shook it out and tossed it back through the open window. Smoothing her dress again she began the walk to her future. Nervously she reminded herself.

'Esse quam videri'. That's Southern Latin for 'To be rather than to seem.'

Her sweetheart had many such wise sayings that came to her during difficult times. She could almost hear him reminding from the grave.

Oh if only.

If only she could be herself and still walk without tripping, smile without grinning and talk without redneckin' it up.

When the line dwindled and she stepped up to the interview table, she was surprised to see that the two brothers in charge of the project were not much older than her. She guessed early thirties maybe. The poor guys apparently had been at it a while as their shirts clung to their bodies with sweat. She glanced at them and sighed as she thought,

Good grief. Why do they have to be so dang handsome?

They stood to their feet and each shook her hand. Neither of them recoiled at the calluses but smiled warmly as she spoke the name of her company.

"We've heard of you Mrs. Miller and Blue Meadow Farm. You certainly do beautiful work!" spoke the youngest of the pair. Both men had black hair and deep hazel eyes, but something about the eyes of the older brother caused her to look away. Perhaps if she concentrated on the younger she could keep from stammering like the bumpkin she knew herself to be.

Lydia tried to speak. "Really? How in the world did you hear of me?"

The older brother continued to smile warmly at her with eyes that seemed to search her soul. The younger continued. "We stopped by the local market and a nice elderly lady gave us directions to the home of… I think her name is Norma? We were hoping you'd come by today. Now let's take a look at your portfolio."

She swallowed hard as she glanced up trying to relax.

Hold your head up girl. You've always been more comfortable with men than women anyway. They're just not usually quite this fetching.

She felt her face flush with embarrassment as if she were in middle school.

What are you girl, thirteen? Hold your fuzzy head up and act like you've got some sense!

Chapter 2

The company name *Stephens and Sons* had become synonymous with charity. Their father had instilled in them the desire to help those who were hurting and the successful family construction business paved the way for the projects he chose.

"We do our best to take care of orphans and widows. That is God's heart!" he often reminded. It seemed the more he did for others the more his business boomed. Finally in his sixties he turned the physical aspect of the charity over to his sons. When he first started building and remodeling homes for those in tragic situations he set the goal to complete at least one project per state. Later he realized he didn't like traveling as much as he thought. The older he became the more he relished being at home with his wife in New York. Their daughter lived nearby and he loved seeing her when she popped in for visits.

His sons however enjoyed the work away from home. The latest adventure had taken them to North Carolina. People had questioned the wisdom of starting a job there in the heat of summer. But the homeowner they had chosen to assist was still recovering from a horrible car accident two years prior. Her neighbors had sent in an application for consideration and Jack Stephens Sr. had known immediately that Denise Parker would be granted a complete home and garden makeover.

Jack Senior's youngest son Johnny was quite outgoing and thrived when meeting new people. Small talk came easy for him and he never met a stranger. With an eye for design and a winsome personality he was the life of every party. His older brother Jack Jr. was larger in stature and much quieter. He brought sound wisdom into the mix and did his best to keep his brother focused. Having been through several personal tragedies of his own Jack poured his heart into the work. He would much rather be on the road than back in his New York apartment where the memories still haunted him.

However the humidity in the small southern town was unbearable. Jack could hardly catch his breath as he and his brother conducted one interview after another. A fan oscillated furiously in the corner of the tent to no avail. He wondered whose idea it had been to do outdoor meetings in that God forsaken place during the heat of June. Looking up from his notes he was surprised to see that last in line was a woman in a cornflower blue dress. Her eyes seemed to be cut from the same cloth. Perhaps the heat would be worth it after all. His brother stood and reached for her hand which prompted him as well. She smiled a beautiful smile then actually blushed when they spoke of her company. As she pulled up the pictures on her phone he noticed her trembling hands. The pictures were impressive but he wondered if she were strong enough to handle the job.

Jack could hardly focus on the interview and was thankful that Johnny apparently was not quite as captivated by the quiet woman before them. As they scrolled through pictures of her work his heart took a nosedive when he subconsciously checked her ring finger. On her left hand was a wedding band. How could he be so foolish?! Of course she was married. And he knew better than to pursue a married woman. Had he not been down that destructive path before?

She stood, shook their hands, smiled shyly and thanked them both for their time.

"Did you get her number Johnny?" Jack heard himself say. They both looked at him as he too felt embarrassed for the first time since middle school. He'd always heard how hot the summers were in the South. Now he knew it to be true firsthand.

Chapter 3- Mid-June

When she got the call that her company had won the bid she was completely surprised. She never really thought she had a chance to be hired for something so high cotton. The town was abuzz with the Stephens brothers coming to their small town for one of their famous projects.

Lydia contacted her two 'sons' who were just as excited. She'd loved them from the time her beloved husband Blue brought them home for supper one winter day ten years earlier. He had such a heart for kids especially those without family. He'd taken them under his wing when he coached their football team. It seemed like yesterday she'd inherited two rough little eleven year old boys: Shawn, whose dad drove a big rig coast to coast for a living, had been left to fend for himself; And Kurtis who was tended to by his elderly grandmother after his parents split up. Each of them definitely needed more adult supervision. Lydia never regretted the decision of raising them though she'd only been nineteen when she became their mother. Now they'd grown into handsome young men about to start their senior year at the local college.

At her kitchen table they poured over plans estimating the cost of supplies and making a few changes. Her boys always had great ideas of their own and loved the dirt as much as she did. So it worked out well for them to help her during the summer months. The three of them made a great team. Plus they knew how hard it was for her financially. Often they waited patiently on their paychecks knowing she was doing all she could to survive. She had nearly lost the farm several times but somehow the money always came in.

"Okay guys. I like our plan! Grab some more lemonade if you want. I'm heading out to the hardware store to place an order for our supplies. They should be able to make a delivery this afternoon. We'll start tomorrow by planting the crepe myrtles. Take the trailer and load up the ones from the lower end of the land. I've already marked them. Don't forget to shut the gate when you leave. Meet me at the project house at six in the morning. Maybe we'll knock some of this out before the day gets blazin' hot."

Shawn was her protective one. More muscular than his buddy he didn't need to join a gym. Hauling brick pavers in a wheel barrow had definitely bulked him up. Lydia had fussed at him about keeping his dark hair washed until finally one day he had it buzzed short. She surprised him by liking it very much and reminded him often not to get scruffy. It was important to him to please the woman who'd been like a mother to him for the last ten years.

"Did you get a new battery for your alarm Liddy?" he asked.

She loved how Shawn watched after her in his own subtle way. "Yep," she replied. "And it works too because it beeped when y'all drove up."

Only last month Shawn and Kurtis had moved out and rented a house closer to the college. The very next week a stranger had ventured onto her front porch scaring the living daylights out of her. He seemed rather shifty and his eyes went where they did not belong. It terrified her that she never heard him coming down the long gravel road to her house. Being in the middle of thirty-seven acres had great advantages and she had never felt afraid of being alone until that moment. After that Shawn installed a small sensor on a tree facing the driveway which gave a chirp inside her house if someone drove by. Sometimes the chirp just indicated a passing deer, but at least she would know if a vehicle approached her home. Plus they'd added a cattle gate at the entrance to her land which she tried to remember to keep locked. Hopefully that would deter any future unwanted guests.

Chapter 4

When Johnny and Jack arrived at the project site on the first morning things were a mess. The front yard was loaded with materials. The fair haired woman was already working. Apparently she had been there a while for she was filthy. Bibbed overalls covered a tank top and Brogans. She raised a gloved hand in their direction then went right back to work.

"I thought we told the crews to be here at eight." Johnny spoke as he slowed the truck observing the mess.

Jack commented with irritation, "We did. I hope this is not going to be a problem. Surely she knows that things have to be done in a certain order on a construction site." Noticing the fresh paint lines in the yard he added, "But at least the utility companies have already marked their turf or we'd have serious issues."

Johnny looked at his brother surprised that he was miffed. Normally he was very easy-going. "She'll be fine Jack. She's probably just excited to get started. What's really on your mind?" He shot him a knowing glance.

Jack tried to cover his inward struggle. "I'm just concerned that maybe she's not the right one for this job. You talked me into it so she's your responsibility." Part of Jack wanted her to be working near them while the better part of him hoped he wasn't about to do something stupid. He hadn't felt this tempted in quite a while.

"That's fine. If Gina and I weren't engaged I might pursue that responsibility more seriously. But anyway, she is MRS. Miller so we won't be going there. Come on big brother. Let's get acquainted."

She looked up with a smile as they approached. A long sweaty braid contained all but a few of the curls. Plucking a light blue bandana from a back pocket she wiped her face. Shyly she spoke.

"Good morning. Did you see all the fencing? I stopped by here yesterday to pick Denise's brain before she left. She mentioned she'd always dreamed of a split rail fence with roses spilling over. When I told the folks at the hardware store of our project they donated this plus all the roses I want! Is that not wonderful?" She smiled with quiet enthusiasm then looked away.

Jack and Johnny glanced at each other knowing what the other was thinking. That was exactly the kind of thing their dad would do.

~~~~~~~

With the morning spent inside demolishing the kitchen the brothers stopped for lunch. The North Carolina heat was definitely taking its toll. The voice of one of Lydia's helpers came from her truck as they also left for lunch. "Follow us if you want some good barbecue."

Before Jack knew what was happening they were in hot pursuit of "some good barbecue." The small restaurant was packed with locals who nodded to them as they made their way to a corner booth where the five of them could barely squeeze in. The sound of meat cleavers chopping pork on wooden blocks came from the kitchen. The floors were sticky and the seats were covered with red Naugahyde. But the place smelled like heaven.

"Well then Mrs. Miller, what do you suggest we order?" asked Johnny.

"Please call me Lydia. This is Shawn and Kurtis. If you're really hungry then get the barbecue plate which comes with baked beans, red slaw and fries. You have to order Cheerwine to drink or else sweet tea. It's a local thing." She smiled brightly and Jack noticed her eyes again.

After following her suggestions they were not disappointed. The five of them laughed easily and enjoyed a break from the heat. Their waitress Ann kept their drink glasses filled and called them honey. She and Lydia had been friends since waitressing together at the same diner while in high school.

Shawn tried to get a rise out of Lydia by commenting that his work boots were sticking to the floor just like they did in her kitchen. He sipped his tea and smiled as he spoke. "Reminds me of the men's room at the race track."

He loved teasing her about her floors because she always made them pull their shoes off before entering her home.

"Next time you're at the house I'll make sure you have a mop in your hand," she countered without missing a beat. "Speaking of restrooms, pardon me children. I must make a pit stop."

Shawn stood allowing her to exit the booth. As he did he noticed Jack's eyes following her and he shot him a look. Jack was actually embarrassed and tried to say something witty but the words wouldn't come. Shawn continued to stare him down when Ann returned with Styrofoam cups filled to take with them. "Lydia's water has an 'L' on it. Tell her I charge extra for monograming."

Shawn finally looked away from Jack as he expressed his thanks to Ann. Lydia returned and tossed tip money on the table. "All right boys, time to get back at it."

"What?!" exclaimed Kurtis. "We just got here! You're a slave driver!"

"Well bless your heart," came her fake sympathy. Though it wasn't that obvious, Lydia loved Kurtis dearly. This overgrown man-boy was such a joy to her soul. With blond wavy hair pulled back under a ball cap he was quickly catching up with Shawn in the muscle department. Kurtis was her sensitive child.

Her crew slid from their corner booth and left. Ann made a note to repair the pleather seat again with fresh red duct tape since guests were in town.

Johnny was still smiling as he finished his lunch. Jack wondered what the rush was. They'd only been there about thirty minutes. He also wondered about the relationship of Lydia and her boys. They'd mentioned something about returning to college in the fall for their senior year. She looked like she might be college age but surely not. Her business had been open too long for that to be the case. At least he thought so. He couldn't quite get the math to work.

Jack was also concerned that his brother might have more interest than he should in her. She really did put them at ease. In his mind he reasoned that maybe she wore the wedding band to keep men from asking her out. She never mentioned her husband. And a local guy had stopped her on the way to the restroom to flirt. But at least she hadn't lingered.

Stop it Jack. What are you thinking?! Run for your very life. Remember your promise.

But he couldn't help but smile at some of the things they had laughed about. Maybe tomorrow he would ask about her husband

.

Chapter 5

While his younger brother snored loud enough to wake the dead Jack stared at the motel ceiling rehearsing how he might bring up the subject.

So what does your better half do for a living?

Do you think your husband might stop by to see your design?

Feel free to invite your husband on site. I'd love to meet him!

He sighed and knew it all sounded lame. He didn't actually WANT to meet her husband. He was probably huge with big chiseled muscles ready to crush anyone who dared approach his wife. And rightfully so. He thought of her with her hair all lightened by the sun… about the color of honey. Not to mention that really nice round rear end.

Lord I'm so sorry. Do You hear these thoughts of mine? You know where I've been. You know I have not been serious about anyone since Ellen left. Please guard my heart. I have no idea why I am so attracted to this woman. Have you noticed how pretty her eyes are? I wonder what her hair looks like when it's not pulled back so tight. And she's funny. I haven't laughed like that since… sorry Lord. How did this happen so quickly? I need Your help. I cannot fall back into my old habits.

Jack fell asleep in the early hours of the morning, half hoping never to see her again but really afraid that he may not.

~~~~~~~

Every day that followed was much the same: hard work, slow progress, and local lunches with friendly banter. Jack continually found excuses to go outside and help the Landscape Artist. Gladly he'd do grunt work just to see her smile. Often he asked her opinion on things that normally he'd finish without thinking. And just as often he was surprised at her different point of view. It seemed she brought fresh eyes to things he'd breezed through for years because it was the quickest way. She easily made him laugh with her weird sense of humor and country talk.

He caught her looking at him one day. He thought she might have smiled just for him but he couldn't be sure. He'd learned from traveling that people in the South tend to smile for no apparent reason. Bravely he invited her into the house to see the progress on the kitchen. She seemed to appreciate the invitation and plunked down on the steps to remove her work boots.

Johnny followed them and began expounding on design decisions. Obviously he was very proud of their work. Stainless steel appliances, shiny red cabinets, and concrete countertops made the new kitchen quite the show stopper. Everything was very sleek and industrial.

"What do you think?" Johnny grinned with delight.

Lydia hardly knew what to say. She really hated the whole thing but didn't want to burst the bubble of her new friend.

"I think Denise will love it," she smiled. As she went back outside Johnny didn't seem to notice that she had avoided the question. But Jack did. As she sat down on the porch steps to lace up her work boots he got brave and sat beside her. She looked up a little startled.

"You don't like it do you?" he asked looking at her. She noticed mischief in his eyes she'd not seen before and found herself thinking.

Good grief… those eyes. It should be a crime for a man to be so pretty. It's a wonder he can even see past those lashes.

She realized he was waiting on an answer. "I'm sorry… what was the question? I didn't know there was going to be a test." She smiled that smile as she walked away. Following her with his eyes he suddenly looked to see if Shawn were watching him.

At least he'd made her smile.

The next morning he was on site at 6:30. He had suggested to Johnny that they get an early start to beat the heat. While Lydia's crew was already hard at work, she was nowhere to be seen. He tried to nonchalantly inquire about her. They said something about a prior obligation at her mother-in-law's house. She only lived a few blocks away so Lydia might be by to check on their progress later. Jack found himself moping as he realized.

18

That's what I've been praying for right? Take her out of my line of sight so I would stop the nonsense. Now today for the first time she doesn't show. I need to clear my head before it's too late

.

Chapter 6

Working in Norma's yard was a blessing and a curse. Not only had Blue's mama been like a mother to Lydia but she had also taught her much of what she knew about gardening. She could pinch a plant off, stick it into the ground and watch it grow to high heaven. Lydia was sure she could produce a lotus blossom from a matchstick. Norma had been so generous to her and many times she wondered if she would've survived without her. Now that her mom-in-law was less mobile she loved for Lydia to come over and work in the yard with her. Dragging around her plastic chair she'd take breaks to rest her bad leg, talking the whole time. Lydia liked the visits unless they became advisory.

"You need to get out and date honey. Blue would not be happy knowing how alone you are. He's been dead seven years. It's time to stop grieving. You'll be thirty on your next birthday. There's nothing wrong with living while you're still young enough to have children."

Lydia turned her head and pretended to be absorbed in the work of moving yet another hosta to the ideal spot.

Give it a rest Norma…

Though she thought it often, she loved the woman too much to say the words out loud. In fact she'd loved Norma since she was five years old. Lydia had somehow missed the school bus and was terribly afraid of a scolding. So instead of facing the music she struck out walking toward school hoping to remember the way. As she hiked alone with her little backpack and copper curls bouncing, Norma had stopped and picked her up. She'd scooted inside their nice car beside of the boy two grades ahead of her. When he said his name Lydia had laughed then felt sorry for it. She tried to make up by saying, "That's a purty name. Everybody calls me Copper. So we go good together. Copper and Blue!"

The shy little boy beside her smiled and they became instant friends. Together they romped the hills behind their homes and shared everything growing up.

Norma interrupted Lydia's happy memory. "We need to get someone to cut those trees hanging over the back of the house. One bad storm and the new den could be ruined."

Lydia looked up from her work. "How 'bout if we take down those two big pines? I know a guy who has a crew that would do that for you."

"Is he single? Wouldn't it be great if you met someone who loved working outside as much as you do! Call him and tell him to come by and give me an estimate. I could stir us up some lunch."

He actually was single. In fact he'd been after her for several months to go out with him. She just wasn't ready. She wondered why. He was very successful and part of a new real estate agency that often hired her to add curb appeal. Maybe it was her lack of confidence or perhaps the fear of the unknown. Dating seemed weird to Lydia and she didn't want to get caught up in that crapstorm. Occasionally she'd meet him for lunch. That was the closest thing she had come to dating.

She was glad Norma had not seen the guys she was currently working with. One glance and she'd have her married and birthing babies. She wondered which one Norma would choose. For a moment she allowed herself to consider the notion.

A large red truck pulled up to Norma's house. It said *Stephens and Sons* on the side. She couldn't see which brother was driving. The heat was killing her and as usual sweat blurred her vision. Had something gone wrong at the project? Surely her absence for one day wouldn't upset the applecart.

Her heart did a flip flop like the day she met him. But there she stood filthier than usual with red mud caked on her Brogans and her tank top sweated through. Knowing she wouldn't be on the Parker job that morning she'd traded work jeans for cut-offs. As she pushed sweat from her face with a gloved hand more dirt and sweat entered her eye. Turning the nozzle she sprayed her face with water from the hosepipe. While drying on her shirttail she noticed Jack making his way toward Norma's chair.

"Norma… this is Jack. He is the manager at my latest project. Jack this is Norma, my mom-in-law."

Jack reached for the elderly woman's hand and smiled warmly. "It's very good to meet you Norma. Your yard is beautiful. It's nice to have an expert in the family isn't it?" He looked at Lydia and smiled.

For once Norma was at a loss for words. How had she not known of this handsome young man in her daughter-in-law's life? When she gathered herself she began apologizing for Lydia's appearance.

"She gets so caught up in her work that she never thinks to check a mirror. My son actually built her an outdoor shower so she could wash off before going inside. Of course I think he had ulterior motives as that shower is certainly large enough for two."

Lydia could have died right on the spot.

"Norma Rae…" Lydia reprimanded with her tone.

Norma knew instantly she had overstepped her bounds because Lydia used her middle name.

Jack didn't know what prompted him but suddenly he was asking Lydia about the outdoor shower. "My parents have a house on Jersey Shore and I've often thought of building them one. Maybe I could take a few pictures of yours for inspiration."

Norma smiled a knowing smile.

~~~~~~~

At the build site a few moments earlier, Jack had worked up the nerve to ask about Lydia's husband. "Do you think he'll stop by to see what we've done? I'd like to meet him." He lied but decided he must have some answers before he gave up on the woman who kept him awake at night.

Kurtis and Shawn looked at each other then finally Kurtis spoke. "Coach was definitely one of the good guys. One morning after working third shift, he was headed home on his motorcycle when a drunk pulled out in front of him. He died seven years ago I think. I still can't believe he's gone."

"Yeah… that's about right." added Shawn. "Blue coached our football and basketball teams so we got to hang out with him and Liddy after school. Then they took us in when we were eleven. He died when we were fourteen."

Shawn went back to work. For some reason he felt he'd revealed too much. He stopped short of saying that Lydia was the only mother he'd ever had.

Kurtis being the romantic one piped up. "If you need her for anything today she's just a few blocks away. I could give you directions."

Shawn gave him the stink eye and added, "But just so you know, she does NOT date."

Jack wanted to scoop Lydia up and promise to take care of her forever. He couldn't imagine all she had been through. Instead he reminded himself to pull back. She was obviously not looking for a rescue.

Chapter 7

No wonder Norma had apologized for her daughter-in-law's appearance. Back at home and finished for the day she peeled the sweaty clothes off in her spacious outdoor shower. Sure it was big enough for two, but Blue had made it large enough that she could put dry towels and clothes on the bench at one end where they would not get wet. It was one of his best gifts to her. Their tiny house only had one bathroom. There was no indoor shower, unless you counted the handheld sprayer over the clawfoot tub. But it had very little water pressure. She used the shower outside even in the winter since he had plumbed it with hot water. Right off the back door to the sunroom she could wrap up and step inside leaving the mud of the day where it belonged. She thought of him every time she used it.

But then she thought of him all the time anyway. It seemed everything reminded her of him, especially the house. They had gone out on a limb when the one hundred acre farm came up for auction right before they got married. Knowing they couldn't afford it all, they talked the owners into dividing the property. Thirty-seven acres would be more than enough to support their dreams. With a shack of a house included, they decided they could surely make do until they could clear some land and build. Looking back, she marveled that they made it through that first winter. With space heaters hooked to the outdated electrical, it was also a miracle that the place didn't burn to the ground. Ironically Blue had been afraid to light a fire in the fireplace because the chimney was questionable. It seemed the former owners had burned pine which coated the inside of it with tar. To light a fire was just asking for trouble. But all those drop cords? They found themselves ending their night time prayers together with "And Lord please don't let the house burn down tonight."

Between work and life they had torn out carpet which stunk so bad it made them gag. They removed the cast iron pipes and the old hot water heater, replumbing the entire house. He always teased her about being "freakishly strong for such a little girl." But her back had hurt till she cried most nights. Thankfully the well was good which saved them several thousand dollars since they didn't have to drill a new one. She still remembered the first time clear fresh water poured out of the new pipes with no rust.

Blue had grinned and made her laugh when he said, "Nothing but the best for my girl!"

Afraid to tackle the electrical themselves they finally had enough money to hire an electrician. He pulled all the wires and had new outlets and a real breaker box installed in two days flat. No more fuses to replace, and thankfully no more drop cords strung across the floor like jump-ropes of death. They were moving on up! That winter they hired a professional to clean and repair the chimney. Not only could they have a nice fire but their night time prayer didn't have to include the house burning down. That same year they invited the boys to live with them. Life was so good!

As she wrapped one towel around her body and another around her hair her phone buzzed on the bench and interrupted her thoughts.

"Hello Lydia. This is Jack. I have a crazy question."

Nervously she answered. "What can I do for you Dearheart?" She covered her mouth and wondered why she'd addressed him as such.

Dearheart? What are you, eighty?

She realized she was channeling her mother-in-law who used the term often.

Jack continued by asking if she knew of a good church in the area.

Lydia was so glad he wasn't calling about a date that she relaxed and spoke to him as a friend. "Why don't you guys go with me? You'll love my pastor. Then you can come to my house for Sunday lunch. I'm not much of a cook but I've got fresh vegetables from the garden. And you could check out the shower."

Jack smiled. His plan had served him well. "I don't know if Johnny will be there or not, but I will. He doesn't care much for church. I'll be sure to invite him with the understanding that he'll have to show proof of church attendance if he plans to dine with us."

She laughed a little too loud she thought. She gave him directions to the church then added, "The second service starts at eleven o'clock. I sit on the left and toward the back. Shawn and Kurt will be there too.

25

You might be able to spot those two goobers easier since they're taller than me."

Jack spoke easily. "I'll find you."

As he hung up it occurred to him that he already had.

~~~~~~~

She smiled as she stepped from the shower onto the deck. Jack's call made her happy. Apparently her appearance hadn't grossed him out too much. The warm sun felt so good that she briefly considered losing the towels and sunning. Nobody was around for miles and if the boys happened by she'd hear them coming long before they got within sight. The sun would dry her hair faster and help with some of those funky tan lines she had going on. She'd done that often when Blue was alive but now, things just seemed different. For some reason lately she had the feeling she was being watched. She figured it was just part of getting used to the boys moving out.

Chapter 8

It was a new experience for her to have a church she called her own, much less to like it enough to bring visitors. Though she and Blue had attended together at Norma's church even before they were married, Lydia always felt out of place. She wasn't sure what that was about. Blue assured her it was her own insecurity that caused her doubts. He was most likely right. They'd been as involved as they possibly could, often having the teens over for cook outs and hayrides and such. She loved that aspect of it all. But after Blue died she found it really hard to go. Folks were so kind, sending cards and tons of food to her home. But somehow sitting in the pew without him was too much to bear. Finally she told Norma she wouldn't be back. She knew she'd be terribly disappointed but Norma had surprised her by saying, "I understand Dearheart. Just be sure to find a place where you can grow. This is no time to do life without the One Who loves you best."

Lydia was pretty sure that the 'one who loved her best' was gone. God had taken him too soon. She was also sure God didn't like her since she'd done terrible things after Blue died. She was fine with that as she didn't much like Him either. For seven painful years she'd been mad at the Lord and knew in her heart that the feeling was mutual.

So when Jack called with his question she was glad that only a few months earlier Kurt and Shawn had practically made her go with them to their new church. A college ministry had drawn them in with pancakes and ping pong and suddenly they were both telling her how much she was missing. Once she tried it she knew they were right. She'd even been brave enough to sit alone. But she didn't have to worry about that as her boys would always find her if she came.

Pastor Dale taught Scripture each week with such clarity that she felt she was being drawn back into the fold. Recently he'd read the story Jesus told of the farmer sowing seeds on different kinds of ground. She found herself relating and praying for help for the first time in years. As she considered giving God another chance, she picked up one of the free paperback Bibles they offered. Maybe she could at least start reading it some in her down time.

Sunday morning the Stephens brothers found her sitting between Kurtis and Shawn. Her boys moved so their guests could sit on either side of Lydia. Apparently Jack and Johnny were used to dressing more formally for church. Each had on a tie and sport coat and looked really sharp. Lydia was glad she'd opted for her other summer dress. Her crazy tan lines had finally evened out enough that she could wear the yellow sundress and white summer heels. She too wanted to look nice for company. Now if only her hair would calm down a bit. It seemed to multiply like kudzu in the terrible humidity. At least with it pulled up loosely she didn't feel quite as much like a maintenance man.

Lydia thought that Jack seemed to thoroughly enjoy the message but noticed Johnny sat very still. It was as though he was afraid to relax lest someone peer into his soul. His usual smile was missing and his back was as stiff as an ironing board. Something was definitely wrong. She hoped maybe they could talk later.

~~~~~~~

Jack really liked the pastor's message. It cut straight to his heart. But that was typical for him at that particular point in his life. He remembered being so calloused to God's Word that even though his dad begged him to remember the God of his youth, he didn't care. Thankfully the Lord had sent a severe wake-up call last year. Otherwise he'd be dead. He was pretty sure that's where Johnny was headed if he didn't make some changes soon. He couldn't believe it when he agreed to come to church with him. Of all mornings to finally get religion! Jack had selfishly hoped he'd opt out as usual so he could have lunch with Lydia alone. He wondered about his brother's interest in her. But maybe Johnny would listen to the message and make the changes Jack had prayed for him so long.

He loved how the pastor related that the past with all its pain could be used to comfort others. It made him realize again that what his own father had taught him was true. He could still make a difference in spite of all he'd done.

He was kind of proud of himself for being able to listen to the message at all. Right beside him sat Lydia like a beautiful summer flower. With her hair loosely tied up it sprang forth with a shower of curls. Why she kept it bound so tightly during the week he'd never know. When he'd first spotted her as they entered the church some guy was standing close to her chatting, making her laugh. He wondered what was so funny that she seemed to be embarrassed. He'd watched her enough on the job to recognize it because she'd cover her throat with her hand as it turned red. Though he'd not had a lot of experience with redheads, not real ones anyway, he supposed that they blushed easily. Otherwise what would someone say to her in church to make her blush? Maybe it was just a part of her shyness. But why would a woman who looked like her be shy? Surely she owned a mirror. The music broke into his thoughts.

Good grief man. You've missed the end of the message while thinking about her again. Sorry Lord.

~~~~~~~~

As they left church Lydia suggested Johnny ride with her as Jack followed them to the house. Mentally Jack was kicking himself for not spelling it out to Johnny how he felt about her. Now it might be too late. Though his brother was engaged, he was certainly not committed.

Lydia however thought perhaps she would have a chance to help Johnny with whatever was bothering him. Down the road a bit she broached the subject the only way she knew how.

"Okay Johnny. Spill it. What's the matter?" A long silence made her wonder if she'd messed up. Again she reprimanded herself for being so socially inept. When finally he spoke he related to her his current relationship with Gina.

"She's gorgeous!" he smiled at the thought. "But I'm starting to have serious doubts. She can be rather overbearing. While I've been here it's actually been a relief to be away from her. What's that about?!" He laughed. "She stresses me so much, but our wedding is coming up in October. She will kill me if I ruin it now. She's been planning this thing for two years! We've lived together for three, but I keep finding myself dreading going home. I don't have a clue what to do."

"Bless your heart Johnny!" And she sincerely meant it. She let his words hang in the air before speaking.

"If you were to play back the things you just dared to say out loud to me as a friend," she chose her next words carefully. "Do you think it would be clear what you should do?" She surprised even herself when she added. "Making a promise to God is kind of a big deal. I don't think that's something you want to do all willy-nilly."

Glancing in the rear view mirror she noticed that she had lost Jack somewhere between church and the turn toward home. Pulling over at the next wide spot, she found his number realizing she needed to add him to her favorites.

"Sorry Jack. Didn't mean to run off and leave you."

His reply made her laugh.

"No problem Dearheart. I'm catching up to you now."

Chapter 9

The long gravel road to her house was dusty with the recent lack of rain. But the view was breathtaking. Wildflowers filled the ditches and one particular field was covered in blue flowers. Apparently those along with her husband's unusual moniker had given inspiration for the name Blue Meadow Farm. Closer to the house cosmos in every shade of purple and pink held their own in a garden against the small white farmhouse. Giant hydrangeas with chartreuse green and white blossoms nodded their heads hello welcoming them to the deep front porch complete with black rockers. Hanging ferns and pots of red geraniums on the wide steps shouted southern hospitality. Black ceiling fans whirred lazily creating a gentle breeze.

As they entered the front door to the den the lack of color was surprising. Nearly everything was white. White clapboard walls with white trim, whitewashed brick on the fireplace, and light pine hardwood floors led into the little kitchen. There they were greeted by old white appliances and a few white cabinets with clear green glass knobs. On the small table was a faded cloth with a green and blue border. The blue Mason jar with a bouquet of cosmos provided a refreshing burst of color. Light streamed through the windows making the room seem larger than it was. Jack noticed immediately the lack of window treatments and loved it. Through the back they could see another space which apparently had been a large slate patio at some point.

"Oh wow. I love the sunroom!" Jack said as he looked through an arched doorway into the space.

Lydia smiled. "Thanks. I love it too. It was Blue's last gift to me."

He realized it was the first time she had spoken to him of her late husband.

"Blue?" Johnny asked.

"That's my husband's name. He was born sunny-side up and came out terribly bruised. He was literally dark blue for a few days so his mama gave him that as his middle name. I always liked it. Anyway, come see my favorite place in the world. With all the windows I can watch the stars at night. I love sleeping here on the daybed. It's like camping minus the mosquitos."

"And out this door is the famous shower he built. It's an engineering marvel." She smiled at Jack as they stepped onto a small deck. "He even painted it white for me so I could spot any critters that might lurk in the corners. That's why there shall always be flip flops on this hook as that's my personal weapon of choice."

He was glad that speaking of her late husband didn't seem to make her sad. And that shower really was nice. He took pictures and hoped to surprise his dad with one at their cottage. Perhaps Lydia could go there to help him with the details. He knew his dad would love her but sighed at the thought of his mom. Though Lydia had such a gracious spirit and humor about her his mom would probably not approve of anyone so country. For a moment he imagined a cocktail party with Lydia in her cut-offs.

Maybe he'd just move south.

~~~~~~~

She invited them to sit at the kitchen table while she prepared lunch. "The boys are at Kurtis' grandmother's today so it's just us three. I'll have it ready shortly." Jack found his way to the stove where she was working. "Can I help you with anything?" he offered.

"Sure. How about peeling the tomatoes? I've got a squash casserole in the oven, a big pot of fresh green beans with new potatoes, and Silver Queen corn. Would you prefer I leave it on the cob or make cream style?"

Though he thought himself rather handy in the kitchen he had never in his life peeled a tomato. And what was cream style corn? He didn't know but it sounded awesome. He noticed that she blushed when he caught her eye.

Lydia handed him a knife. "I'm afraid it's not very sharp. I don't know how to do that. There's a sharpie whet stone thing in the knife drawer if you need it."

Jack proceeded to make the knives so sharp that the tomato skin melted away like 'buttuh.' The peeling and slicing of a fresh cantaloupe completed the meal. Without their noticing, Johnny had slipped outside to the front porch. There he sat rocking slowly, staring across the meadow.

Lydia opened the screen door and invited, "Come on in Johnny. Let's have a nice lunch together and act like we've got good sense."

He smiled and obeyed his hostess as he wondered.

Had he finally come to his senses? Now if he could just follow through.

~~~~~~~

After lunch she pulled a hot peach cobbler from the oven. The aroma was wonderful but they were too full to enjoy it just yet. Lydia offered to take them around the property on the Four Wheeler. While they still sat at her little kitchen table suddenly Johnny took her hand and said to his brother, "Lydia and I have an announcement."

Jack's heart dropped to his stomach as he waited for Johnny to continue. He stole a glance at Lydia. As usual he couldn't read her.

"We've decided I should break up with Gina," announced Johnny.

Lydia smiled and looked at Jack, "Actually I had nothing to do with his decision. Johnny spoke his fears out loud and I just reminded him to listen to his own wisdom." She pulled her hand from Johnny's and hoped Jack didn't think she was a meddler. She had never met the woman, but when a man dreads seeing his own fiancée, there's definitely something amiss.

She noticed Jack had a strange look on his face, something akin to relief. Gina must be one wicked chick if these two nice men would be relieved to be done with her.

"I'll be right back. I'm going to change into my Four Wheeler riding attire. One can't be traipsing all over Blue Meadow Farm in one's church frock."

33

When she left Jack leaned toward Johnny and whispered, "You scared me half to death just now. You did that on purpose didn't you?"

Johnny grinned back at him, "Sorry. I couldn't help myself. Do you think she has any idea how infatuated you are?"

Jack sighed. "Is it that obvious? I'm hoping to enlighten her soon. I can't leave North Carolina without telling her how I feel. But I also don't want to lose her. I'd rather have what we have now… which I'm not sure what that is… than to scare her off. But we've only got about four more weeks here."

"I understand." Johnny nodded then added. "Actually I don't. I can't wait to get rid of Gina. She is going to go psycho when I cancel the wedding."

"Don't forget how you're feeling right now. You know how she manipulates you into changing your mind every time you get close to calling it off." Jack warned his little brother.

Johnny sighed. "I know. I need to get home and get this over with."

Jack smiled. "You can't wait to get home and I can't bear the thoughts of leaving. Aren't we a pair?"

Lydia emerged ready to take them on a tour. Johnny said he'd rather just hang back and relax on the front porch, so Jack and Lydia brought the Four Wheeler from the barn. Off they went down the dusty road with Jack driving. Lydia liked being so close to him though she held to the seat instead of around his waist. When he took off with a sudden burst of speed, she held him tightly so as not to slide off the back.

Perfect! he smiled to himself.

~~~~~~~

The man in the woods scowled as he watched. Today was supposed to be their day. But who were these new men? Now he'd have to wait. But he could do that. The reward was in the watching. He loved it and had a feeling she did too. It was their special game. Soon he'd start giving her more clues. The fear in her eyes the day she'd opened her door to him was fun. Perhaps he'd take more time to build the anticipation.

Chapter 10   July

Lydia and her crew eventually took Jack and Johnny under their wing. Lunches together at the diner found them laughing easily. It wasn't long before Lydia invited them to eat supper at her house each evening as well. It was actually a big step for her but they'd been so appreciative of the Sunday lunch that she decided it was the hospitable thing to do. And since her boys came anyway, two more guys around the table would be a piece of cake.

If only she could cook.

Johnny started opting out having Jack drop him off at the motel. He was dog tired at the end of each day so why continue the torture with food at Lydia's? Jack was happy just to be with her in her home no matter how bad her cooking was.

During one meal which included a particularly dense meatloaf Shawn spoke up.

"Liddy this is really bad."

Kurt punched Shawn in the arm. Jack was shocked at the words and wondered if she'd cry. Instead she burst into laughter. In fact she could hardly speak for laughing so hard. "It really is bad! Sorry guys!" She looked at Jack adding, "It has to be awful if Shawn won't eat it."

By then they were all laughing. They were surprised when Jack offered to cook for them next time. Lydia high fived Shawn and commented, "I love it when a plan comes together!"

She got up, raked the food into the compost bowl and put on a fresh pot of coffee. "At least I made Buttermilk Brownies. Maybe y'all won't starve completely to death."

Kurtis started washing dishes as Jack dipped ice cream onto the chocolate squares that Lydia served. Shawn stepped between them and scoured the refrigerator. "Where's the lemonade Liddy?"

She reached in front of him and pulled the jug from the top shelf. "It's hiding there in plain sight honey." She glanced at Jack and they shared a smile. That smile of hers nearly melted his heart. But she quickly looked away. When he tasted the dessert tentatively Lydia understood. She was rewarded however with his enthusiastic approval.

"Oh wow. You have definitely redeemed yourself with this dessert Lydia. You made this?" Jack had always been a fan of chocolate.

"Yep. It's an easy recipe. I know it's a surprise since I'm a terrible cook, but I actually do okay baking." She was glad that he liked it so much.

"Oh yeah! We're going to make a great team." Jack spoke not really thinking. He was so busy bearing down on his dessert that he didn't notice the uncomfortable look she shot Shawn. Kurtis however was smiling as he rinsed the plates. Being the tender hearted one he silently prayed for her to let go of the past and be happy for a change.

~~~~~~~

Jack could definitely cook. Every night after that he picked up groceries on the way then made himself at home in her little kitchen. The boys were thrilled but Lydia kept her distance. She often reminded herself that he'd be gone soon and that she sure didn't want to get attached. She found herself laughing though at the crazy conversations they had each evening. Sometimes they pulled out cards and played for hours. At least it was easier to play with four instead of three.

And those eyes. She tried her best not to look into them.

About a week or so in, she came home later than usual and found Jack waiting on the front porch. It was a bit unsettling. Her boys always went by their house in town to get cleaned up before arriving. That gave her time to bathe before supper. But there sat Jack. She couldn't very well strip off in her outdoor shower with him there. And she really hated trying to wash her hair inside where there was no water pressure. She decided she needed to give him the talk. He'd already been all up in her business more than anyone besides the boys. She wondered what the man was thinking.

~~~~~~~

Jack waited on the porch thinking about her. She had the kindest heart he'd ever seen often doing things for those around her. Jack noticed more than once how she'd leave lunch to run cookies by to an elderly person in town. Almost daily she spent part of her lunch break checking on folks. Sometimes she'd take her crew and tidy up a yard, do a quick mow job or just push their trash to the curb. Her boys did those things without complaint as though it were the normal thing to do. No fanfare; just caring for those that others had forgotten. The only way Jack knew about it was that sometimes Kurtis would mention things at dinner. He was definitely a lot more sensitive than Shawn. Raised by his grandmother before he moved in with Lydia, he too had a heart for Lydia's "little old ladies." Jack rocked in a rocker wishing she were there.

Soon Lord, he prayed. *Please warm her up to me and show her that she can trust me.*

He heard her truck coming down the gravel drive and his heart leapt. She parked around back near the deck and he wondered whether to stay put so she could let him in the front door or to walk around to meet her. He'd love to gather her up and carry her over the threshold but he didn't think they were quite to that point. He smiled at the thought realizing again how crazy he was being. He'd heard of love at first sight, and had even used that same line to his advantage before. But this had taken him by complete surprise. She came through the front door and sat in the rocker beside him.

As usual the words were hard for her to say. She rocked slowly wondering how many times she'd ended up hurting a guy because she didn't stop things before they became serious. How could she do it? The back door had been left unlocked again so Jack could've gone in and made himself at home. But he didn't. That was a point in his favor. Maybe she should just let it go. He'd be gone soon anyway.

She rocked and stared across the meadow in front of the house. He wondered if he should lean over and kiss her. Something inside caused him to hesitate. Instead he broke the uncomfortable silence. "I picked up chicken to do that oven baked recipe that you liked so much last week. You know… the one with the crackers? Sorry I got here early. It just takes longer to bake and I know you like for us to leave before dark."

He looked at her and smiled. She smiled back that smile he loved so well.

"Sounds great," she nearly whispered. Perhaps she'd just let him enjoy his time with them while he was there. No need hurting the man's feelings when he hadn't made any kind of advances anyway. Besides, he was a really nice guy not to mention a fantastic cook.

But she still had the shower issue.

"Hey Jack?" She looked at her hands which were rough and dirty from a very long day at work.

"Yes dear?" He asked smiling.

She laughed as she wondered.

Why does he say stuff like that?

And why did it make her laugh and even hope a little?

"I need to um…" She couldn't say the word. She didn't want some mental image of her nakedness popping up in his brain.

"Shower?" He asked as if it were nothing.

She didn't speak but her face gave away how uncomfortable he was making her. His laughter surprised her and she looked up as he rose from his seat.

"Lydia dear." He pulled her to her feet. Suddenly he hugged her and walked her to the front door. "I'll stay in the kitchen and promise not to look at your little bare feet under the shower door. I just need to get this chicken started if we're going to 'roll out of here before dark' per your request."

They stepped inside the door into the tiny den. He stood close and considered kissing her for a brief moment. But they both heard a noise at the same time and looked toward the kitchen.

She glanced at him nervously. "Did you hear that?"

"It sounded like the back door. Stay here and let me check." Jack walked through the house as Lydia shut the front door behind her and locked it. Looking through a window she could tell that Shawn and Kurtis weren't around. Fear gripped her heart and she realized how thankful she was that Jack was there.

Jack returned to where she waited. "I didn't see anything. Does the wind ever catch your door and make that sound?"

She shook her head no. "That's weird. My door was unlocked when I got home. You didn't do that did you?"

"No… how would I unlock your door?" Jack wondered. He took her arm as they walked toward the kitchen.

"I've got a spare set of keys in the shower for the boys and I thought maybe they told you. I'm almost sure I locked the door this morning. But I've been awfully tired lately. I probably just forgot." She pulled her arm away from him and headed into the bedroom to retrieve clean clothes.

Jack had a bad feeling about the whole thing. He couldn't imagine her forgetting to lock her door. But things were certainly different in the South. A lot of folks there never locked anything, except their gun safe.

When she came from the bedroom with clean clothes and towels in hand he was surprised that she headed outside to shower. He wanted to stand guard but had promised her he would get dinner started.

"Lydia?" He spoke behind her as she walked through the sunroom toward the back door. "Do you have a lock on the inside of the shower door?"

She stopped and looked at him. "No…" she answered. "I tried to put one in but couldn't get the latch to line up, so it doesn't work."

Jack followed her to look in the shower. He was relieved to see the spare set of keys there behind the flip flops. Unscrewing the circle end of the fastener from the shower frame he made quick work of reinstalling it so the latch would fit securely.

"Please use it Lydia… every time." Jack said it with such kindness that she suddenly felt very protected and cared for, even more than when the boys were around. She rewarded him with a smile.

"Thanks Jack." Then she had to add with a twinkle in her eye, "But don't look at my feet."

Chapter 11

Jack felt like they were making headway in the relationship department. She looked especially pretty the next morning on the job. She seemed to hang back allowing her crew to do the digging. She even had on a decent pair of jeans and a blouse instead of the dirt stained clothes she usually wore. Though her hair was twisted into a loose knot on top of her head, it looked soft and had strands of curls escaping. He considered again asking her out. Shawn's warning kept him wondering though. As they enjoyed lunch together later that day, Jack couldn't help but look at her. He was surprised when her eyes followed a nice looking young man who took a seat at a table across the room. Jack sized the guy up and decided that he was probably a couple years younger than himself.

Shawn interrupted Jack's thinking as he muttered, "It's time Liddy. Either fish or cut bait."

Kurtis and Shawn stood on cue and let her out of the booth. Jack watched as she walked to the far wall toward the guy at the table for two. He stood and embraced her longer than Jack liked. She joined him at his table as though it was the most natural thing in the world.

Her crew sat back down and continued eating. Jack wanted very much to ask who he was and what she was doing over there. She had taken her drink but not her sandwich. Maybe she was just saying hello to a friend. He tried to look away but couldn't. Even Johnny had gone silent.

The guy ordered his food then as the waitress left he reached over and took Lydia's hands in his own. She didn't pull away. Jack wanted to punch him. "Fish or cut bait…" What did that mean exactly? He worked on his lunch trying not to stare. The guy was talking and continued to hold Lydia's hands. She wasn't smiling or pulling her hands from his. She was looking into his eyes not saying a word.

Jack was kicking himself. He looked at his barbecue salad with a side of ranch dressing and missed what happened next. Lydia and the mystery man were walking out. The guy had ordered his food to go and she carried their drinks as he stopped at the register to pay. They exited through the screen door and Jack lost sight of them.

I didn't move fast enough. I knew I should've kissed her last night!

He looked helplessly at Shawn. He should've known better. Shawn wasn't giving anything away. Kurtis was no help either. Johnny sighed and shook his head. Jack ate the barbecue off the top of his salad along with the tomatoes and left the lettuce in the bowl. What had possessed him to order a salad? Of course it wouldn't hurt to lose a few pounds. At thirty-three he was no longer a spring chicken and that guy Lydia walked out with was trim AND young.

It seemed an eternity passed before Shawn and Kurtis finished. Kurt wrapped Lydia's sandwich taking it with him. Shawn tossed a tip on the table and they waited at the register to pay. Johnny said under his breath, "Sorry Jack," and looked at his brother sadly. Jack noticed the boys had walked outside so he paid and left as well. They'd probably take Lydia's truck back to work as she had left with Mr. Young and Restless. Jack sighed heavily and almost bumped into the guy as he rounded the building toward his own truck.

They did the Pardon-Me-Shuffle as each made his way around the other. The guy stopped and looked at Jack briefly as if he wanted to speak. Hearing the roar of Lydia's old truck they both watched as it went by. Shawn was driving, Kurt rode shotgun and Lydia sat in the middle with her two best friends.

Johnny spoke to Jack as they headed back to the job site, "Well THAT was interesting. At least she didn't leave with him."

Jack had no idea what to make of it. He hoped something would come up at dinner to give him a clue. When he returned to the Parker project Lydia had changed at some point and was already on her knees working on a flowerbed. She didn't look up when he spoke but Kurtis did. He gave Jack a smile and a nod. Jack hoped he would be a source of information later.

~~~~~~~

Jack decided to take a chance and call her. She didn't seem to like him getting to her house early so he might as well ask. Maybe she'd volunteer what had gone on at lunch. He realized that as much as he'd been over at her house that guy had never been invited. The only time she would be free to date him would be on Saturdays as they also joined her for church and Sunday lunch. But even on Saturdays Jack had often been invited to go with her and the boys to things in the community. There had been the town of Faith's Fourth of July celebration, church softball, and a cornhole tournament for Norma's friends who were going on a mission trip. But none of it had landed on Saturday night. He had to wonder if that's when she was going out with the guy. But Shawn had told him specifically that she didn't date. He tried to remember if that was the same person that made her laugh at church when Jack first visited. He didn't think so but he couldn't be sure.

He remembered one of their early days on the job together. She had smiled at the phone call she received. She'd walked up the drive to her truck, removed her muddy boots and stepped out of her coveralls by the tailgate. Jack couldn't look away. Of course she had clean shorts and a tank top on underneath. That was one of the few days she'd missed lunch with them. It was before Jack knew she was widowed so he had wondered if she were meeting her husband. Maybe it was that guy instead. That sort of thing had happened off and on in the weeks since they'd met. But surely she wasn't seeing someone who never came over at night. The puzzle pieces weren't fitting together for him.

He got her voice mail.

"Hi Lydia. Just wanted to check to see what time I should come. I don't want to intrude. I plan to make my dad's famous chicken salad and it takes a bit to stew the chicken. If this is not a good night to do that, just let me know."

He barely stopped short of saying, "I love you." He'd thought it so much in his head that it almost came out of his mouth. He quickly hit the end button and thanked God for engaging his brain before his words gave him away.

His phone received a text later with "6." That was all. Apparently she was screening her calls and didn't want to talk to him. But he was glad for what she didn't say. It could've read,

"I have a boyfriend. Don't call me again."

Or "I have plans tonight and they don't include you."

Or "You are too old and chubby for me. Bless your heart."

Jack decided that six was a good message.

Chapter 12

She liked the fact that he asked. That way she could make sure to be clean and dressed when he got there. And she happened to LOVE chicken salad. Since he'd brought groceries with him the day before she could get the chicken started stewing when she finished her shower. How hard could that be?

Tossing the big bird into a large pot of water she turned it on high and walked outside to sit on the deck. The heat and gentle breeze would have her hair dried much quicker than if she stayed inside in the air conditioned house. She didn't much like air conditioning anyway. It seemed to make her body hurt. That's why they'd never added it to the sunroom. Sitting on a white plastic chair, the warm deck was perfect even though she could feel sweat already starting to form. As she combed out her hair she got that crazy feeling again that she was being watched. For some reason she felt compelled to move inside and even lock the door. It was a good thing she did since the chicken had boiled over. She lowered the temperature and wondered if she should add salt. Glancing outside she saw nothing unusual but remembered how protective Jack had been telling her to latch the shower door. She decided that she would continue doing so on a regular basis. If for no other reason it made her feel secure.

The alarm chirped informing her that Jack was on his way down the drive. She checked the mirror in the bathroom and wished her hair was dry. Maybe once he got there they could take a walk or do something outside. She wouldn't be so wigged out with him near. As she answered the front door she heard the chicken boiling over on the stove again.

"Sorry. I was trying to help but I might've messed up." She spoke as she hurried to the kitchen to lower the heat under the stewing bird. "C'mere and see if this is okay." She invited Jack as she removed the lid with a pot holder and peered inside the big pot.

Jack recognized the clothes as the ones she'd had on at lunch. He liked how the blouse showed her curves. Unlike the t-shirts she normally wore it fit her very well. So did those soft worn out jeans. As usual when indoors she was barefoot. He looked inside the pot trying to act interested in the chicken.

"Did you add salt or pepper?" he asked looking at her with those eyes.

"Nooo… did I ruin it already?" She glanced at him wondering and wished she'd left the cooking to him.

"Oh no," he answered sensing her insecurity. "Thanks for getting it started. We'll add it now." He looked around and she brought shakers from the table.

"Do you happen to have herbs of any kind? Rosemary would be my first choice." Jack was looking at her again. She wished her hair was dry and that she'd thought to add make-up. Good grief the man was handsome.

"I DO have herbs." She brought a long pot from the sunroom and sat it on the counter near him. "I grow them because I love the way they smell. I have more outside but I don't have a clue what to do with them." She smiled and stroked one of the spikey plants. "Rosemary is my favorite too. I heard it prevents dementia so I try to sniff it often. I don't believe it's working though since I keep forgetting to sniff it." She laughed easily.

Jack gazed at her and laughed as well. "Here, let me show you something that will jazz up your life. Do you have twine or cheesecloth handy?"

She opened a kitchen drawer which had all manner of stuff inside. "Please feel free to dig through here. If I have some this is where we'll find it." She pushed things around in the junk drawer and was rewarded with a tiny ball of string. "Well lookie here! Who knew I had such a well equipped kitchen. Proceed with the jazzing."

Jack's heart was happy at how relaxed she seemed. The boys weren't even there yet. He took the twine from her, snipped a few herbs then tied them together. Dropping them into the pot he explained, "That's called a 'bouquet-garni.' It will make the chicken as well as the broth taste fantastic. I tied it together so it's easy to remove at the end. We'll freeze the broth and you can use it later to season vegetables or make soup. Do you have peppercorns or an onion we can add?"

"I do…" Lydia searched a cabinet finding a pepper grinder. "I don't know how to get them out of there. No telling how old they are so…" She was examining the gadget she'd never used. Jack removed the top and poured some of the whole peppercorns into his hand. He sniffed them then held them out for her to do the same. She commented, "They must keep their goodness a long time. Did you say you need an onion?" Pulling a white porcelain dishpan from the cabinet under the sink she handed him a large yellow onion. It had started to sprout. "Is it okay to use that? It's kinda wiggly."

He laughed at her funny word. "Let's cut it and see." As he did it fell apart on the cutting board and a milky liquid oozed out. "Hmmm… let's skip the onion. I think it's past its prime." He tossed it into the empty compost bowl on the counter. He washed his hands then took a wooden spoon and pushed the chicken around in the pot. Returning the lid he lowered the heat then proclaimed that it would take about forty five minutes or so to get done. "Did you know that if you had stainless steel sinks you could rub them to get the onion odor from your hands?"

Lydia looked at him and commented. "I did not know that. But did you know that I really hate stainless steel?" She remembered the new kitchen at Denise's and nearly shuddered at the thought. Jack laughed and shook his head.

He surprised her by asking, "Do you want to take a walk? I love your barn and I only saw it that day we took the Four Wheeler out. I think that was the first time you had me over." He nearly reached for her waist to pull her close. But he still wondered what was going on with Mr. Young and Restless.

"Sure. I need to walk up there anyway to check on my fountain parts." She took a scrap piece of paper from the junk drawer along with a pencil and wrote "Barn" leaving it on the table. Jack was glad that she and her boys had a system just in case.

He realized he was still unsettled at the noise they'd heard the day before. He started to ask her about the extra keys but decided not to. If he got brave enough to ask anything it would be about the guy at lunch.

She didn't bother to lock the door as they left. Walking up the dirt road toward the barn he realized how hot it was about the same time she did. "Let's take the truck," she offered. "It's still awfully hot and I hate to get all sweaty before bedtime." She turned toward the truck and Jack smiled. She noticed his mischief and looked at him with something akin to a warning as he entered the passenger side.

"What?" He laughed.

She waited before she cranked the truck still looking at him. When finally she started the engine he added, "Because who in their right mind would want to get all hot and sweaty before bed?"

She couldn't help but laugh. But she tried really hard not to.

Once they were at the barn he was surprised at the nice breeze that greeted them there. Situated on a hill with a few large shade trees around it was actually very pleasant. The wind caught her hair and twirled it behind her. She walked ahead of him into an area with stacks of odds and ends. Most of it was metal pieces of rusted junk. As he gazed at the old stuff she exclaimed with pride, "This is my treasure chest."

He hardly knew what to say, but somehow felt privileged to be there. "Wow…" he tried to sound impressed.

She looked at him and laughed. "Now you know how I felt when Johnny showed me that godawful kitchen."

Jack was caught by complete surprise at her honesty. "I designed that kitchen!" He looked away hoping to get some sympathy.

It worked.

"No you didn't… did you?" She walked toward him and touched his arm. "I'm sorry… it's… very bright and cheerful. Denise will probably like it a lot which is all that matters."

Jack finally looked at her and she recognized the mischief.

"You're mean." She laughed as he smiled at her. "I think you might be a rascal."

He loved it. Plus it had gotten him out of trouble for not appreciating the treasure she was so proud of.

She began gathering parts tossing them into the back of her truck. He stood there looking around trying to watch her without getting caught. Her hair was all down and quickly drying into a mass of ringlets. He'd often wondered how it looked when she didn't pull it back so tight. It seemed to be growing bigger by the minute.

His heart beat hard at the sight of her and he realized he'd not allowed such feelings to surface since his wake up call the previous January.

Seven months Lord. I think that might be some sort of record. Maybe this time I can get it right.

He wondered if he could bring up the subject of the guy at lunch. She continued to pick through the pile as though she was looking for something specific.

"Can I help you find anything?" He asked and silently wondered about her design choices.

"I need a watering can… or a… cool! Look at this!" She held up what seemed to be an ancient galvanized vessel with a long thin spout. It still had a paper label on it though it was faded and peeling. "I knew when I found this it would come in handy one day. Now look for a rose… a metal thing that goes on the end to make sprinkles." She continued to dig around, checking a few shelves against the wall.

"Like this?" Jack asked as he held up an object.

"YES! Perfect!" She took it from his hand and blew out the dust.

Instinctively she checked for snakes as she pulled a large tin tub from a nail on the wall. If her old friend Blackie fell out of there she figured Jack would probably soil his undies. She smiled at how he seemed to be tiptoeing around everything checking for critters.

Jack had never seen her so happy before. He gazed at her too long smiling at her happiness.

"You think I'm nuts don't you?" She glanced at him wondering.

Jack spoke quickly, "No, I think you're an artist with a lot of creativity that most people will never be able to understand."

She looked up from the things she carried and turned her head sideways. "That's code for crazy, right?" She laughed and tossed the rest of the stuff into the truck bed.

Her phone buzzed in her pocket.

"Hey Kurt. Yep. Sounds about right. Okay… yep… tell her I said hey." She shoved the phone back into her pocket without explanation then pulled it back out to check the time.

"It's been about forty minutes on the chicken." They climbed into the truck. She was so happy at the treasure she'd found. Jack was wishing he'd taken an opportunity to pull her close and express how he felt about her. The boys would be there soon and they always left after him.

"Oh. I forgot the pump." Lydia turned off the engine and exited the truck. She brought back a small black box with a hose attached. She placed it between them on the bench seat. "Now I can see if this is going to work before I set everything up over at Denise's. That way you can tell me what you think. It might be too redneckish to use."

The thought of giving his opinion on something she was obviously excited about made Jack nervous. He decided maybe he could fib if it made her happy. It wouldn't be like the lies he'd told women in times past. Thank the Lord he'd chosen to be done with that lifestyle once and for all.

She said it as if it were no news at all. "Kurt and Shawn stopped by to help Norma after work and she asked them to stay for supper. So I guess that means more chicken salad for us!" She smiled at him as she started the truck.

Jack's heart did a happy dance… and so did Lydia's.

Chapter 13

Back at the house she parked the truck close to a hose bib and lowered the tailgate. "Do you need help with the chicken salad?" She asked.

Jack really didn't but he could tell that she was about to start her project without him. He had visions of them doing dinner together as well as her fountain. He didn't want the one time they finally had the evening alone to spend it separately.

"I'll take the chicken out of the broth to cool then come outside to watch you work your magic." He was proud of his quick thinking. He was definitely out of the habit of manipulating a situation with a woman to his advantage, though that had been a specialty in times past.

"Sounds good." Lydia answered not looking at him. Jack could tell she was more interested in her treasure than his company. For the first time in his life he wondered if a woman was attracted to him.

When he returned he found her washing the fountain pieces. She filled the tub with water then plugged up the pump. Submersing it she looked at him and smiled happily. "Still works!" Taking a tall shepherd's crook from one of her flowerbeds, she lifted the hanging begonia from it and nestled it into periwinkle ground cover. Unhappy with how it looked she turned a clay pot upside down and elevated the begonia to an area more pleasing. Removing the hanger from the pot, she seemed satisfied when delicate white flowers spilled over the sides brightening a shady corner.

"This is a practice run, so try to visualize it set up in the space between her pathway to the front porch and the carport." Pushing the shepherd's crook into the ground, she pulled the hose from the pump up and into the watering can she had hung there. Water filled the sprinkler and began to pour through the spout into the tin tub.

"WOW! That is really pretty." Jack exclaimed so enthusiastically that she tipped her head sideways to look at him.

He laughed and felt the need to explain. "No really! I LOVE that! It sounds like rain and looks great!"

She looked back at the fountain and still seemed unconvinced. "I'll put a nice fern in front of the pump so you can't tell how the water is circulating. But I need you to be honest Jack. Is this too dumb looking?" She stared at him and wondered what he was really thinking.

"I'm serious Lydia, I LOVE it! I want one for my rooftop patio at home. It's so soothing. My mom would love it!"

She spoke without thinking. "You live with your mother?"

Jack laughed so hard that she laughed too. "NO. I DO NOT LIVE WITH MY MOTHER. Sheesh! What kind of man do you think I am?" He was still laughing.

"Well… I didn't know… you seem awfully… domestic." Now she was smiling mischievously.

"Domestic?! What a thing to say!" Jack was actually a little hurt, until she added, "In a ruggedly handsome kind of way." She smiled at him and he nearly melted.

Quickly changing the subject she asked, "So how would a manly man who knows how to do all kinds of things keep the watering can tipped at the correct angle?" Her attention had returned to the fountain.

He stepped over closer really hoping he had a solution. Otherwise he could lose his man card as quickly as it had been granted. "Maybe if we put something here… hmmm. Do you have electrical tape?"

She walked inside and checked the same junk drawer where they'd had earlier success.

"Yep." She returned and handed it to him with a smile. "And it's black like the shepherd's crook so maybe it won't show." She stood close and watched holding the can while he worked. When he finished she was very pleased that the bottom edge of the sprinkler rested easily on the head of a screw he had pulled from his pocket.

"Cool! Way to improvise! I love it!" She held a hand up to high five him. He had something more romantic in mind, but gladly accepted her praise.

Together they stood watching the fountain for a minute then headed into the kitchen to pull chicken from the bone. As they sat at the table Jack started laughing. "See this bag?" He pulled a small paper sack from the cavity of the chicken. "You're supposed to remove that before stewing. That's where they tuck the gizzard and liver and such." He turned the plate and reached into the top of the chicken cavity as well. "And this… is the neck."

"Oops. I did not know that." Lydia smiled and laughed softly. "Is it ruined?"

"No… we'll strain the broth anyway to get the peppercorns out." Jack looked into her innocent eyes.

"Well I'm glad at least one of us is domestic." She smiled at him again thankful that she hadn't completely messed up a whole chicken.

Once they deboned the chicken he set about chopping celery and walnuts and slicing grapes in half. She stood beside him at the kitchen counter stirring it all together as he tossed things into the big bowl. Once the mayo was added plus salt and pepper he took a fork and offered her a taste.

"Oh wow… that's really good." She was glad when he took a clean fork to get his own sample. She was not a fan of double dipping. "Do you think it needs more grapes… or mayonnaise?" he asked.

She pulled another fork from the drawer and tasted it again. She liked how close he stood to her. "I think it's perfect just the way it is." She looked at him and felt her face flush so she turned away to gather plates. "Do we need crackers or bread? Whatcha thinkin' there handsome?" She spoke the words before she thought then realized she'd often said the same words to her beloved Blue. How had those words tumbled out of her mouth?!

Jack laughed and said, "Whatever you prefer Dearheart." He didn't seem to notice how uncomfortable she'd just made herself. Gazing into an upper cabinet he found a box of Townhouse. "These are my personal favorites. Very buttery!"

They sat at the table and he suddenly took her hand and bowed his head. "Thank You Lord… just thank You. Amen." He purposely let go before she had time to pull away. "Mmm… this is pretty good if I do say so myself! Not bad for a man who obviously lives with his mother."

Suddenly Lydia was comfortable again. And the chicken salad was definitely the best she'd ever tasted. She went to the refrigerator and poured Jack a tall glass of lemonade and water for herself.

"You are so disciplined, drinking water all the time. I wish I could get used to doing that." Jack complimented her as he took a long drink. "But I have to say that as long as you have lemonade, there is no way I'm passing it up! I need your recipe."

She was glad they were back to normal again so she felt comfortable teasing. "Can't give it to you."

"Why not? Is it an old family secret?" Jack actually wanted to know how she made it. "Are you sure you can't share it? Surely we're close enough to divulge our innermost secrets now." He tested the waters to see how she'd react.

She smiled and answered, "My family secrets have nothing to do with lemonade. Believe me… you don't ever want to get caught up in that crapstorm." She looked at her plate and he wondered what in the world she was inferring.

Her phone buzzed in her pocket and she praised God for the rescue. When she looked at the name on the screen she hit ignore and put her phone away.

Jack really wanted the night to go well, but he also wanted her to let him into her world. Surely she was ready by now. How many weeks had it been that they'd shared meals and laughter and smiles?

He waited a bit then spoke. "May I ask what went on at the diner today? Are you dating that guy that was holding your hands?"

She looked at her plate and tried to swallow. "I don't date Jack." She couldn't think of what else to say. He couldn't just leave it like that so he tried again.

"So… the very well dressed attractive young man who looked into your eyes and held your hand in the diner today is just a… friend?"

She laughed and actually looked at him. "Would you like his number?"

Jack had to laugh at that too. "I don't know. Does he live with his mother?"

Lydia laughed easily then added, "His name is Tate. Well… that's his last name. He sells property so we end up working together off and on when I'm not tied up on a huge project like the current one. He hires me to add curb appeal. It was time to have that 'Let's just be friends' talk. I'm not into dating and he kinda won't leave me alone about it."

"Would you like me to speak to him for you?" Jack asked and for some reason it made Lydia laugh again.

"Nooo… I spoke to him. He'll let it go when he realizes I'm not going to answer when he calls anymore."

Jack looked at her wondering whether to be glad that she had dumped the guy or sad that she actually had a no dating policy.

"Sooo… why don't you date? I mean… what if a really nice guy wanted to get to know you better? What should he do about that?" Jack was hoping he hadn't just ruined their evening.

She looked into his eyes with warmth he hadn't seen before and said, "If it ain't broke then why fix it?"

Jack tipped his head and looked at her wondering. "You mean spending time together without all that silly kissing and hugging? Cause there's just no need in getting all hot and sweaty before going to bed."

Her mouth dropped open and she smacked him on the arm. At least she was laughing. "You're embarrassing me. I think it's time for you to leave!"

She rose to escort him to the door but he stood and pulled her close. With his arms around her waist he didn't try to kiss her, but held her to himself stroking her back until she relaxed. He loved the fragrance of her hair and the nearness of her body. Finally she rested her head on his shoulder and held him as well for a moment. Feeling the tears coming she pulled away and patted him on the chest.

"See you tomorrow Jack." She did her best to smile.

He wondered at her tears as he let go and walked toward the front door. They stood on the front porch and he said softly, "Thanks for having me over Lydia."

She couldn't answer. Jack stopped and asked, "So does this mean my calls will go straight to voice mail from now on?"

She swiped at a tear and whispered. "Not a chance."

When he stopped his truck to look back at her one more time the tears poured freely. Oh how she missed her beloved Blue. But could it really be time to move on?

Chapter 14

The new landscaping Lydia's crew had worked so hard on was fading fast. If she kept watering it Denise's bill would be sky high since she depended on city water. But if Lydia left it unwatered all their hard work could literally turn to dust. Deep in thought she stood surveying the front yard. Jack spoke to her from behind making her jump.

"I'm sorry," he said laughing. "I wasn't trying to sneak up on you. You sure were lost in thought." He was still laughing.

She sighed deeply. "I'm worried Jack."

He thought about pulling her close and assuring that whatever was troubling her could certainly be handled better if she had a man like him in her life.

Instead he asked, "What's wrong?"

"It hasn't rained in weeks. I've had to turn the sprinklers on a couple nights in a row just to keep things alive. If I keep doing that her water bill is going to be outrageous. I don't know what to do." She looked at him truly worried. "I don't want to burden Denise but I sure hate for everything to die when this project is over."

Jack stood too close which of course set Lydia to blushing. Why did she find it so hard to talk with this handsome man who made her laugh? As long as they were working near her crew or sharing lunch with the guys she found it easy to be herself. But this one on one sharing made her terribly self-conscious. Again she wondered what was wrong with her.

She moved away and pointed out crispy leaves on some of the hosta as Jack followed. He still stood closer than she was comfortable with. Suddenly she was terribly hot and felt faint. He was speaking but she didn't hear.

"Do this. Water everything as much as you need to and I'll make sure to pay her water bill after this is over." She wasn't looking at him so he touched her elbow and turned his head trying to get her attention. "Okay Lydia?"

She seemed startled at his touch.

"Are you okay?" he asked. "You seem awfully distracted this afternoon."

"Sorry Jack. What did you say? Water it?" she tried to answer.

"What's wrong Lydia? Have I missed something?" He hoped he hadn't somehow hurt her feelings.

Finally she spoke and moved slowly away. "I think I need to take a break."

He took her elbow and tried to walk her toward the house. "Let's get you inside to cool off. Do you have water nearby? This heat is terrible."

"Could you walk me to my truck? I left my water there. My legs are so weak. I probably just got too hot." She wasn't looking at him but was glad when he took her arm. When they reached her old Chevy she pulled the beach towel over the driver's seat and got in. Jack closed her door, walked around and slid into the passenger side. He was glad she'd parked under a big shade tree. He handed her the monogramed cup of ice water she'd left there a few minutes earlier after lunch.

"Sip slowly," he advised.

She did then leaned forward onto the steering wheel with her head on her hands. Instinctively he reached over and rubbed her back. He was glad that she didn't jump. Instead she seemed to relax.

Her back was killing her. But his touch… his care for her… for a moment she thought of how good it would be to have him stay. His caress was definitely doing something to her wounded soul.

Suddenly she felt it as the old beach towel filled with blood. She caught her breath and spoke sharply.

"Get out Jack." She hadn't meant to sound harsh, but she could not let him see it. She would die. Her crazy body would go for months not having a regular period then the flood gates would open completely unexpected. It had probably been six months since the last one.

Jack sat there stunned. "Lydia! Are you having a miscarriage? Let me get you to the hospital!"

"Get out Jack. I'll be fine. Please… just get out." If she didn't get moving soon she'd be too weak to drive.

Jack sounded stern as he answered, "No! I'll drive you to the hospital. Slide over here, I'm coming around!" With that he was out of the truck which gave her the moment she needed to start the engine and put it in gear. Thankfully he had shut his door but he was already around to the driver side. She spoke to him as gently as she could. "Jack… just tell my boys I wasn't feeling well and left for the day. I'll be fine."

"Lydia please let me get you to a doctor. You should not go through this alone!" Jack was pleading with her and obviously didn't get it.

"Dammit Jack! It's just my stupid cycle for crying out loud. There'd have to be sex to have a miscarriage, okay?" With that she peeled out of the yard leaving a cloud of dust and a very nice man standing helplessly watching her leave.

On the way home she realized that he thought she was the type woman who would sleep around. Apparently the continual gossip in town had reached the guys from New York.

"Whatever," she decided. She'd learned in sixth grade to accept the label "Trailer Trash."

~~~~~~~

When she finally got home she thought she might die and wished she'd hurry up. The shower outside helped some but her back hurt exactly like the miscarriage she'd had early in her marriage. Memories of that terrible day also flooded her soul. She stood sobbing as the hot water pounded her body. Why had she dared to hope? Jack had seemed different than the local yokels. Why did others always assume she was trashy? She'd only had one lover in her life and he was her husband. She looked at the wedding band on her hand and kissed it as she had every day for the last seven years.

"Sorry Blue. I should've never given the guy a thought. I only liked him because he reminded me of the best of you."

59

It was true. Jack treated her gently, never supposing that because she worked hard physically that she wasn't a woman. He respected her opinion and complimented her work. And really even a few minutes earlier he'd just wanted to take care of her even if he did assume the worst.

She saw her phone light up on the shower bench. It was Jack. She'd have to deal with him if and when she ever turned the water off. The pain was nearly unbearable. For such a "strong self-sufficient woman" it sure didn't take much to knock her off her feet. If she didn't long to have children at some point down the road she'd just have surgery to take care of all that mess.

She was startled to hear a truck pull into her drive and right up next to the shower. One of her boys was probably worried. She'd never left a job without telling them why. She turned off the water and grabbed a towel. Thankfully the door was latched. However, she just then realized she did not have clothes in the shower with her.

"Lydia?"

It was Jack's voice.

"Yes?" she answered.

"Are you okay?" he asked quietly.

"Yes," was her firm reply.

"I'm going to wait on the front porch until you finish. Then I need to talk to you."

"Crap," she whispered louder than she meant.

"I heard that." he actually laughed.

"Sorry." she sighed. "Go to the porch please. Then let me know when you're there."

"How shall I do that Dearheart?" There was a smile in his voice.

"Perhaps you could call from there with your big man voice so that I can tell that you are not standing in view of the shower."

She turned the water back on. "It might be a while. You don't have to stay if you don't have time."

Jack called to her from somewhere toward the front of the house. "I can't hear you. I'm on the front porch."

She laughed weakly and finished. Wrapping the towel back around her she unlatched the shower door and peeked out. Creeping into the house through the back door she dressed as quickly as she could in cut-offs and a t-shirt. Walking through to the front porch she found him there on the swing. He stood up and looked at her with those eyes as he spoke.

"I owe you a big apology. Can you please forgive me?" He stood with his hands in his pockets and reminded her of a little boy.

"It's okay Jack. I didn't mean to sound so ugly to you." She was still in so much pain she thought she might cry. "Come on in and let's grab some lemonade. I need to take a handful of painkillers.

He surprised her by taking her into his arms and holding her for a bit. She liked it but wasn't sure. She still didn't know this man very well and he certainly didn't know her or he wouldn't be holding her.

When she didn't return his embrace Jack thought maybe he'd completely blown it. But then she smiled weakly and said, "There might be chocolate chip cookies too if you're into that sort of thing."

He found the lemonade and cookies as she searched the medicine cabinet in the bathroom. When she returned with only one pill he asked, "I thought you were going to take a couple. Are you out?"

"I am. But maybe one is all I need." She knew better.

"As soon as I give you my speech I'll go to the drugstore." He poured her a glass of ice water and led her to the daybed. Then he really surprised her by grabbing pillows from the wicker furniture and stacking them on one end. "Lie back and put your legs up. Keep these under your knees and that might take some of the pressure off your back. Do you have a heating pad?" He lifted her legs onto the cushions.

She felt her neck getting very red. She was sure glad she'd taken time to shave her legs the night before. Who was this man and how did he know these things? He seemed to read her mind when he answered, "My poor sister Julie has a terrible time every month."

Lydia laughed and started to remind him again that he was quite domestic. Instead she asked, "So what's the speech? Or you can just save it and I'll call Kurtis to make the drugstore run."

"No no! This is a very good speech. I worked on it all the way here." Jack smiled and pulled the ottoman near the daybed. He sat down and began his rehearsed apology. "I know you said everything's okay, but it's not. I need you to know that I have never thought anything but good wholesome pure thoughts about you." He paused. "Except maybe for that time I drove up to Norma's and you were standing there in your cute little cut-offs and tank top spraying yourself with water. Mercy! I thought I had died and gone to country music video heaven. But anyway, I think you are a very nice lady and I really want to get to know you better. However there's this dilemma." He paused and tried to remember exactly how he wanted to put things.

"I've been trying to ask you out, but just the other day I overheard Shawn tell a ruggedly handsome man that you do not date under any circumstances. He made it very clear that you would keep a great gulf fixed between you and any man who dared broach the subject. So I, being the honorable church going man that I am, decided to be very careful not to push you away. But the more I've prayed diligently about this decision the more I'm inclined to believe that by doing so, we are both missing a chance to enjoy a very special… deep… personal…" He struggled and couldn't think of the word he'd so carefully planned.

"Friendship?" she asked.

"Friendship! Yes! That's the deep personal word I was searching for. Because relationship might sound too… you know…"

"Deep and personal?" she asked smiling this time.

"Exactly! So for now your new best friend Jack shall retrieve the Advil from the closest market. And since I know where the spare keys are I shall take them with me. You won't even have to rise to let me in." He was still speaking very proper in his nervous mostly prepared speech. It seemed to be going well but he couldn't be sure. He was relieved when she spoke.

"You're right. That was an excellent speech. I just hate that Shawn scared that other guy off. Say he was ruggedly handsome?" Her eyes twinkled with mischief.

"Oh… words cannot describe! But in lieu of him, I shall have to stand in. Need anything before I leave?"

"Not a thing. Thank you. But do lock the door." She was still wigged out by the noise they'd both heard.

She tossed the sheet over her legs suddenly chilled. Jack wondered how she needed covers since it was at least a hundred and ten in there even with all the windows open and the ceiling fans going. But he helped spread the sheet over her feet and turned to go. "Oh. Do you have a heating pad?"

"Nope." She relaxed, closed her eyes and hoped the cramping would ease off soon. That one little brown Ibuprofen was not touching the pain.

Chapter 15

Jack found the closest drugstore which was no small feat. His quest took him in the opposite direction from where he'd come and into another county. But he was rewarded with not only a heating pad but also Advil gel caps which his sister had sent him searching for many nights. He hoped they would help Lydia. He might even convince her to let him cook dinner. As he thought about it he decided not to ask. He pulled into a Food Lion and picked out the meal. Farther down he found fresh peaches at a roadside stand. A jar of money stood guard marked "honor system." Apparently he was to place the cash in the jar and take the produce he needed.

"Gotta love the South," he smiled.

When he returned to her farm he found the daybed empty. She called from the bathroom, "Jack?"

"Yes dear?" he called back. When she didn't answer he realized he was sort of making himself at home. He wondered if she'd appreciate his taking charge as he tried to help or if she'd slap his face. He'd garnered both reactions from women in times past and Lydia intimidated him more than any woman he'd ever known except for his mother.

When she came from the bathroom through the kitchen she noticed he was trying to start a pan of oil for frying. "That burner doesn't work. Neither does the back right one. But both left ones do. Were you able to find a drugstore? I forgot to tell you that it's actually closer to go the opposite way into the next county."

Her eyes were surrounded by dark circles and her hair had been twirled into sort of a bird nest. She reached into the refrigerator for the pitcher of water.

"I did!" he said as he switched on the left front burner. "Those gelcaps work better than anything else Julie has found, even prescription. There's a heating pad plugged up waiting for you. I'll have dinner ready in about forty-five minutes." He moved the frying pan to a working burner as she walked toward him.

He had a feeling she was about to fish or cut bait.

She reached out and gave him side hug. "Thank you Jack. And I have to say…" She walked away but added, "You're a little bit ruggedly handsome." She smiled back at him as she went to the daybed.

~~~~~~~

He was right about the gelcaps. She'd never had anything work that well. She actually felt like sitting at the table and eating the nice meal he prepared.

"These are wonderful. What are they?" She loved the taste but had never had anything quite like it."

"They're homemade eggrolls. It's simple really. Something I made up on the fly. There's sausage and mushrooms and spinach and cream cheese in an eggroll wrapper. It only takes a few minutes to fry them once you figure out which burner works." He smiled as he dipped his into a sauce.

"What's the sauce?" She was completely amazed at the flavorful combination. Surely he didn't just make that up on the fly.

"The sauce is orange marmalade and brown mustard. Do you like it?"

"Oh my word Jack! Where'd you learn to cook like this?" She was glad the cramping had eased off so she could enjoy the food.

"I finally got hungry enough to start trying my hand in the kitchen. Of course the cooking channel doesn't hurt. I can always get ideas from there."

"There's a cooking channel?" She shook her head. She didn't even own a television.

After dinner he cleared the table. "Hey Jack?" she called.

"Yes dear?" he slung the dishtowel over his shoulder and began filling the sink.

"I don't feel like doing dishes and I can't let you do them for me. So can we just sit out back before you have to leave? I don't want you rolling out of here after dark." She was being honest. He kinda looked like he was moving in and it scared her a bit.

"It won't take but a second and I'll have the kitchen clean for you." He added plates to the soapy water splashing suds on the floor. He opened cabinets looking for paper towels. Instead he found a basket of clean up rags under the sink and began wiping up the suds.

"Jack?" she asked trying to be kind.

He turned and saw the look. Putting the towel on the stove handle he dried his hands and walked toward her. "Sorry. I was on a mission. I want you to be able to rest and feel better and I thought it would be hard for you to do that without a tidy kitchen. I tend to make a pretty big mess."

She looked at him with a look he hadn't seen before. "I will gladly trade a clean kitchen for time outside please."

Extending his arm he walked her through the sunroom onto the back deck.

She spoke softly to the man with the eyes that made her heart do weird things. "The sun will be setting shortly. A breeze kicks up about this time in the evening so it will be pleasant out here in a few minutes." She smiled at him as they pulled a couple white plastic chairs from the deck into the grassy backyard. The view down the hill toward the pond was still pretty considering they'd had no rain. A large weeping willow leaned heavily over the south end of the water and for a moment she could picture Blue as he planted it for her. It had grown so tall and graceful branches spilled bright green all around like a fountain. She heard the honking overhead and pointed upward. On cue about a dozen Canada geese flew over in formation and landed gracefully on the pond. She noticed Jack was still sweating from cooking and was glad that the air began to stir.

"That feels good," he said with a sigh. "How do you get used to this heat?"

"It's one of those Southern things. I sure hope we get some rain soon or Denise's yard is going to be toast." She pulled a band from her hair and shook it loose. "Oh! Feel that? Maybe a storm is brewing!" She spoke as if it would be wonderful.

He longed to pull her into his arms but knew better. She reminded him of the deer he'd passed on his way back from the drugstore, observing with caution ready to bound into the woods. He watched as she twisted her hair back up.

"Don't plan on coming in tomorrow Lydia. It won't kill the guys to work without you." Jack leaned over trying to get her to look at him.

She wouldn't return his gaze. Of course she planned to work. She was feeling better all ready. Besides, no telling what mayhem would happen without her there to keep things in check. She didn't much like Jack instructing her as to what she should do.

He could tell he'd crossed the line again. "Sorry Lydia. I don't know why I get so protective. Sometimes I think it's about having a little sister." He finally looked away and fell silent.

She wondered why they couldn't just sit and watch the sunset without all the words. She stole a glance at him and realized he looked rather dejected. Why did she have to be so dang hardheaded anyway? What was she afraid of?

Love?

Maybe it was because he reminded her of Blue. He too could get pretty bossy and protective. Sometimes she felt smothered, but at least she'd never wondered if she were loved.

Finally she broke the silence.

"Sorry Jack. I think I've been a hermit so long that I'm socially inept. And Shawn is correct. I don't date so frankly this new friendship we're forming feels weird to me. I can't help it. I am a redneck bumpkin who hasn't a clue!" She laughed hoping he would too, but he didn't.

"Careful pretty lady. You are talking about a close personal friend of mine!"

With that he rose and said, "I hope I don't see you tomorrow."

She stood as well and asked, "Where you going? The sun hasn't set." She was surprised he was leaving without being told.

"You said you wanted me to roll out of here before dark. I'm just trying to be a good boy."

Crap! She thought.

Jack noticed her look of disappointment. Stepping near he circled her waist looking into her eyes until finally she looked up at him. Leaning down he kissed her lightly.

"Good night Dearheart. Sleep well."

Her heart pounded and her face flushed as she thought,

Lord have mercy.

Chapter 16

The cramping lasted all night especially every four hours when the Advil wore off. She lay awake thinking of Jack wondering if he'd ever been married. Surely a man like him had not stayed single that long.

A man like what?

She wondered at her own question. A man as sensitive as Blue but who could also cook; a man with such a great sense of humor who got her weird jokes and laughed freely; a man as handsome as her beautiful Blue, but like him didn't seem to have a speck of vanity. If he got up the nerve to ask her, she would definitely consider breaking her no dating policy. She might even consider breaking a few other rules as well.

But since she'd sent him home before dark, she probably wouldn't have to worry about it. She gave up trying to rest. He'd been right. That kitchen mess was driving her crazy. She got up about three in the morning and cleaned it all up. Another dose of Advil and the cramping slowed to a minimum. Finally she relaxed on the daybed falling into a deep restful sleep. The next time she realized she was in the world was about eight thirty; over two hours past her normal arrival to work.

She thought about calling Jack, but again it felt weird. It wasn't like he was her boss, although technically he was. Looking at her phone she pulled up his number then changed her mind. Why should she call? What could she say? She hated talking on the phone almost as much as she hated shopping. Maybe she'd text him.

"Good Morning Jack." She took it out and started over. "Slept well. Thanks for everything." Nope. She backed that message out also. What if someone saw that and read into it things she didn't mean.

Finally she sent a text that she felt kinda good about. She hoped he'd like it.

~~~~~~~

When she didn't show up for work Jack was completely surprised. He wondered if she had gotten worse or if she was just so mad at him that she was forming a great gulf betwixt them as Shawn had warned. She hadn't pulled away from his kiss though. He smiled recalling her hair when she shook it loose. How good she felt in his arms… and that kiss.

He thought about calling her but he was already pushing the limits. Plus she might be sleeping like he'd suggested.

No, that's the least likely scenario.

So when he got a text from her about a quarter til nine he nearly laughed out loud. It simply said,

"Day trip 2 beach w/ BFF next Saturday?"

Jack smiled so big his brother asked him about it.

"Just a text from a friend," he smiled happily.

"Umm hmmm… a red headed foxy friend?" Johnny was truly happy for his brother.

~~~~~~~

She still felt terrible but usually could push through the pain on the second day. This time seemed a lot worse. Maybe it was the heat or more likely because she'd worked so hard on the landscaping at Denise's. She'd done her best to outshine any other company the Stephens brothers had used before. She really wanted them to be proud of her work when it was finished.

Once she decided to get dressed and go in, she realized that the load of laundry which contained every pair of work jeans she owned had been left in the washer since she got home the day before. Opening the lid a very foul odor greeted her there. "Gross," she mumbled closing the lid. They were soured from the heat. Switching the wash to hot water and adding more detergent she searched her room for something appropriate to work in around the guys.

She sighed as there was nothing left. Her back was hurting so bad that she decided maybe it was a sign. Perhaps she should take the day off. Right on cue her phone buzzed.

"Hey Kurtis honey. Everything okay?" she asked.

"Yep. Just checking on you. How's the cramps? You feeling any better?" He inquired as if it were regular chitchat.

She could've died. How dare Jack inform them of her personal issues?

"So Jack's filled everyone in?" She was mad.

"Nah. I haven't seen Jack. I just know that if you stay out of work it's because of girl stuff. Hey what're you planning about that fountain? You still thinkin' about adding that?"

She didn't know whether to be glad he didn't hear it from Jack or aggravated that Kurt knew her personal calendar better than she did.

"Liddy?" Kurtis was waiting on an answer about the fountain.

"Yep. Let's do it. But the stuff I plan to use is here at the house. I think I'm going to hang around here today. I'll bring it tomorrow. How's the last of the walkway coming? Were y'all able to get it good and level?"

"Yep. You'll be proud of us. We're almost done. I just wanted to check before we put in the pavers at that end. We're going to have to bury the electrical for the fountain somewhere."

"Ohhh… that's right. Good catch. I'll come on in so I can look at it." She was glad they needed her but still wondered what she could wear. Often she'd lamented that she'd rather go butt naked than to shop for clothes. She might have to eat those words.

~~~~~~~

She heard the washer finish so she tossed the jeans in a basket and headed out to the clothesline. That stupid basket was heavy. Her back reminded her again why she was home. But if she could get the jeans hung out maybe a pair would be dry by lunch.

As she also hung the clean beach towel she was reminded of her skirmish with Jack. How quickly he'd forgiven her even though she'd yelled AND cussed. Then she'd reprimanded him for trying to clean her kitchen… AFTER he'd cooked supper.

What a man. How quickly she'd assumed the worst about him again while talking with Kurt. What in the world was she thinking? She recalled his gentle kiss and smiled. How long had it been since anyone had held her? It felt really good. But he'd be gone soon. Her heart hurt at the thought.

Maybe she should pay more attention to him before he had to leave. Their little day trip to the beach might be just what the doctor ordered. She and the boys often took off on Saturdays driving the four hours there just for the surf. She hoped Jack would feel the journey was worth it.

Her phone buzzed.

"What's up Shawn?"

"Hey Liddy. You alright?" Shawn was never much of a conversationalist. He and Lydia understood each other with very few words.

"Yep." she answered.

"Just checkin' on ya. Need anything from the store? I'll send Kurt. He knows about girl stuff."

Lydia sighed. Apparently everyone knew about girl stuff but her.

"I'm good," she sighed.

"Alright." With that he was gone.

She searched her dresser for something she could just throw on to run by the job. Already ten-thirty the day was mostly spent. If she waited til those jeans dried she wouldn't accomplish anything.

Do the best you can with what you've got and forget about the rest.

The words of her mother came as she dug through the clothes that had been there since high school. She pulled on one pair of shorts after another; on and off feeling somehow too exposed.

Finally dressed she sighed. "Holy cow woman! You have done added some poundage!"

She tried stretching the V-neck Carolina shirt so it wouldn't be quite as clingy. A pair of blue plaid shorts would have to do.

She sighed as she looked into the dresser mirror. She couldn't see the bottom half of her body so she tried standing on a footstool. She wasn't sure but she thought she was okay. She didn't like showing her legs unless she was at the beach. She stepped off the stool and took her hair down from the night time pony tail.

Why did she care what she looked like all of a sudden?

Whatever. He can like me or he doesn't have to.

She tossed the things for the fountain into her truck then covered the driver's side with a clean towel. Someday she might splurge on a seat cover. But for now this would be fine not only to cover the torn vinyl but also to keep her legs from scorching on the hot seat.

Settling in she realized that same hot seat felt really good on her back, but not nearly as good as when Jack had stroked it while she was in so much pain. She sat still for a moment remembering his gentle touch. Perhaps she could warm up to his deep personal friendship after all. She smiled at the memory of his funny speech… and that kiss.

Driving by Denise's she was disappointed that Jack and her boys weren't there. Apparently they'd taken an early lunch.

When the cat's away… she mused.

Chapter 17

"Whoa… Carolina girl…"

Jack looked up seconds after the guy at the next table commented to his cohort. Lydia walked through the door and smiled that beautiful smile. It seemed to be for him he thought. What a difference a day had made! Her blue eyes sparkled and her hair fell all around like a Pantene commercial. She took his breath away. He slid down to let her into the booth.

"I see we're dining early today." Lydia sat by Jack and was glad he'd made room.

Kurtis commented, "You look like you feel better. Did you bring the stuff for the fountain?"

"Yep. That's the reason I'm here." Lydia hoped the subject of her physical well-being would not become a lunchtime topic with the four men at the table.

Shawn noticed the guys beside them were still looking at her so he delivered his famous death stare. Jack knew it well but this time he appreciated it.

Ann stepped up and commented as she brought the guys' food, "Lord have mercy honey. You trying to start a riot? Whatcha havin' today?"

Lydia wondered about her comment and ordered a footlong hotdog, all the way without onions. Jack had come to understand that a hotdog "all the way" in North Carolina meant mustard, chili, slaw and onions. He'd quickly acquired a taste for the same and had just received one minus onions. He took a plastic knife and cut the footlong in the middle, sliding one half toward Lydia on the paper wrapper. "You owe me," he smiled at her.

"Yes I do," she smiled back. "So how's it going?" Lydia looked at her guys and Johnny who was grinning like a mule eatin' briars. "Did you remember to soak all the plants last night?"

"Yep." Shawn answered between bites of his hamburger.

"It's looking a lot better," added Kurtis. "If we can start that fountain after lunch we'll be almost finished. I know you're not doing well so you just tell us where you want things and we'll do the rest."

There was that subject again. She could feel her face flushing. "Sounds good. Shawn how's your burger?" She tried to redirect the topic of conversation.

Shawn and Kurt looked at her wondering. Shawn spoke up and said, "Same as every other day. Mustard, chili and white slaw. Only I'm not planning on kissing anybody so mine's got onions." He shot a glance at Jack.

Once again Lydia could've died. Johnny laughed out loud. Right on cue Ann delivered another hotdog with an announcement. "Footlong, no onions divided in half for the lovebirds. Enjoy yourselves."

Lydia looked down hoping her neck wouldn't show.

Jack winked at Ann hoping her words would come true.

~~~~~~~

As they finished up Jack announced that he'd be riding with Lydia as they needed to think about the logistics of the fountain together. He picked up her ticket and left a tip as they took their monogrammed go cups. Lydia felt they were somehow suddenly a couple.

Weird. Seems like just yesterday we became close friends.

"Want me to drive?" Jack asked as they approached her truck.

She wondered what he was thinking as she replied. "I got it."

She forgot to spread the beach towel before she got in. "Yeow! That seat is hot!" She jumped back out and straightened the towel. "I'm not used to driving in shorts," she laughed.

Jack was already in the passenger side and helped with the towel. "You look fantastic." He tried not to smile too big and he really tried not to look at her legs. So her words startled him.

"I know we're not supposed to lust and all... but there's something I want you to see." She paused just long enough for him to wonder where she was headed. Hands down she was the most modest chick he'd ever met. She turned onto a road behind town and pulled into a yard full of stuff. Sometimes it was hard to tell if someone was having a yard sale, as they called them down there, or if it was just how they lived. But the whole area looked rough. A bluetick hound came bellowing from behind the house as Lydia parked and looked at Jack.

"Can you play along for a minute? I haven't been brave enough to come down here by myself."

Jack could certainly understand that. He wondered what made her brave enough to come then.

A man lifted himself slowly from a metal chair which used to be green. He raised a hand toward her.

"Hey little lady. What can I do ye for?" He smiled a greasy smile.

Lydia slid out of the seat and tossed the beach towel back through the open window. "I noticed that old Camaro back there and wondered if you'd ever thought of getting rid of it?"

He spit a stream of tobacco juice to the side and wiped his mouth with the back of his hand. "Uh..."

He was pondering. "Ah hain't never thought 'bout it..."

"Is it a '68?" she asked. "It looks longer than a '67..."

Jack wondered what he was doing there and hoped the dog sniffing at his leg was not about to enjoy lunch at his expense. It suddenly stuck its snout into Lydia's crotch from behind. Without thinking she knocked it silly.

The old guy didn't seem to notice. Jack praised God that no construction workers were harmed in the making of that particular scene.

"I'll 'ave to talk to my boy and git back to ya. It's his prah-jeck. I had it since it wuz new. It's a '67. We need to get it to a barn so it don't keep rustin' out chere in the yard like 'at. Gimme your number an' my son'll give ye a holler." The old guy motioned them into the house.

"We can't stay… got to get back to work. Here's my husband's business card. Give him a call if you ever decide to sell."

Jack followed her lead and handed the guy his card. "Thanks man. I'd love to restore this for my wife. She's is such a sweetheart!" He suddenly pulled Lydia next to his side and kissed her on the cheek.

The old guy laughed, "I hear ya. Y'all stop by any time. Maybe my boy'll be here. He got 'em a big ol' camper van so he might be willin' to part wid dis un now."

Jack let go of Lydia's waist and wondered why he kept pushing her. She obviously was not enjoying his playfulness.

Lydia walked over to the old Camaro and lifted the tarp daring to dream.

Back in the truck she was rather quiet Jack thought. He tried again not to look at her legs and remembered her earlier comment.

"So when do we get to the lusting part?" He was careful not to look down. Thankfully she laughed.

"You missed it? Back there was the lusting part." She smiled then explained. "I'm a sucker for old vehicles, especially a '67 Camaro. That's what Blue and I got married in."

She stopped speaking and blushed suddenly worse than ever. She stammered as she tried to explain. "Beep beep beep. Back the Camaro up. We got married in a CHURCH. We drove a Camaro before and after. Good Lord I am a mess today."

She laughed nervously and he sensed that was a cover for the pain she still carried from the loss of her husband. He understood. He'd have a hard time too if he ended up without her.

~~~~~~~

She thought of Blue and the first time she rode with him in the Camaro. He was so proud of it. Though it took them a few awkward years of dating others to eventually end up together as more than friends, some of her favorite memories with him had been made in that car. A year before he died he'd come home one day to inform her that he'd sold it. She was so mad that she said some terrible things to her quiet gentle man never giving him a chance to explain. The next day a truck pulled up to deliver windows for the sunroom he planned to build with the money he made from it. She would never forgive herself for hurting the man who loved her better than he loved his most prized possession. The sight of the old Camaro under the tarp ignited her deep longing for Blue again and she wondered what she was doing with Jack.

As they roared up to Denise's together in her old truck she realized the others had beat them back to the house. It embarrassed her to think of how it must look; she and Jack steeling away together during the day. Her back was suddenly killing her again. She'd forgotten to take anything at lunch. Opening the glove compartment she grabbed a few pills and downed them with her water.

"How many are you taking?" Jack asked. She looked at him and thought.

What business is it of yours?

Thankfully she didn't say it out loud.

"Three. Why?" She stared at him almost daring him to instruct her.

"Sweetheart those things will eat a hole in your stomach. Be careful okay?" Jack said it gently but she still didn't like it.

"Did you just call me Sweetheart?" She looked at him and turned her head sideways. "We are NOT a couple Jack."

"BEEP BEEP BEEP… back the Sweetheart Bus up! I don't know what you HEARD but what I said was… something less endearing like…" He couldn't think of anything so he just exited the truck.

She got out too and slammed the door as she murmured. "Stupid beach towel."

The godawful heat hit her like a hammer. She suddenly remembered the dog and the man with his nasty tobacco. That hotdog all the way without onions came right out.

There she stood in the road, hurling in front of God, Jack and everybody. When finally she finished, she opened the door of the truck, spread the beach towel, got in and cranked it up. Down the road she flew letting the tears pour freely. What the heck was wrong with her?

It wasn't until she hit the gravel road toward the house that she realized the fountain parts were still rolling around in the bed of the truck.

Chapter 18

Her phone didn't buzz. No text came. No one pulled up as she took the clothes from the line. She brushed her teeth and washed her face, put the laundry away and made a pitcher of lemonade. But it didn't matter because no one was there to drink it. She grabbed a bag of peas from the freezer and placed them on the back of her neck. Collapsing on the daybed she kicked the extra pillows to the floor and turned on her side the way she was used to sleeping. Her head throbbed and her back cramped and she wished she could just be done.

How could she ever move on without her beloved Blue? She'd tried to take a few steps toward that lately inviting Jack on a daytrip the next weekend, even sitting with him at the barbecue joint where everybody in Rowan County would have them married. She could just imagine the chatter. It was only a hotdog for crying out loud.

She gagged at the thought.

What possessed me to check on the Camaro today? Why didn't I ask Shawn instead of Jack? Shawn's great at sizing up vehicles and would've gladly gone. Why DID I ask Jack? Then I told him about Blue's. It seems almost... unfaithful. That's exactly what I am. Unfaithful! I'm cheating on Blue with this man who reminds me of him.

"I'm so sorry Blue." She whispered through the tears.

She kissed her wedding band and tried to sleep. Oh how she longed to join him.

~~~~~~~

Her phone buzzed and she woke hoping it was Jack. But it wasn't.

"Hey Jesse… how're you doing?" She asked in a sleepy voice.

"How's my favorite little red-haired girl next door? You don't sound very good." Jesse's deep voice as always was music to her ears.

"It's been a rough day. How do you always know when to call?" She smiled at the thought.

"Oh… I just thought I'd see if you needed anything." He waited while she tried not to cry.

After a long silence she said, "Same ol' stuff I always need."

When she couldn't continue he spoke softly, "It's been a long hard trial hasn't it?" He waited knowing she was trying to rein in her emotions. "You know I'm right next door Darlin'. I'm praying for you night and day."

All she could muster was, "Yep."

"Hang in there girl. God loves you and I do too." He waited and could hear her soft sobs.

"I don't think God even likes me, much less loves me. But at least I can always count on you Jesse-man." She hung up without saying "I love you too." Those words were reserved for only one man in her life. Unfortunately he was no longer available.

~~~~~~~

She sat outside by herself that night and watched the sun go down. It was glorious. Her daddy would've loved it. She wondered where he was and if he were looking at the sunset too. She thought about calling him but knew she'd burst into tears at the sound of his voice. He hated when she did that so she had quit calling him long ago. For a moment she remembered his care for her as a child. Though his words were rough and he never said so, she always knew she was loved. His curly black hair spilled into his sparkling blue eyes and he gazed down at her smiling. She stood on his boots and they danced in the kitchen. He had taught her to play guitar pretty good and to shoot a gun though she didn't much like it. But something changed when the cotton mill closed and he lost his job. A short while later her mama became so sick that she seldom had the strength to function. She fought hard but passed away when Lydia was just coming of age. Her father nearly grieved himself to death and began traveling for extended periods of time.

Lydia closed her eyes and recalled Blue's tender love and protection. She'd loved the boy all her life and would've married him at seven years old when he asked the first time. But they waited til she graduated high school. Though she was only eighteen and he was twenty-one, to her it felt like they had waited forever. Then five short years later he was gone.

She wondered if her father would ever forgive her. Maybe if he knew what really happened the night he caught Blue in the trailer he would understand. Instead his hate filled words still echoed causing her heart that old familiar ache. Apparently her own father believed the label the kids at school had given her.

The scent of rain floated on the gentle breeze. She prayed for it to come but knew God had no reason to answer her.

Returning to a dark house she switched on a lamp, locked her doors and toasted an eggroll in the oven. Perhaps she could take more Advil with something in her stomach. She cut back to two and drank a glass of milk thinking sarcastically, *"No need to eat a hole in my stomach!"*

Why did the man exasperate her so? And why did she keep looking at her phone hoping he would call? She sighed as she thought.

Maybe because I'm crazy.

The eggroll was really good. She heated up another and wondered if he'd still want to go next Saturday. Hopefully she could escape the emotional roller coaster by then and show him a good time before he left.

Suddenly the thought of his leaving made tears slip down her face again. She sighed and realized what a wreck she was.

~~~~~~~

She taunted him often like that. Sitting outside by herself with no fear. She would learn that she needed him. Besides that man might show up spoiling their big day. He had interfered with the plan several times lately. But it didn't matter. Waiting had become part of the fun. Watching her made him feel powerful and in control. He would start their private game again soon.

Chapter 19

Jack lay staring at the motel ceiling like he had when he'd first met her. He remembered begging God to bring them together. Perhaps he should stop begging and start listening. While Johnny snored loud enough to rattle the windows Jack whispered a prayer hoping this wasn't the end of whatever he had with Lydia.

"Lord," he began, "For a day that started so well, it sure hasn't ended great. As You know it was a tiny bit discouraging that calling the woman I love 'Sweetheart' made her throw up." He laughed. "Please help her tonight. Help her rest well and get her strength back. Protect her and send her comfort."

He paused at the thought. He would have loved to comfort her but she kept pushing him away. It made him sad to think that she'd rather be alone than to give him a chance. Never in his life had he been resisted so thoroughly. For some reason it only attracted him to her more.

"I think she's still going through a lot of grief. It will be awfully hard to walk away but I guess it would be better now than down the road when… actually I can't imagine loving her more. Please help us Lord. I love her so much already and I don't even know why." He laughed at his own honesty. "She's driving me crazy!"

~~~~~~~~

She awoke during the night to the sound of rain, wonderful rain! And not a gully washer either! It was a soft steady soaking rain. The yard would have just what it needed to settle in and thrive for Denise. It made her heart happy to think of it. Somehow it seemed God had heard the cry of her soul and come to her rescue. She kneeled by the daybed not knowing what to say, but feeling such gratitude that she just stayed there a bit finally whispering "Thank You God. That was really nice of You."

She noticed that the pain in her back had eased off as well. It was about three-thirty in the morning so she tried going back to sleep. She lay there wondering if a text would wake Jack. Texts on her phone just showed up without fanfare. She'd hate to wake him but for some reason felt an urgency about the situation.

Looking at her phone she tried to remember if she'd ever heard a text come in to his. They'd spent a lot of days together working side by side. But she couldn't be sure if a text would wake him or not. She closed her eyes and tried to sleep. The rain sounded so good that she finally drifted off.

Blue pulled her close and whispered, "Let's lie here together and listen to the rain. Isn't it wonderful?" He smoothed her back and kissed her tenderly. She looked into his eyes and saw nothing but love. He held her next to his side and stroked her hair until she relaxed and fell into a deep peaceful sleep.

The phone fell from her hand and landed on the slate floor with a clank. She sat up knowing what to do.

~~~~~~~~

Jack tried to sleep but still held onto hope. Finally he prayed again, "This is me signing off Lord. If I don't hear from her, I'll know You want me to walk away. I love her, but whatever You think."

His phone lit up with a text. "I'm sorry Sweetheart."

"Wow Lord. You're good!" Jack smiled as he took his phone to the bathroom and closed the door.

"Should I call her back Lord? It's 4:27am. But she did just text me. However I keep responding like a lovesick puppy. Should I make her wonder what I'm thinking til morning?" It was as if the Lord spoke to his heart, *"Love keeps no record of being wronged."* So he held his breath and called her.

"Good morning Lydia. Thank you for your message." Jack spoke softly into the phone.

She spoke softly too as if afraid to break the moment. "I hope I didn't wake you. Was your dinger off?"

"My what?" He smiled.

"Your dinger? Did I wake you?" She asked softly.

Between her deep southern drawl and the strange word Jack was still unsure what she was asking. So he answered, "I was actually praying for you." He was still gun shy about using the term sweetheart even though she'd seemingly just given him permission.

"You are so kind." She sounded different to him, kind of sexy. Maybe it was her sleepy voice but he liked it. He wished she would say more but he'd learned that her words were generally few. He should probably just let her get back to sleep and talk to her later. He started to say so but she surprised him.

"Do you want to come over?" She invited in her sleepy voice. It was soft and slow and he felt weak in the knees. His heart leapt in his chest and he wondered what she meant. Maybe he would just go find out.

He heard himself whisper, "I'll be there soon."

He hung up thinking his prayers had been answered but knowing his own weakness. He knew better than to go, but also knew that if he didn't it would be all over but the crying. He dressed as fast as he could then scratched a note for his brother.

"I'll be back with the truck before you need to be on site."

~~~~~~~

Lydia decided she'd been a good girl for too long. Everyone assumed she was sleeping around so why not give in to a man who obviously desired her? She wouldn't let him get that far anyway. They'd just kiss and stuff. He knew what time of the month it was so this would be a good chance to take things farther… but not all the way.

Something in her soul whispered, *"Careful Darlin'."* The voice sounded like Jesse's.

She sighed and wondered what she was thinking. The loneliness was overwhelming. Maybe it was the dream and how good it had felt to be held. Maybe it was Blue letting her know that it was okay for her to love again. Maybe it was God giving permission by allowing the desire to return. Maybe nothing would happen at all. Maybe Jack thought he was coming for pancakes.

That was a great idea! She'd make pancakes so she didn't seem desperate which suddenly she realized she was. In fact she was near panic by the time he got there.

She opened the door and smiled that beautiful smile he loved so well. Her wild curly hair spilled from where she had it gathered on top of her head and she stood there barefoot in shorts and a tank top.

"Come in out of the rain! Isn't it wonderful! I'm making pancakes."

Jack breathed a deep sigh of relief. He had a speech ready but kinda hoped he didn't have to give it. But it sure would be nice to hold her, if he hadn't completely read her wrong.

Lord help me with my promise, he prayed.

He wondered why he'd come. But one look at her and he knew exactly why he'd come.

"Just warming up the syrup and then we'll eat if you'd like. Are you hungry?" She looked at him as she stirred the syrup heating on the left front burner. He pulled her into his arms. His heart beat so wildly that he couldn't make his speech. Instead he kissed her thoroughly.

Thank You Jesus! They thought in unison.

He continued to kiss her while the syrup came to a boil and nearly poured right over the top of the pot. Reaching behind her he turned the burner off and kissed her again. He held her close and stroked her back.

"Good gracious Jack," she whispered into his neck. "You ARE a deep close personal friend." Jack laughed then led her to the table where the pancakes waited.

"Syrup Sweetheart?" He thought it might be safe to call her that.

"Yes please." She gazed into his eyes trying hard to remember why they were wasting time on pancakes.

Jack completely surprised her when he took her hand in his, kissed it and then bowed his head. "Thank You Lord. Thank You for answering my prayer."

She didn't bow because she couldn't take her eyes off him. When he looked up he asked her simply, "How does it feel to be an answer to prayer?"

"What in the world are you talking about?" She tipped her head and looked at him with new eyes.

"I was just about to give up on us so I asked God to have you get in touch with me. Your text came to me before I said 'Amen.'"

"No it did not…" She couldn't believe it.

"Oh but it did. Have you ever texted someone that time of day? The Lord has a plan dear Lydia. And I'm pretty sure it includes us!" He leaned over and kissed her again for good measure. She didn't pull away at all. Instead she wrapped her arms around his neck and whispered softly. "Jack honey, I'm sorry for being so hateful."

He smiled loving how near she stayed. "You called me honey and I like it!" He whispered as he kissed her neck and rubbed her back. "Only when you say it, it sounds like huuunnney."

Then pulling back he added, "While these might be the very best pancakes I've ever had in my life, I'm going to leave now so that you don't come to your senses in about an hour and wonder why you invited me over. Before this goes any farther dear woman, you've got to know in your heart that…" He swallowed hard before he said it, "I happen to love you very much."

He kissed her again then added as he rose from the table, "And that is the ONLY reason I am leaving."

He rose and walked out the front door. She stood on the porch watching him run to his truck through the downpour. The rain hit the tin roof in thunderous applause. He stopped the truck and looked at her again.

For the first time in a long while they each felt very loved.

~~~~~~~

Jack slipped back into the motel room and Johnny never moved. He was glad for that. It was still too early and he knew his brother wouldn't understand.

As he sat at the small table with his coffee and his Bible open he found the passage in 1 Corinthians 13, the love chapter. Beside it he marked the date and prayed again for Lydia.

My beloved Lydia.

The thought made his heart happy though he knew they had a long way to go and a lot to work through. But God's answer to his prayer by way of her text confirmed what he'd known in his heart from early on. She was someone very special and worth the wait. If only he could stay strong.

Chapter 20

As Lydia tossed the pancakes into the compost bowl she sent texts to Shawn and Kurtis giving them the day off since it was raining. Poor Jack. Those pancakes were awful and the syrup had scorched. Yet he referred to them as the best he'd ever had in his life. Bless his heart. She laughed as she realized he was just being kind.

With a hot cup of coffee in hand she headed to the front porch to watch it rain. She wasn't sure if there was anything on the job site that she could do that day, but she'd definitely stop by. She smiled at the thought of seeing Jack.

Her paperback Bible from church called out to her from an end table as she walked through the den. A deck of cards had been left on top apparently a few days earlier when she and her boys had played after supper. Norma Rae would have a cow if she saw that. In fact Blue would've rolled over in his grave had he not been cremated. She picked up the Bible letting the cards slide off and took it with her to the porch. The rain pattered softly making a happy song. She thought about praying but didn't know the words. Stretching out on the swing long ways she opened the Book.

The words on the page made her heart happy. "Love is patient and kind…

That's Jack up one side and down the other.

"Not jealous…"

Blue was terribly jealous. But so was I.

A high school memory interrupted her thoughts. She'd nearly jerked a girl's arm clean off and slammed her against a locker for flirting with Blue. She laughed at the image of the girl's face as she priss-tailed away in her little cheerleading outfit. "Take your pompoms elsewhere you hussy! I will snap you like a twig!" Lydia had warned. She laughed at what a wild child she'd been all her life. That incident alone had cost her three days suspension and she'd only been in ninth grade.

"Or boastful or proud or rude. It does not demand its own way…"

Oops. That's a biggie for me Lord. I like what I like and I don't care for change. You probably need to help me with that one.

"It is not irritable and keeps no record of wrongs…"

Oh dear Lord You know what a b… umm… witch I am at times. This last episode with all the hormones has nearly driven me crazy and probably everyone around me. Poor Jack! The man has definitely seen me at my very worst and yet… he loves me.

Tears slipped down her face.

He loves me. How in this world can the man love me?

She tried to read but the words were blurry. Finally she was able to see the rest.

"Love never gives up, never loses faith, is always hopeful, and endures through every circumstance."

Good gracious Lord! Those are some beautiful words right there!

She read them again then dog-eared the page so she could come back to it. She wondered if she read the words every morning if it would remind her not to be so ill.

Lord I need Your help. I think Jack deserves better than me… he definitely deserves better than me. But maybe it's time I love again. Could You please work on the witch in me? Actually, kill her off and bring out somebody better. Is this okay to ask because I think… I think You might be listening but I'm still not sure.

That old sense of shame engulfed her like a dark cloud. She shook her head and said, "Never mind. I'm not worth the trouble."

She jumped when her phone buzzed in her pocket and spilled coffee all over 1st Corinthians 13. Hoping it was Jack she hurried to answer.

"Good morning girl. What're you up to today?" The deep voice greeted her like the gentle summer shower.

"Hey Jesse. Just sitting on the swing watching it rain. Don't you love it?" She wondered how the man always knew when to call. They'd go for weeks and not talk then out of the blue he'd check on her.

"I DO love it!" He answered cheerfully. "Since it's raining I figured you'd take the day off. I thought about coming over and sitting on the porch with you a minute. I won't stay long though. I've got to run to Charlotte. Hey… would you like to ride along?"

"Where are you headed?" She was thinking about it. Jesse had been such a good friend. She'd shared things with him that she'd never been able to tell anyone else. He was the kind of person who always brought out the best in her.

"Metrolina Greenhouse. I always feel like I'm cheating if I go there without you." He laughed that laugh she knew so well. She loved the place but had never been there without him.

"Come over and have a cup of coffee with me and I'll let you know then." It was always good to see her friend Jesse.

~~~~~~~

Jack wondered whether to call her that rainy day or not. Their early morning together had been a breakthrough. Obviously she wanted him. She'd suddenly made that very clear. But where did they stand? He'd even gone so far as to tell her he loved her. What had come over him?

Since her crew hadn't shown up he assumed it was due to the rain. Communication was certainly not her strong suite. But really with the small amount of work she had left, there wasn't a need for her to come in while the rain continued to pour. But should he call?

He knew he tended to push her more than he should. He'd just been with her a few hours earlier. It seemed like forever since he'd left her there waving good bye from her porch. It reminded him of his favorite western *Quigley Down Under* when Tom Selleck had to leave his girl to go kill the bad guys. His girl had watched hoping he would turn to look at her and he did. Jack couldn't help it. He was a romantic even if he wasn't a cowboy.

His phone dinged in his pocket. "Oh… my dinger." He laughed at Lydia's word and praised God it was her.

"Hello Sweetheart. May I call you Sweetheart?" Jack smiled and walked away from the crew.

"I would love it if you called me Sweetheart," she answered. "Hey, are you where anyone can hear you?"

"Let me go to my truck." He ran through the rain glad she wanted to speak in private. "Okay… I'm wet now, but entering the *Cone of Silence*." He laughed and wondered if she had ever seen *Get Smart* reruns. "What's up pretty lady?"

Lydia struggled to find the words. Finally she admitted. "This whole sweetheart stuff is weird to me. Nice, but weird. I don't know if I should ask permission or just go do what I want all willy-nilly." She paused not really meaning to use the word permission. She didn't think Jack was the jealous type, but then he'd never seen Jesse. But she also didn't want to give up a good friendship just because she was interested in Jack.

"Ask permission from me?" He laughed. "I can't imagine that you would ever do that!" Then he suddenly wondered what it was she planned to do. Maybe she would say.

"Oh good. I'll be in Charlotte today with a friend. I don't know what time we'll get back. Here he comes now. Gotta go Jack. Have a good day."

He sat there wondering what he'd just given his non-permission to.

The day dragged by without her. Johnny noticed Jack's lack of motivation and sang under his breath, *"Ain't no sunshine when she's gone…"* He laughed and said, "Suck it up brother! You didn't really expect her to leave here and follow you all over creation did you? She's a homegrown country girl with roots so deep in this red clay she would be miserable anywhere else. And you KNOW better than to take her home to mother."

Jack wondered why his brother was being so mean. Maybe he was jealous, or maybe he was just recalling Jack's other failed relationships.

Or maybe he was right.

Jack walked away and called her. But she didn't pick up. He decided not to leave a message.

Chapter 21

During the drive to Charlotte Jesse was able to get Lydia to talk about her recent bout with depression. She'd trusted him often to be a confidant and friend. He was definitely someone she could count on. She wondered why she didn't think to call him on those days when she struggled with that terrible dark cloud.

On the way home she considered telling him about Jack. He eventually broke the long silence with a comment that gave her reason to speak of him.

"You seem pretty happy today for a girl who's been battling those old demons we have to whip together sometimes." He looked at her inviting her to share.

"Yep." She wondered how much to tell him. But she'd learned years ago that he could be trusted. "There's this guy…" She paused not knowing exactly how to put it. Jesse knew everything about her. Everything. Often she'd been more honest with him than she'd ever been with Blue.

"There's a GUY?" He smiled. "I take it he's a good guy."

"Yep." She didn't know where to begin. "I think I might love him." Of course her neck turned red and her face flushed.

"Tell me about him." Jesse already knew the scuttlebutt around town, but wanted her to share it with him from her own perspective. He was not disappointed. Lydia began talking, giving Jesse the lowdown from the time she first met Jack, to their workdays together and their jokes and misunderstandings. She even shared the terrible embarrassing moments and how he'd made her so mad taking care of her too much. Jesse shook his head. "I bet that did not end well," He laughed.

Lydia was laughing too at the stupidity of it all. "NO, it ended by me telling him that we were not a couple and then I threw up in the street. Poor Jack."

"So have you at least sent him a text or something?" Jesse felt sorry for the guy and knew she was not likely to call.

"Oh yeah. That's a whole nother thing. He SAID he was praying I would get in touch with him and my text came before he said amen. Do you think God does stuff like that?" She asked knowing that if anyone had a handle on God it would be Jesse.

He answered thoughtfully. "Not usually but sometimes when the need is urgent he'll answer fast that way. Remember the prayer you prayed as a little girl that He answered so quickly? Maybe this prayer of Jack's was answered like that. So what happened?"

She decided she might as well confess it all. "Well, that was around 4:30 this morning. He called me after the text and I asked him to come over." She knew Jesse would be disappointed in her. He said nothing for a while. The wipers on the truck beat a rhythm in the rain as they drove down I-85.

Finally he asked as he changed lanes. "And?"

"He came." She didn't know how to say that she was all over him like white on rice. So she just added, "But he left before anything happened that would cause you to open the door and push me out." She tried to lighten the mood and apparently did because Jesse added, "Or kill him in his sleep?"

"Right." She laughed a nervous laugh because she knew it could happen.

"I let him kiss me Jesse. And I have to say that I liked it. I had no idea how lonely I've been and all of a sudden I'm feeling things I haven't let myself feel."

She paused remembering the morning. "I think I would've let him stay." She was embarrassed at the confession, but knew somehow that Jesse would understand.

"But you know what he did?" She looked at Jesse as she told him the rest. "He told me he was leaving because…"

She swallowed hard at the words. "He told me he was leaving because he loves me." Suddenly tears were slipping down her cheeks again.

"Dang hormones!" She laughed as she wiped the tears away.

Jesse looked at her. "Wow. I think I like Jack." Jesse smiled that smile that made her feel so secure. "There you were completely vulnerable with a man in your house that you obviously care about. And he leaves because he loves you? What a guy!"

Jesse helped her even more when he added, "Think about it. You finally seem open to his affections and then you invite him over at that time of day. If he doesn't come he risks a woman scorned. If he comes he might end up taking advantage of the girl he cares about. How can he win? He did the only possible thing he COULD do. Yep. I definitely like him."

She sat there soaking in Jesse's words realizing even more what Jack meant to her. How glad she was that Jesse had happened by on that particular day. Since she'd embarrassed herself thoroughly by spilling her story she decided she had nothing to lose by asking.

"Jesse I don't have any idea how to go about these things. I haven't dated since high school. I don't know what's expected nowadays."

She laughed at her own bumbling. "I sound like I'm about eighty but I'm serious. I'm afraid of the whole dating mess. I don't think I can be that girl. But I don't want him to just go back up North and me to stay here pining for what could've been if I had let him move in with me or something. It seems like that's what everybody does now. Maybe a practice run isn't such a bad idea. I mean, what if we hate each other? It would be terrible to vow before God that I'll love him til death if it turns out he's gross."

Jesse waited before he spoke. "Darlin' you're worth more than that. A practice run is the worst idea in the world. If Jack is as smart as he seems, he'll feel the same way. Skip the dating scene if you want, but don't skip getting to know him. Take your time just doing life. Watch how he treats others. But don't give yourself to him until you both vow before God to love only one another. He must be a one woman man in order for you to rest in his love. A marriage covenant is a beautiful thing designed by God. Do things His way and I promise, you'll have no guilt or regret later on."

He spoke with such authority and wisdom that she was glad she'd spilled her questions to him. As usual Jesse could be trusted to speak the heart of God straight into her soul. She'd need to introduce him to Jack soon.

Jesse followed his advice for her with a very difficult request.

"Promise me Lydia." He looked at her waiting. When she looked away he tried again. "Please don't do anything out of loneliness. I can't stand the thought of you being hurt. Make him wait, just like you did Blue. That turned out pretty good didn't it?"

"Yeah… but we were kids." She continued to look away not daring to meet his gaze.

Jesse took her hand and added one more thing before he was able to let it go.

"Honey, you barely know him. He seems like a good guy but please ask the Lord for wisdom concerning him. God seldom does anything in a hurry so take it slow Chickadee."

Finally when the silence got to be uncomfortable she added, "I'll think about it."

Jesse treated her to a really good supper but still had her home by seven. After talking with him about Jack, she had a much better handle on her feelings. Wishing Jesse and Jack were friends she added, "Here… put Jack's number in your phone. I want you two to get to know each other soon." He did, then hugged her goodbye from the side and kissed her on the top of the head like always. He lingered a bit longer than usual and she could tell he was worried about her. She looked up into his kind gray eyes and promised not to let so much time pass between their visits.

When she pulled out her phone to check Jack's number she realized she'd missed his call. She wondered if she should call him instead of shooting him a text. She surprised even herself when she hit the call button without hesitation.

Her heart did a happy leap when Jack answered with, "Hello Sweetheart. How was your day?"

She smiled into the phone. "It was good! In fact it was very good. Got some things cleared in my brain. How about yours?" she asked.

He waited then dared to say it. "I really missed you. May I come over and spend some time with you tonight? I know it will be dark soon but I really want to see you."

"I'd love it. Hurry and we'll watch the sunset together." She smiled at the thought.

"Want me to bring something to cook?" He was hoping she hadn't eaten.

"I've already had supper, but if you haven't I could make you a BLT." She opened her refrigerator doubting that she had lettuce.

"I'll be there in a bit. I love you Dearheart." He didn't want to wear out their new term or forget the old.

"See you soon." She hung up happy he was coming. He hung up wondering how long it would be until he heard her say the words he longed so much to hear.

Chapter 22

He was glad to smell bacon frying when he stepped onto the porch. When she opened the screen door she put her arms around his neck and gave him a hug. "I really missed you today." She smiled and hurried to the kitchen to take the bacon off the burner. "Sorry I don't have lettuce. So it'll just be a BT sandwich."

He watched as she peeled a very ripe tomato then joined her at the counter. "Did you make this bread? It looks fantastic."

"I did. But I pulled it from the freezer this morning so it's not hot out of the oven. But at least that makes it easier to slice. I hope it tastes okay. I'm still learning." She tilted her head, looked at the lopsided loaf and added, "Obviously."

Jack looked in the drawer and found a long serrated knife making nice thin slices.

"Mayo?" She asked as she watched how easily he sliced the bread.

He looked at her and wondered why they were making sandwiches. Pulling her close he held her to him stroking her back. "Yes please." He leaned down and kissed her head. Hmmm… there was the faintest fragrance of a man in her hair… or was that his jealous imagination?

His heart took a nosedive. "So tell me about your day. Say it was really good?"

"It was. We went to Metrolina Greenhouse in Charlotte, actually in Huntersville. It's a massive operation that provides all the plants for places like Walmart and a bunch of other big companies. It's like Nirvana! I get so many ideas every time I go down there. But it wears me out because I have to see it all. No corner is left unexplored."

He'd never heard her string together so many words at once. Apparently she'd had a VERY good day. He couldn't leave it alone.

"So who is 'We?'" he asked trying to be nonchalant about his fears.

"Me and Jesse. He's a really good friend. I basically talked about you all day. His ears are surely worn slap out." She laughed as she asked again, "Did you say yes on the mayo?"

"Yes please." He looked at her and wondered.

Who is Jesse and why hasn't his name come up before?

He was trying to figure out a way to interrogate her further without sounding completely over the top jealous when she asked, "Do you still want to go to the beach next Saturday? We could plan our trip tonight." She sounded so hopeful and happy that he decided nothing was worth spoiling the mood.

"Sounds great," he answered. And he purposely dropped the other questions in his head. As if the Lord whispered confirmation to his heart he recalled the portion he'd read that morning. *"Love is not jealous… keeps no record of wrongs… never gives up… always hopes."*

"Wow. This sandwich is really good!" He dug in. "But next time hold the mayo." He smiled that mischievous smile she'd learned to recognize.

"Hey. If you ever make one for me add cheese and grill it butter! And I wonder why I waddle!" She laughed as he shook his head and wondered.

Woman… do you not own a mirror?

~~~~~~~

At some point while he finished his sandwich and lemonade, she went to her truck and retrieved a map from under the seat. He couldn't remember the last time he'd seen a real map. His Pop was still a big fan but even he had quit using them to chart a road trip. She unfolded and spread the tattered page on the kitchen table.

"These are our choices." She pointed to several coastal towns in North and South Carolina. "It depends on what you prefer. The South Carolina beaches are actually closer but they're also more crowded. The North Carolina ones can take as much as an hour longer to get to, except for the Outer Banks which are way too far to go down and back in one day. We only go there for an extended stay. Myrtle Beach in South Carolina is considered Mecca to most vacationers, but Garden City a bit farther south is very nice. North of Myrtle is Ocean Drive and Cherry Grove. That's where the boys usually go."

He tried to pay attention but couldn't take his eyes off her. She explained where they could get great seafood, where the best boardwalk was, something about hot doughnuts, the best places to shower before coming back, something about not swimming near the pier. It was getting kind of fuzzy but he liked it. Obviously she loved the beach. Finally they were getting somewhere. For so long he'd wanted her to talk to him and now she was sharing and he couldn't keep up. He smiled at her excitement too much and she stopped talking.

"You're laughing at me!" She frowned a fake pouty and crossed her arms.

"No Sweetheart, I'm smiling because I'm so happy. I've just never heard you use so many words at once." Jack laughed. "It's your fault." He tried to fix it. "You're so pretty with your curly hair and your blue eyes and pouty lips and your... I'd better stop before I work my way down."

Her mouth dropped open then she gave him a warning look.

"I'm not kidding Lydia. I can't pay attention for wanting to kiss you and hold you and call you Sweetheart."

"You're a rascal. Oh my goodness! We're missing the sunset! Come come come!!!" She jumped up and rushed through the sunroom to the windows facing west. "Hurry hurry!"

"Oh never mind. It's too cloudy anyway. Well at least it's still raining."

He met her in the mostly dark room and pretended to be interested in the rain.

"Hey Jack," She turned from the window toward him. "Thank you for this morning. You..."

She couldn't find the words and was trying hard not to tear up. "You are such a good guy. And the way you treated me helped me to trust." She reached for him and hugged him tight.

He held her and stroked her back for the longest time then offered, "Let's finish planning our day trip."

They sat at the table and decided which route they'd take, the things they'd do, etc. The forecast promised a beautiful day.

When she said goodbye to him on the porch that night she kissed him but kept it minimal. Her heart beat so hard she was sure he could hear it. Everything within her wanted to tell him to stay. Remembering Jesse's words of warning she tried to guard her heart. She felt like she'd known Jack forever but really it had been only a matter of weeks. What had come over her soul that caused her to feel these things she hadn't allowed in years? Her heart nearly melted when he stopped his truck as he pulled away. Putting the passenger side window down he looked at her one more time before he left, just like Blue used to do.

Chapter 23

She and her crew put in the new fountain and finished the brick pathway in the light rain. When the weather cleared they would tidy up and their part would be finished. Lydia stood back and took it in with great satisfaction. She hadn't seen Jack that morning but they'd been working so hard that he could've walked by without her noticing. But that wasn't likely as surely he'd speak before going inside.

She sent her boys home telling them she'd finish anything left. Walking up the new paved drive to the road she wanted to get a perspective from a distance. Passing one of the design assistants Lydia smiled and nodded good morning.

The woman stopped and spoke. "Surely you know that he has a different girl on every job." The woman turned on her heel and walked toward the house.

"What did you say?" asked Lydia. The woman stopped and added, "Have you ever heard the saying, 'A girl in every port?' Well that's a good description of Jack. Don't be fooled Sweetie. He can't be trusted."

Lydia's neck turned red as Queen Boobs-A-Lot sauntered away. Memories of slamming the cheerleader into her locker came roaring through her head like a locomotive. Instead she walked up the incline to the street and peered down toward the house. Trying to calm down she took advice she'd been given at some point from Norma Rae.

Deep breaths Dearheart... in through the nose... out through the mouth. In through the nose... out through the mouth.

In case the woman was watching from inside she decided to smile. Pretending to receive a call she laughed with her phone to her ear.

Ha ha ha... yep. Funny! That is soooo comical that I can hardly stand it.

She finished her little comedy routine and shoved the phone nonchalantly into her back pocket about the time it buzzed.

"Hey Jesse. I was just thinking of calling you. Are you working in town today? Good. Can I meet you for lunch somewhere? No… not there. Okay. Perfect. Be there in ten."

Sitting on the tailgate of her pickup she pulled her mud caked work boots off and tossed them into the back of the truck. She smiled for no apparent reason still hoping that chick was watching. She wasn't, but Jack was. She pulled wet coveralls off, smoothed her dry clothes, and stepped into her cowboy boots. She shook her hair out and twirled it onto the top of her head. Her truck roared to life as she left to meet Jesse.

Jack had seen her crew leave earlier and hoped he and Lydia could get away for a private lunch somewhere different for a change. But apparently she had other plans.

He pulled out his phone and called her. She was already rolling out of sight.

"Hey Jack," she answered. "What's up?"

"I thought we'd go somewhere different for lunch today. But I didn't catch you in time. Where are you going?"

"Olive Garden. I'm meeting a friend. I didn't see you come in so I made plans. I'm sorry." She wondered what to do. She wasn't going to lie to him but she needed advice from Jesse before she ripped that chick to shreds or doubted Jack's character. Now she was stuck.

Almost as a warning to her heart she remembered the words she'd read again in her coffee stained Bible that morning. *"Love does not demand its own way, is not irritable."*

But did she love him? It could be time to fish or cut bait. Suddenly she and Jack spoke at the same time.

"I'm sorry. You first," she offered.

"I was just going to ask if you were meeting Jesse again?" Jack's tone was rather cold.

"Yep. And I was just going to ask if you'd like to join us. I want you to meet him." She needed to get this show on the road one way or another. The woman's words were very disconcerting.

Jack was quiet on the other end. When finally he spoke he surprised her. "No that's fine. I don't want to intrude. I'll find someone here to have lunch with." He hung up abruptly. Lydia looked at the blank screen on her phone and thought.

Whoa… whatever Dearheart.

But her heart hurt a little.

Jesse waited for her at Olive Garden. The hostess seated them at a booth in a far corner and Lydia was glad for the privacy. She could talk to her friend without being overheard. Once they placed their orders Jesse looked at her with steel gray eyes that seemed to study her soul.

"Spill it girl. What happened?"

"What makes you think something happened?" she asked.

"Because your face is glowing and not in a good way. Plus it's lunchtime and there's no Jack. Is he on his way?" Jesse could read her like a book.

"I invited him but he declined. I need your wisdom Jesse. You know I told you that I think I might love him. He is the nicest man and we have the best time together. But one of the women on the job told me he has…" Lydia used air quotes as she spoke the words, "A girl in every port."

"She said he can't be trusted and that he has a different woman on every job site. I don't believe it, but I also don't know what to do with it. I don't actually know the man. Should I ask him about it or just try to forget it, or maybe hire a hit man?" She laughed. "I could call my daddy. Or I could do what comes naturally and just whack the woman in the head with a shovel and bury her in the garden over at your house. That's where all the other wicked chicks are."

Jesse offered. "Let's call fire down out of heaven!" Lydia laughed louder than she wished she would've.

Too bad the woman from work wasn't there to see her. She'd be jealous on so many levels. Maybe she already was. That was Jesse's guess.

"What does your gut tell you?" he asked.

"My gut keeps warning me not to move too fast and that I've only known him about six weeks. But my heart wants to hope that Jack is truly a good guy. Honestly he reminds me of all the things I loved about Blue. He's protective, respectful, hardworking, and Lord have mercy. When I see him my heart does this little thing… Oh my goodness. There he is!"

She smiled and waved but Jack didn't wave back. Instead he turned and left wondering how God could've steered him wrong after he'd been so careful to keep his promise. Perhaps this was payback for his many infidelities.

~~~~~~~

She rose to try to catch him, but he was already out the door. Jesse spoke as she stood looking through the window watching Jack hurry to his truck. "Give him some space. Remember how you feel when you're about to blow a gasket. Sometimes if people would just leave you alone you wouldn't end up saying things you regret."

She knew he was right. She watched Jack spin out of the parking lot. She'd never seen him mad. He was definitely steaming. It surprised her to see that side of him.

Jesse gave her one more piece of advice. "Keep praying honey. God knows better than any of us how this should play out. Be sure to ask Him for wisdom regarding Jack then be open to His leading. We can't see the whole picture, but the Lord does."

She nodded and thought carefully on his words.

When lunch came she asked for a box knowing she wouldn't be able to choke down a bite. Hoping to catch up with Jack she ordered something for him as well. Jesse enjoyed his pasta and again picked up the tab. Lydia left the tip, hugged her friend and stopped long enough for him to kiss her on the head.

"How long should I wait before I try to talk to him?"

Jesse advised that she send a text when it had been about an hour. When she got inside her truck she pulled out her phone and realized it had only been forty-five minutes. So she decided to text him when she got back to the site if he wasn't there. She found herself praying.

Lord please help. I think I've hurt one of the nicest men I've ever met. But as Jesse said, give me wisdom about Jack. I want so much to trust him. But should I? Help me please Lord. And thank You for Jesse. I don't know what I'd do without him.

Chapter 24

Jack's truck was on site. She had to park down the road a ways so instead of venturing inside where there could be a showdown, she sent him a text.

"In truck under shade tree. Meet me?" She tried to relax a bit as the gentle rain turned into a downpour. About thirty minutes later she sent another.

"Please."

When another thirty minutes passed she tried again. "I brought make-up pasta."

When he didn't answer that one she waited a while longer and sent the last. "I miss you already. Sorry I didn't say the words."

She waited another thirty minutes and left. At the end of the block she stopped and called him. Surely he'd had time to cool off. It had been nearly three hours. But he didn't pick up. So she whispered the words to his voice mail trying her best not to cry.

"I love you Jack. Sorry I didn't say the words."

~~~~~~~

Jack thought he might scream. If the woman bent over in front of him one more time he might have to put his shoe on her rear and shove her into the next room. Why had his brother hired this person? It seemed she was helpless when it came to small finishing touches.

Just climb the ladder and screw in the bulbs for crying out loud! It's not that hard!

She laughed loudly and flipped her blond hair as she took his arm pointing out all her design choices and laughing at his opinions.

"JOHNNY! GET IN HERE!" His sudden call for his brother startled her and she actually quit speaking. "Come help this woman with the details!"

Jack was sick of it. And he was starving. Why had he turned away when Lydia waved at lunch? It would've been the perfect opportunity to meet the guy she was so infatuated with. Who was that jerk anyway with blonde hair in a ponytail and muscles pushing his short sleeves out of the way? Jack was quickly discovering that he really disliked blondes.

Johnny asked with surprise, "What's wrong with you Jack? We always have loose ends to tie up like this." Jack pushed past as he informed him that he was through for the day.

"You'll need to find a ride to the motel when you finish. I've got something I need to take care of." He walked briskly up the drive to his truck which waited where Lydia usually parked.

Why didn't she come back to the job to at least talk about it?

As he slid into the seat his phone stared back at him from the console. He'd missed a ton of messages and a couple calls. Hopefully one of them was her.

On the passenger seat was a container of food. He dove in as he read his texts. As best he could tell she'd waited a couple hours for him hoping to talk. When he pulled up his voice mail one was hers. Precious words were recorded for him there. He played it over again and knew he'd hold onto it forever… and hopefully to her as well.

~~~~~~~~~

He didn't want to take time to call her but what if he pulled up and Jesse was there? He decided he'd deal with that like he should've at lunch. He thought a minute then picked up his phone.

"Hello Sweetheart. May I come over?" He knew he was going there no matter what she said.

"Yes please do," she answered.

The rain poured and he couldn't drive fast enough. He tried to prepare a speech but he had no idea what to say. He couldn't remember ever being so jealous. Maybe because he'd never been so much in love. His heart beat faster at the thought of her saying that she loved him.

He turned into her long gravel road. The gate was already open. He stopped and closed it behind him so they wouldn't be interrupted by one of her boys.

Sorry Lord, he thought as he got back into his truck. *I'm really gonna need some help tonight. You know full well where my thoughts are headed.*

She waited for him on the front porch swing in that blue cotton dress. When he'd passed her that morning she'd been about knee deep in a trench in muddy coveralls. Wet hair was plastered to her head and she was working so hard she never noticed him standing there watching. That had been hours ago for now her hair was washed and dried and falling in those ringlets he loved. Her tanned legs and bare feet stretched out on the swing where she waited. She stood and embraced him as though she'd never let go.

Jack spoke first. "So I got a message, from this girl I love… and she said something I've been longing to hear." He looked into her eyes. They matched the dress she wore so well, flowing softly around her curves.

"Really? What in the world did she say?" She couldn't take her eyes off the man she'd prayed for all day.

"She SAID," his eyes filled with mischief, "I can't remember. Maybe she will say it again for me in person someday."

"Oh Jack." She paused. Her heart was beating so wildly that she had to whisper it.

"I love you."

She hugged him again and added, "Don't forget it because for some reason I have a really hard time saying the words." His laugh was music to her ears.

Taking his hand she led him. "Come sit with me on the swing. Did you find your food?"

"Not til just before I came here. I'm sorry I didn't return your texts. My phone was in the truck. I was stuck all day with that woman who picks out pillows and stupid stuff that makes me crazy. Let me run get the pasta. I'm starving."

He bounded down the steps then returned to sit beside her. She asked as he dove into his food, "So this woman… does she happen to be blonde?"

"Yes but Lydia please don't be jealous. Believe me there is nothing to be jealous of. I'd like to put my foot up her… sorry. What I MEANT to say is that Johnny hired her so he can deal with her. I'm not going to let him employ her again. Every time she's on the job I feel like I'm losing my mind!"

"What's her name?" Lydia was trying to make sure they were speaking of the same person. Jack thought a minute then paused. "I have no idea. She's said it a million times. I keep calling her Carol but I think maybe Cathy? I don't know. It doesn't matter. As soon as the Parker project is finished I hope I never see her again. Why?"

"Well… she had some very unsavory things to say about you earlier today. But I was able to forget them after talking to Jesse." She was practically whispering. Jack knew from previous conversations that she tended to get quiet when things were personal. "That's what lunch was about. Jesse is my counselor… as-in… I sometimes struggle with serious depression. He's literally saved my life several times. I want you to meet him."

"So the guy with the hair and the muscles is a counselor? Seems suspect to me." Jack looked down at his pasta hoping not to start a fight. But if they were going to be a couple he wouldn't much want her meeting Jesse for lunch and spending days at a time with him.

"I'll introduce him to you soon and you'll see. It might help to know that he has a wife that he loves with all his heart." She knew he had no idea that earlier that day Jesse had helped her to trust Jack again.

"That does help." He had a drop sauce on his chin. She took a paper napkin and dabbed his face, "Here, let me get some of that make-up sauce."

He looked at her like a lost puppy and she couldn't imagine loving him more. Her heart beat wildly and warned her to walk away for a minute.

"Lemonade, tea or water?" She asked as she rose from the swing.

"Lemonade please." He watched as she left. She returned a short while later with her own box of pasta and their drinks.

"You're having dinner early?" He asked as she sat down beside him trying not to rock the swing too much.

"I didn't eat lunch either."

Jack realized why. "I'm sorry Lydia. What were you saying before about that woman?"

Lydia wondered how much to say. She ate a few bites then gave a minimum amount of information. It didn't matter. The woman was probably just jealous.

"She said that you can't be trusted. But apparently she doesn't know you like I do. This is really good Alfredo sauce, very creamy. Do you like shrimp? Here, taste this." She held out a bite of food from her box.

Jack ate from her fork. "Wow. That IS good. I think I could make that."

"You're hired!" She smiled at him and turned her attention to her food hoping the subject was changed.

"Can't be trusted? Why would she say that? I'll have to ask her about it." He didn't like the woman anyway, so what did he have to lose?

"Probably wise," Lydia added hoping to move on. "Tomorrow's Friday! If it stops raining tonight I'll be able to finish my part at Denise's in the morning."

"Good. Then you can rest up for our adventure on Saturday!" Jack closed the lid on his finished meal. He sipped the homemade lemonade reminding himself again to get her recipe. His Pop would love it.

Lydia broke into his thoughts. "I'm actually hoping to do a few jobs for a couple of my regular customers. They've been pretty patient with me,

111

but I'd hate to lose them." She didn't dare reveal to him that waiting on her check from his company had put her in quite a financial strain. She was used to getting paid on the spot from her regular clientele.

Lydia took another bite then handed her box to him.

"Don't you want the rest?" Jack asked.

"Eat up honey. I'm fuller than a tick." Lydia handed it over.

"That's gross." Jack laughed.

"Sorry." Lydia suddenly felt embarrassed. Jack noticed and leaned over to kiss her. The two tall glasses of lemonade which balanced precariously on the swing between them quickly keeled over. She jumped up but not before it got her dress and ricocheted back onto Jack's jeans.

"Oops." She laughed. Liquid dripped through the slats on the swing to the porch floor. "You grab the glasses and I'll get the hose pipe." Stepping into the soft rain she pulled the garden hose from the side and warned Jack to move as she sprayed lemonade away.

"Need me to squirt you down?"

"No. I'm good." Jack held food containers and empty glasses looking down at his very wet clothes.

She laughed pulling the hose with her as she walked toward the front. Standing on the bottom of the wide steps which divided the porch, she sprayed mud from her bare feet. "Pull your shoes off and step inside. I'll find you some pants."

Dropping the hose she stepped lightly onto the porch door mat and wiped her feet. "What a mess!" She laughed easily then thought to add. "Be sure you heard me right. I said pull your SHOES off."

Jack laughed too. "Got it. Pants off, passionate make-up sex. I'm on it baby."

She stepped down to the waiting garden hose and sprayed him good. Laughing he jumped inside the house. "Don't blame a guy for trying!"

He looked to see if she was laughing. Thankfully she was. The day was shaping up nicely. Old Jack came out of nowhere and entered his thoughts.

It'll take more than a little shot of water to clear sex from the agenda tonight baby. The evening is very young and I get the feeling you're ready. By tomorrow morning you'll be asking, 'Jesse who?'

Chapter 25

She knew exactly where to look for pants. She'd kept one dresser drawer reserved for things of Blue's that she couldn't part with. Pulling a pair of jeans from there she handed them to Jack with a black t-shirt she hadn't thought about in a while. *"Live to Ride, Ride to Live"* was written on the back around a Harley Davidson. She'd bought it for her husband when they were hoping to get a Harley. When he'd purchased a used Yamaha to save money it had felt silly to wear the shirt. He joked and said he'd use it to polish his V-Star. To her it was too sentimental to put into the Goodwill bin with his other stuff. Jack could wear it, but he'd definitely have to give it back. She stopped just short of saying so when she handed it to him.

"Take this to the bathroom and change in there. I'm going to find some dry stuff too." She opened another drawer and peered inside. Jack stood looking at her knowing better than to draw her into his arms and pull her toward the bed.

But he did anyway.

She surprised him by pushing away.

"Nope! Not wise honey."

Grabbing clothes from her drawer, she went to the bathroom and locked the door as she changed. Her heart pounded at the thought of him.

When she emerged she was wearing a pair of worn out jeans, and her old softball jersey. Her hair was pulled up on top of her head but a thousand curls still escaped the clasp. "This humidity makes me look like Medusa." She laughed as she spoke to Jack from the kitchen. Silently she hoped that she hadn't hurt his feelings. But the words of Jesse as well as that woman, whatever her name was, swirled around in her brain. She must be careful lest her loneliness cause her more heartache than she might be able to recover from this time.

~~~~~~~

Jack stood by the double bed that apparently had been Lydia and Blue's. How could he be such a jerk? But that wet dress had clung to her and their day had been so bad. He'd allowed himself to go where he'd promised God he wouldn't.

"Sorry God," he prayed. "I really need help." As he pulled on her former husband's jeans he prayed again. "This is not funny Lord." He buttoned and zipped the jeans but it didn't matter. They nearly fell right off. The shirt also swallowed him whole. Being six one he'd never felt small in his life. But Blue could've broken him in half. Maybe that was his way of speaking from the dead. Jack shuddered as he cinched his own belt around the jeans to hold them up.

Gathering his wet things he walked into the kitchen with his pants dragging the floor and sagging in the rear. Lydia covered her mouth with her hand to keep from laughing. She took the wet clothes from him and tossed them into the agitating washer.

"No wait! Don't wash them, just dry them!" Jack desperately wanted back into his own clothes. He thought to himself that that was truthfully something he'd never wished for with any other woman.

Again… not funny Lord.

"Too late honey. I've already started the wash. I'm doing a load of my jeans anyway." She took some sort of stick and pushed the clothes around.

"What are you doing?" asked Jack.

"This lets me know how much room I have left in the load." She spoke to him as if everyone did such.

"Is that a Southern thing?" he asked. "Where do you get a stick like that?"

"No… I think it's a Lydia thing. This stick came off a new plunger." She turned to look at him but couldn't without laughing.

"It's not funny." Jack said.

"Sorry. I tell you what; you don't laugh at my laundry stick and I won't laugh at your fashion statement."

"But you are still laughing." Jack was not enjoying standing there feeling like a boy in her former lover's clothes. But he had to smile when he thought of how the Lord had put him in his place so quickly and without striking him dead as he deserved.

"I think I hear your dinger," Lydia said stopping the washer to listen. Jack heard it too from the bedroom. He went to retrieve his phone from the bed but he'd already missed the call from his brother. Whatever that was about could wait. He checked the time and figured it was likely about a ride home. Johnny would just have to think for himself for a change.

Time to grow up boy. I told you to find a ride and you probably weren't listening as usual.

The words his brother had spoken about Lydia not leaving home were still bothering him. He got the feeling that things hung in the balance somewhere between all or nothing. If he was smart he'd mind his manners and help her trust him as he'd decided from the start. And surely things with his mother would work out.

"LIDDY! WE'RE COMIN' IN IF Y'ALL ARE MAKIN' OUT!"
A voice startled Jack. Someone was coming through the den.

Jack quickly sat down at the kitchen table hoping they didn't notice his clothes. Suddenly he realized the boys could have caught them in a very embarrassing situation if Lydia had consented. She most likely would not have forgiven him. He thanked the Lord silently as he thought of what a close call it had been.

"In here guys!" Lydia called back as she closed the washer lid content that the water to laundry ratio was correct. Kurtis passed Jack and hugged her as if they'd not seen each other in a week. Shawn followed but wasn't much on hugging. He still gave her a little side hug then looked at Jack.

"What happened man, run into a shrink ray?"

Lydia covered her mouth and turned back to the wash. Before Jack could think of anything clever Kurtis moved on to the reason they were there. "Y'all want to ride with us to the beach Saturday? I can take the Jeep."

Jack wondered what she'd say. He'd caught himself thinking of how he could conveniently suggest they stay overnight because of being so tired. If they rode with Kurt and Shawn then that couldn't happen. He was glad for Lydia's answer.

"No thanks. I want Jack to myself for a day. He'll be leaving soon and I miss him already." She turned away feeling she'd revealed too much.

"See, I told you." Kurt punched Shawn who added, "Okay. Maybe y'all can come find us and play volleyball or something."

Kurtis piped up hopefully, "There's a street dance in OD this Saturday. A couple of really good bands will be there and we can practice our shaggin'."

Jack wondered what language Kurt was speaking.

"That's gonna make for a long night Kurtis. If y'all stay, be careful not to let some hoochie-mama put a noose around your neck." Lydia warned.

"Let's just play volleyball. I don't know how to dance good." Shawn whined. "Besides if we stay that late you won't be able to haul your butt out of bed in time for church Sunday. And you know you want to catch up with that girl that talked to you last week."

"Oh yeah." Kurt smiled at the thought. "Alright. Volleyball, swim, pizza, home; just like every time. So why's the porch wet?"

"We had a lemonade mishap." Lydia tried not to laugh at the thought. Shawn opened the refrigerator and pulled the milk jug marked lemonade out. "Are we playing cards tonight?"

"Sure," Lydia agreed. Earlier she'd decided to text the boys not to come, but since the day had taken a few unexpected turns, this would be better than being with Jack completely alone. Realizing she was taking the lead without consulting Jack she looked at him and asked, "Is that okay with you or did you want to go somewhere?"

"What, in my little shrink ray body? No, I'm good. Play cards!" They laughed as Kurtis retrieved the cards from the den and reviewed the rules of rummy.

~~~~~~~~

"Okay guys. One more hand then you're outta here!" Lydia spoke to the group. They finished up, hugged her good-bye and fought about the interpretation of the rules all the way to Shawn's little truck. Jack was happy to see they were leaving before him finally. Lydia watched from the porch til they were out of sight. Jack stood by her side realizing she'd missed a spot when hosing off the lemonade. The bottom of his left foot was definitely sticking to the floor.

"Let's check your britches." Lydia turned to go inside. Jack followed shaking his head at her words but choosing not to comment. As she opened the dryer she sighed with disgust, "I forgot to turn the dryer back on for the second tumble!"

Jack reached in to feel the clothes. They were too wet to wear. Without meaning to he sighed deeply.

"I'm sorry Jack. Here, let me pull everything out but yours and they'll be dry shortly. My stupid dryer has an element burned out. It takes several cycles to get jeans dry but I forgot because I usually hang them on the line. Sorry honey."

"No Sweetheart. I'm the one who is sorry. Please forgive me Lydia." Pulling her close he stroked her back. "I'll just go in this if you don't mind and bring them back to you tomorrow. Maybe I won't wreck on the way and get laughed at." He hung his head in mock shame then peeked to see if she were feeling sorry for him.

It worked. She laughed. That was all he needed to know they were okay. As she walked him to the door he pulled her close and asked, "May I kiss you good night? It would make up for all my pain and suffering."

Laughing she drew him into her arms and kissed him tenderly. "Sleep well. I'll see you in the morning."

"Which is not long from now. Thanks for letting us stay a while. That was fun playing cards with the guys." He kissed her again then pulled his phone out to check the time. He noticed he had a text from Johnny and looked at it as he walked down the steps. "Oh no."

"What's the matter?" Lydia asked.

"Johnny sent me a text not to come to the room tonight." He paused suddenly realizing he'd revealed things to Lydia he wasn't ready to share.

"Has he got a girl with him?" Lydia asked. Jack didn't answer.

"Do you need to sleep here tonight?" she asked then immediately regretted it.

"Hang on. What I meant was… Do you need to stay here tonight… in the guest bed… by yourself… while I sleep on the daybed… as usual?" She laughed nervously hoping with all hope that this was not something Jack had worked out with his brother ahead of time. She felt her face flush as she thought.

Please say no, please say no. I didn't mean it. I wasn't thinking…

He took a deep sigh. "May I please? I promise to behave. I'll even cook breakfast." He looked at her with those puppy dog eyes, but she really wasn't buying it.

"I'll be long gone before you ever roll out of bed Jack Rabbit. Alright. But no kissing! There shall be no kissing! We've already said our good nights."

"Yes dear." He tried appearing remorseful again but she wasn't looking.

"Let me get my stuff out of the bedroom and you can turn in when you want to. I'm headed to bed. Some of us have to get up and work for a living rather than stand around discussing the virtue of certain pillow patterns!" She sounded miffed.

"Lydia, I… I did not plan this… if that's what you're thinking. I don't have to stay. I can get a room in town probably at the same motel we're staying at."

She thought a moment then answered. "It's okay. This will be a good test for us in case we decide to go somewhere together. Come on. You can help me make the bed. It doesn't have sheets on it."

"Does the single bed in the front bedroom have sheets? I can sleep in there. I don't have to take your room."

"No, you don't want to sleep in there. That's where Shawn lands when he stays over and I haven't washed those sheets in a while. Come on. It's fine. That's not really my room anymore. I've slept on the daybed for seven years."

She laughed trying to hide the pain of the words she'd just spoken.

Pulling clean white sheets from the cedar chest she began making the bed. He tucked them under the corners on the opposite side silently watching her.

She spoke without looking at him. "There's a fan on the dresser you can use to drown out the noise if you want."

"There's going to be noise?" he asked hoping to lighten the tension. "This is the quietest place I've ever been in my life!" She relaxed and laughed at that. Taking his hand she led him to the sunroom where the windows were open. "Listen to the crickets and tree frogs." He paused and heard a crazy symphony he'd never noticed before. He looked at her longing for more but didn't dare.

"One more thing Jack. Not that I would do it on purpose, but don't come in here in the middle of the night. I sleep with a loaded gun and I'd hate to accidently blow your head off." He could tell that she meant it. She returned to get her things from the room he'd be sleeping in while the words settled into his brain.

Note to self: Do not follow through with plan to set alarm in order to kiss her awake. Make pancakes instead.

~~~~~~~

"All yours," she called as she left the bathroom. He watched her walk through the kitchen to the sunroom. Her hair was up in a nighttime pony tail and she wore what looked to be her high school PE shorts and tank top. Baby blue was definitely a good color for her showing off her pretty tan. He couldn't remember ever seeing a redhead with a tan. He liked it very much.

"Good night Sweetheart." He called through the kitchen wondering if she could hear. She didn't answer. When finally he crashed in the middle of the double bed he sank like a rock into the feather topper. Crisp cool sheets comforted his weary body as the ceiling fan whirred above.

But it was so dark.

And so quiet.

He waited for a bit, switched on the lamp then got out of bed to turn on the small fan. He didn't need it to drown out the noise. He needed it to drown out the silence. Back in the middle of the bed he slept harder and better than he'd slept in ages.

Lydia sent a quick text to Jesse.

It simply said, "I promise."

~~~~~~~~

That man had spoiled his plan again. He was getting tired of him intruding on their time. She'd even dressed in the bathroom and he hadn't been able to see. Now his night was ruined. He might have to lay low for a while til that guy disappeared. She'd go back to dressing just for him again once the other man was out of the way. He could wait. Their day would come.

Chapter 26

Jack somehow slept through his alarm and didn't even stir til Lydia started her old truck. Trying to remember where he was he missed waving to her from the porch. That was a good thing too since he wasn't able to pull those big jeans on and move fast enough not to lose them on the way.

"Aw man. I was going to make pancakes." On the kitchen table were his jeans and shirt dried and folded. He looked for a note, even checking under the table in case it had blown off. But there was none. He checked his phone in case she'd left a message but she hadn't. He wouldn't read too much in to it. She'd always been at work long before he got there. Why should that day be any different? As best he could tell they were still on for the beach in the morning. That would be nice. But he had a feeling something was amiss.

He dressed and made the bed. On a whim he checked her daybed for a gun. To his dismay he found one.

Gotta love the South, he thought again.

But it made sense being out there all by herself. He was actually glad she had one. It must've been hard getting used to living without her husband. He folded Blue's clothes and put them back in the drawer where she kept them. There was a wedding picture framing the two of them on the front of a photo album. Lydia looked much the same only a little thinner. He wondered if she'd even graduated high school. Blue's shoulders were huge. He probably played football in college somewhere. His brown hair was rather long for a wedding day Jack thought. His eyes went back to Lydia in her wedding gown. This slip of a girl even then had that beautiful smile and sparkling blue eyes.

He glanced around the room knowing he was prying. Opening the album there were happy pictures on every page of two kids growing up; a smiling little boy with kind blue eyes, and a scrappy red haired girl in braided pigtails. In one of the pictures she had a black eye. Jack laughed as he imagined her whipping some boy's butt for trying to kiss her. He flipped through the pages smiling at her tomboy life. She seemed to always be barefoot and have on tattered clothes. Sometimes they were fishing, other times in a tree, sometimes with Norma and her husband.

Toward the back there was a picture of Lydia's parents. Her mother was beautiful with short dark curly hair and a smile like Lydia's. Her dad however had a look that said 'Don't mess with me.' It made Jack shiver. He'd seen the same look on Lydia's face a few times and it was completely intimidating. Last night was one of them. It was easy to see that she'd also inherited her daddy's tall lanky frame and bright blue eyes. Though he looked tough as nails his eyes sparkled with something akin to mischief. Jack wondered where he was and if Lydia had any contact with him. He flipped the page. She smiled from a white Camaro in her wedding gown with Blue leaning near. They looked so happy.

Those two would have made beautiful babies, he thought.

He closed the album to return it to its place and realized two photos had either fallen out or had been stuck in the drawer separately. In the first Lydia was in torn jeans, a white tank top, and a black leather biker jacket leaning against a motorcycle. He was actually surprised as he observed more closely. She looked really harsh. There was no smile and her eyes had no sparkle. Instead she glared at the photographer. On the back was written in a handwriting that wasn't hers, "Death Wish."

The next picture was the flip side of her personality. It was a shot of her standing in the kitchen pulling a white cotton gown close to her very large belly. Her smile told the story as it reflected the joy of her pregnancy. She'd thrown her head back laughing. Even though her hair was a good bit shorter it still fell in a mass of curls. He wondered how long ago that had been and what had happened. His heart hurt for her again. She'd never spoken of the baby.

Feeling guilty he placed the album on top of the pictures the way he'd found it and closed the drawer. "Lord please help us," he prayed. Immediately the verses from first Peter came to mind that he'd read when they first met.

"Husbands give honor to your wives. Treat her with understanding... She may be weaker than you are but she is your equal partner in God's gift of new life. Treat her as you should so your prayers will not be hindered."

It was very convicting. He knew he'd not spent much time with the Lord lately. And he'd also allowed himself to think old thoughts and fall into wrong habits. He shouldn't be walking so close to the edge that the Lord had to get his attention. His Pop had reminded him often, "Son, there are two ways to learn. You get to choose. Enter the school of hard knocks, or rest in the almighty arms of God and hear His heart. One is a whole lot harder than the other."

Something prompted him to get on his knees by the bed there. He stayed for a while not even knowing why. He'd never had the Lord speak actual words to him before. But this came pretty close; almost an instinctive warning of sorts. In that moment on his knees he asked for strength to love and protect this crazy chick the Lord had brought into his life. Even while he prayed he wondered why he felt so torn.

~~~~~~~

Driving in to work Lydia was glad to see the sun. But doubts filled her soul as she considered the days ahead. How quickly she'd grown close to Jack since June. The end of July was fast approaching and he hadn't said a thing about the future. The Parker project would be finished in only a week. She sighed and consoled herself that at least she hadn't slept with him.

Her phone buzzed and she saw that it was her daddy. Though she didn't usually talk and drive she knew she'd better pick up. The man seldom called and immediately she felt the familiar ache in her heart.

"Hey Daddy. What's up?" She tried to sound breezy.

"I don't know. You tell me. I hear there's a man hangin' out with you lately. What's all that about?"

She sighed and wondered what to say. "I'm not real sure. Why? Do you know something I need to hear?" Immediately she wondered why she'd invited him to give his opinion. But for some reason it seemed the right thing to do.

He sighed. "If I did would you listen?"

She was quiet for a bit then laughed. "Probably not. I'm ever bit as stubborn as my mama." She was glad when he laughed too. With the phone still at her ear she waited through his silence. The man was impossible to talk to. Finally he uttered with an unusual amount of care. "Be careful Copper. I've got a bad feeling."

His words surprised her. "Thanks Daddy. I will."

He hung up. She wondered where he was and decided that she might start trying to ask when they talked. Though she couldn't prove it, she was fairly certain her father was a hitman. Hopefully he was not currently in North Carolina or she may not have to wonder about her future with Jack at all.

Chapter 27

She tidied up a few details on the job that morning, rinsed the pathways, took a leaf blower and dried them just to get the full effect. Stepping back she snapped a few pictures. She wondered if the woman who'd spoken the ugly words was in the house. She thought about taking her out for lunch then burying her in the garden.

Johnny came out of the house and gave Lydia a hug. "The yard looks fantastic! You did an awesome job. Of all the projects we've done this is by far my favorite landscape. The roses are beautiful!" He gushed and she wondered if he had any idea that Jack had accidently divulged his current indiscretion. Lydia didn't much like him hugging her.

"Where's Jack this morning?" Johnny asked.

"I guess he's still asleep? I don't really know for sure." She was trying her best not to lie or let on that she knew Jack didn't go back to the motel room the night before. How dare Johnny ask her as if…

The timing couldn't have been worse. Jack came down the drive, kissed her on the cheek and smiled broadly. "Good morning Sweetheart! Don't you love this beautiful sunshine?" Of course Johnny had to point out that Jack was wearing the same thing he had on the day before and grin like a possum.

"That's because I couldn't get into my room last night remember?!" Jack called Johnny on it right there in front of God and everybody. Lydia walked toward her truck hating the drama.

"Where are you going?" Jack called behind her.

"I told you I have a couple jobs this afternoon. I need to get on it before the day gets any hotter." By that she meant before SHE got any hotter. Her temperature was definitely rising.

"I'm coming to help you." Jack turned to follow her.

Johnny commented, "That's fine. I'll help Cassie with the last of the details inside." When Johnny turned to go into the house Jack stopped dead in his tracks. "Did you say Cassie?" He walked closer to his brother and whispered, "Is that who you took back to the motel last night."

Johnny smiled and murmured, "Mmm hum…"

Jack walked into the house and found her. "Cassie?"

She looked up from her work and smiled. "Yes?"

A sudden wave of recognition hit him. They had been an item last fall when Jack was mostly wasted. He hadn't even recognized her. Sure she'd lost a lot of weight and dyed her hair blonde. But it was her.

"Cassie… I don't know what to say. I didn't recognize you. I am so sorry." Jack wasn't exactly sure what he was sorry for but somehow he'd managed to be a real jerk. Her reply got his attention.

"It's okay. Your brother more than made up for it last night. But of course if you're available later we could pick up where we left off last year." She smiled up at him and stroked his chest.

He stepped away. "No thanks. Please just… fluff your own pillows and leave me out of it!" He left her standing there with her mouth open. As he walked up the drive toward Lydia he wondered how much Cassie had told her.

~~~~~~~~

Lydia pulled her truck up and sat waiting on Jack. She started to just leave him. She wasn't excited about explaining him to some of the old ladies that she worked for. What would she say? She had no idea where she and Jack stood. Though he'd been such a gentleman at first the whole business of staying last night seemed a bit too convenient. Not to mention how strong he'd come on to her before the guys got there. What if she'd given in to him?

And after all the warnings she'd given her boys about women! She thought about her text to Jesse and looked at her phone to see if he'd responded. She smiled at his reply: A happy face AND a heart. She decided to text him back with a single word she was feeling, not only for the current day, but for the days ahead.

"Pray," she wrote him. She knew she could count on it. Her own prayers might not be heard but she was sure Jesse's were.

Jack walked up the drive and got into her truck. He had a weird look on his face.

"What's wrong," she asked. She waited before starting the truck. Jack was quiet and seemed to be struggling. She couldn't tell if it was anger, or worry, but it wasn't good whatever it was. The man was never at a loss for words.

"We need to talk," Jack spoke without looking at her.

"Like… I can drive us to the next job and we can talk on the way talk? Or find somewhere quiet because I'm about to drop a bomb talk?" Lydia waited knowing in her heart it was going to be the latter.

Jack finally looked at her and she knew. Shifting the old truck into gear she drove them to an area referred to by locals as "The Forest." A deeply shaded paved road connecting two small communities would provide privacy but keep her within close vicinity of the yards she planned to work on that day. Jack still hadn't said a word. She pulled from the road and turned off the truck, hoping she could get out of the mud when he finished.

"Spill it Jack." She looked at him expecting to get dumped and not much caring.

"I have really messed up Lydia." Jack began. "I need to tell you some things I'm not at all proud of."

She waited in the silence. It took a bit but finally he began. "My parents raised me to know the Lord, to honor Him. But I got a girl pregnant in high school." He sighed heavily then continued. "Long story short, I married her, we lost the baby, and got divorced all in the matter of a few months." His sad eyes looked at Lydia and her heart hurt for him.

"After that I ran as hard and as far as I could from both God and my family. There have been lots of women on lots of different jobs, something that grieved my Pop terribly. The business took a huge hit and he nearly stopped the charity. But last January God really got my attention and I've made a complete turnaround. I promised the Lord

I'd stop the womanizing and leave my future in His hands. I begged Him to bring a good woman into my life and I honestly believe that's why I met you. There have been no other women since January when I made my promise."

"But here's the worst." Jack continued with great effort. "Cassie, the woman that spoke to you about me, was one of those women. I stayed so wasted most of the time that I haven't even recognized her until just now. She and I spent a few nights together last July. I don't have the words to tell you how sorry I am."

He finally looked at her with deep sadness in his eyes, "Can you forgive me Lydia? She means nothing to me."

Lydia couldn't look at him as she tried to process the information. Of course the man had a past. Who didn't? But his had caught up with him right when Lydia entered the picture and she wasn't sure she'd heard the worst of it yet. Then it occurred to her.

"Is that who Johnny was with last night?" She looked at Jack expecting an answer. He slowly nodded yes.

She started the truck and spun the tires in the mud until they were back onto the pavement with a screech. They rode in silence back to the Parker job site where she stopped at the top of the drive to let Jack out. She sat waiting for him to exit the truck. Instead he tried again to let her know the difference that had taken place in his life.

"Lydia, last January, God saved my life. I had a death wish and He spared me. I know it was so that you and I could have something special together."

She glared at him and had that look he'd seen in the picture that cut through his soul like a hot knife. By saying the words "death wish" Jack had revealed he'd been prowling through her private things. The thought of it made her too angry to speak.

Jack tried again to dig his way out. "Sweetheart, please calm down. Maybe we can work through some of this on the way to the beach tomorrow."

She laughed sarcastically under her breath. "Nope and get the... just get out of my truck." It was all she could do not to give the man a good southern cussing.

As Jack walked toward his own truck he could hear the words his dad said to him when he had finally come home.

"You are forgiven Jack. But there will always be consequences to sin; some of them harder than others."

He had a feeling the consequences were about to hit the fan. The possibility of losing Lydia was suddenly very real. And she hadn't even heard the worst of it.

Chapter 28

She worked all afternoon on jobs around town, burying her anger as she dug in the dirt. Most of the elderly ladies just needed someone to visit with them. They loved chatting with her as she trimmed bushes or moved plants. She did her best to listen to them ramble on about the heat, their ailments, their grandkids and sometimes about life. She was afraid to stop by Norma's because the woman always picked up on her sadness. But she hadn't been by in a few days and wanted to check on her.

Norma was outside, talking to Jack. Lydia just kept on driving even though she knew they'd seen her. She wondered how Jack would explain his way through that.

How dare he? If he's hoping to charm my mom-in-law in order to win me back he's got another thing coming.

Again she thought about the shovel in the back of the truck.

Calling it a day she headed home. She was hungry and tired and her back hurt worse than usual. The rain had stopped so a good hot shower would be just what she needed, except for the hunger... and the love. She thought briefly about calling Jesse but decided against it. He had a wife. How could she allow such a thought to fly across her brain even for a moment? It was then she remembered the dream she'd had about him the night before. She shook the mental image from her head as her mama's words warned her from the grave.

It's one thing to let those birds fly over your head. It's a whole nother to let them build a nest in your hair.

She realized she was no better than Jack. Instead of calling Jesse she turned her truck around and pulled through Cook-Out's. There weren't many things a double fudge chocolate milkshake couldn't cure.

~~~~~~~

Leaving muddy work boots on the deck outside the sunroom she went inside to gather clean clothes and towels. She noticed a note on the table from Jack and walked by without picking it up. In her room she opened the bottom drawer which held the remainder of Blue's things. Lifting the photo album she checked in the back of it for the two final entries. They were missing. There in the drawer on top of a baby blanket they waited as if never handled by Jack. But she knew better. "Death Wish" was not something one said every day. She'd only heard it one other time, and that was from Jesse. He'd dared to take that picture to warn her of where she was headed if she didn't get help. That was the second time he'd saved her life.

She picked up the other picture and looked at it for a while.

"Why Lord?" she whispered tucking the two pictures into the pocket in the back of the album.

Why do You have to be so mean?

Retrieving her Bible from the den she angrily tossed it into the drawer and kicked it shut.

You belong in there with the other stuff that breaks my heart.

~~~~~~~

He watched excited to see that she was finally alone. So far she hadn't noticed her extra keys were missing. When she did, wouldn't it be fun? He imagined her running panicked into the house only to realize he was outside holding the keys. He leered and could hardly wait.

~~~~~~~

The shower was soothing until she heard someone drive up. She sighed and thought,

What's the use of having that stupid gate if everybody and their brother knows where the key to the padlock is?

She latched the shower door, dried off and dressed as quickly as she could. No one had made their presence known and it wigged her out. She opened the shower door and peeked out hoping it wasn't Jack.

Kurtis' jeep was parked near the porch. Walking around to the front of the house she found her boys waiting for her.

"You know it wouldn't hurt to give a girl a call before you came." She sounded miffed and they wondered why. Shawn mumbled louder than he meant to, "I thought that was LAST week."

"I heard that Shawn." Lydia walked onto the porch and plunked down on the swing so tired she thought she might cry. At least she didn't have to go to the beach in the morning. Pulling the towel from her head she leaned back on the pillows that were finally dry from the lemonade mishap. She almost laughed as she thought of it but stopped herself. Rearranging the cushions with two at one end, she stretched out her legs on the swing long ways and put the other under her knees.

That DOES help. She thought of Jack again.

"Brought you something," Shawn handed her a milkshake.

"Oh wow. Thanks." She slurped her favorite supper through the large straw thinking,

Hey bartender! Make mine a double.

"Do you mind if we stay here tonight? It's closer to leave from this side of town and we forgot to get our towels last night anyway." Kurtis asked. "Or will we be bothering you and Jack?"

She looked at him sideways. "You guys are welcome to stay here any time you want. In fact, we ought to get that other bed back down from the attic so you don't have to sleep on the couch Kurtis." Lydia was glad they hadn't asked earlier in the week or she might've given a different answer about them staying over.

Kurtis realized she hadn't answered the question about Jack. But before he could figure out how to ask again if they were in the way, Shawn blurted out, "Is Jack staying here tonight so we can get an early start?"

Lydia took a deep breath hoping she could say it without crying.

"I'm done with Jack."

Shawn and Kurt looked at each other then leaned forward in their rockers to look at Lydia. She closed her eyes hoping her back would ease off.

"So y'all aren't goin' to the beach?" Shawn was slow on the uptake. When she didn't answer, the two boys picked up their rockers and re-situated them in front of the swing looking at Lydia.

Shawn couldn't believe it. "What's going on? You were smilin' all the time and happy again." For years he'd protected her from guys who showed interest. Now finally when there was one he approved of she'd shown him the door.

"And Jack is a really good guy!" Kurtis added.

"That's what I keep hearing. It just didn't work out okay? Can y'all please let it go?" Lydia heard the tone she was using and felt bad that her boys were coming under her wrath a lot lately. "Sorry guys. It's been a crappy day. But I'm glad you're here. I could definitely use the company." She lied. She'd much rather just take a handful of Advil and go to bed. She thought of Jack's protection again and nearly smiled in spite of herself.

Kurt was sure they could work it out. "So did y'all have a fight? I could call him and we could play cards and maybe you'd make up. It's no good being alone all the time Liddy. Jack always makes you laugh."

She stood and walked between their two rockers to the front door. "I'm turning in early. You guys know where your sleeping stuff is. I'll fix breakfast for you and wake you about, what time?"

They stood too and moved their rockers back to the other side of the porch. "If we get up around 5:30 and leave by six we'll be there by ten." Kurtis wanted to make sure they had plenty of time on the beach.

"Don't you want to come with us?" Shawn asked.

"No honey. I need some space. But I'm glad you're here tonight." She tried to open the front door but it was locked.

Swear words learned at home during her childhood tumbled through her brain. It was all she could do to keep them at bay. She sighed a heavy sigh and leaned her head on the door.

"I got it!" Kurtis ran around the house to let her in. As he opened the front door for her from the inside he announced, "There was a note on the table. It might be from Jack." He handed it to her as he held the screen door open. She stuck it in her back pocket and walked wearily to the bathroom.

Can everybody please get out of my business? She murmured to no one in particular.

With three Advil and two milkshakes in her system she collapsed on the daybed. Even with pillows under her knees and a heating pad set on medium her back still kept her awake. She began to seriously consider getting out of the landscaping business. But what could she do? She hated dressing up so that immediately nullified most jobs she could think of. She would not under any circumstances go back to waitressing. She had hated that job while she and Blue were married. Remembering the picture she'd not thought about in quite a while she turned on her side pushing pillows to the floor.

All she'd ever really wanted to be was a good mother.

Chapter 29

Not wanting to deal with his brother Jack cleared his things from the motel room, sat in his truck and called his dad.

"Hello son. What's going on?" His father always had wise counsel. Jack nearly choked up at the sound of his voice.

"Hi Pop. It's been a rough day." Jack relayed to his father the events of the last few days trying to spare the details about Johnny. "It seems those consequences you spoke of have finally caught up with me. And I've hurt Lydia. I don't know that she'll give me another chance."

"I'm so sorry son." His dad grieved with him as if he were going through the loss himself. "All we can do now is pray. Maybe God's not through with this love affair yet."

"Oh Pop, please don't say affair. I'm so sick of it all." Jack leaned back on the truck seat and closed his eyes. "If only I knew something to do for her to win her heart back. But I don't think she'll ever trust me again. I had planned to tell her everything but I didn't want to scare her off so soon. The timing got shoved forward though." He sighed deeply again.

"I don't even know where I'm sleeping tonight." Jack laughed absentmindedly.

"So… you were staying at Lydia's?" His dad was surprised.

"NO! She wouldn't have it… I mean. Just forget about that part Pop. I'll find something. There are plenty of motel rooms here I think. I just haven't had time to check yet."

His dad wasn't exactly sure what was going on but he had a feeling it involved Johnny. Though he was considered the "good son" by his mother, his father continually prayed for his youngest boy's heart.

"I'll be praying Jack. Remain faithful. Don't let loneliness or discouragement wreck your purpose. I love you son. Please stay in the Word."

"I love you too Pop. Give Mom my love." Jack hung up wondering what to do next.

~~~~~~~

The house was quiet except for all the fans. Lydia got up to go to the bathroom. The clock on the stove said 3:30 as she walked through the kitchen. Once she was in the bathroom she pulled the note from her jeans which hung on the back of the door. Apparently Jack had a lot to say before he'd left yesterday morning. His handwriting beckoned.

"My Beloved Lydia,

I have many things to confess. First of all I accidently found your wedding album when I was putting away Blue's very large clothes [which by the way, made me feel like a little boy.] I couldn't help but look at your beautiful smile on your wedding day and wish it were for me. Blue was a very lucky man.

At some point two pictures fell out. I have to say that one of them was very scary. {{{Shiver}}} The look on your face as a biker babe is one I hope to never see. But even then you were smokin' hot! Smiley face.

The other picture fills my heart with so much love that I can't help but hope.

Lydia, you are the only girl for me. Can we please try to make this work? Before you jump for joy at the wondrous opportunity to deal with me on a regular basis, I have many things to confess to you in person. The mistakes I've made still haunt me. I too had a death wish, but I've been given a second chance. I want very much to do well. I believe that's possible with you by my side.

All my love, Jack

PS: Even Jackasses need love and lemonade. Don't forget the lemonade. Can I puh-leeeese have your recipe?"

Lydia laughed at her crazy Jack.

Him and his speeches.

She read the letter again and dared to hope.

She looked at her phone and remembered a similar morning only a few days ago. She wondered if Jack were lying in bed praying for her. She started to text him but decided it could wait til morning. At least now maybe she could get some rest.

"Lord," she prayed. "If I were You I wouldn't listen to the likes of me. But please help. My heart hurts."

Settling into the daybed she situated the pillows under her knees again. Her phone lit up with a text.

"Praying for you Dearheart. Hope your dinger is off."

She laughed. Kurtis was right, Jack always made her laugh. Now if he could just quit making her cry.

Though she didn't text him back she decided that she'd talk things out with him once the boys left. What did she have to lose?

~~~~~~~

After a very nice two hour nap the alarm went off. Feeling like a mother of middle schoolers, she made breakfast and sandwiches and snacks for her boys as they slowly readied themselves for a day at the beach. She thought to herself that she WAS a mother in some ways. These guys had no one who cared or even knew where they were half the time. But she and Blue had taken them in and raised them as their own. At least she'd been a mother to Shawn and Kurtis. With a hug and another warning to stay away from the hoochie mamas she watched from the porch til they were out of sight. It made her heart happy that they'd nearly begged her to go with them. How many college boys would want their mama tagging along?

Summertime at six seventeen a.m. brilliant color stretched across the eastern sky. She stepped into the front yard to get a better look. Her heart soared at the beautiful sight. She thought of the Artist. Jesse reminded her often how God splashed His love across the sky twice a day just to remind her of His love. If only she wouldn't mess up so bad thinking those words and wishing to die. An old familiar cloud began to engulf her. She nearly jumped out of her skin when her phone buzzed in her sleeping shorts pocket.

"Hey Jesse-man," she answered. She walked barefoot through the wet dew to the front porch as they talked.

138

"Just wanted to say have a good day with Jack. Are y'all down the road yet? "

"Nah… I called it off. I'm at home." Lydia wasn't sure how much to tell. The last time they'd talked Jesse had helped her give Jack the benefit of the doubt. A lot had changed since then. Lydia still wasn't sure.

Jesse sounded surprised. "Called it off? It's a perfect day for a swim in the ocean. I know for a fact that saltwater cures a world of pain, sometimes even better than cookies!"

She smiled at her friend and wondered what he would think of Jack's confession to her.

"Hey Jesse, how would you deal with someone's past? Like… if you loved them… and they had mistakes that they were dealing with." She couldn't even put into words her question.

Jesse knew she was struggling and wanted to help. "If you for instance, had things in your past that were really bad, and let's say someone loved you. I would think that they would help you get through the hurt by loving you the best way they knew how. They sure wouldn't ditch you in your time of need." Jesse waited and hoped his words would sink in.

"Don't misunderstand me honey. Just like you've helped me get through things with Kenya, and I've helped you get through losing Blue, Jack needs you. Sometimes God allows us to go through trouble so that we can learn to comfort others. In light of that, you should be an AWESOME comforter!" He laughed then asked.

"Have you got a Bible handy?" To her shame she answered no.

"Next time you do look up 2 Corinthians 1. It gives us a wise perspective on trials. God doesn't comfort us to make us comfortable. He comforts us to make us COMFORTERS. Jack probably needs your care more than you can imagine."

"Thanks Jesse. I'll think on that."

"I love you too." Jesse laughed at her non-words. "OH! And thanks for your promise. Stay strong Chickadee. I'm praying for you."

"I will Jesse." She hung up and thought about calling Jack. But it was still so early. She might as well wait and give him a chance to sleep in since it was Saturday. If he was like her he was probably up half the night worrying. She yawned and stretched long ways on the swing. The morning air was pleasant and cool.

Her phone lit up with a text from Jack. "Wish we could talk. Need coffee."

She texted him back: "Yes on coffee."

He rolled up approximately three minutes later. She went inside and pulled on jeans with her t-shirt. He waited on the porch swing until she returned. Handing his coffee to him she sat on the other end of the swing with a fresh hot cup in hand.

She finally broke the silence with a sigh and a tentative smile. "Ah precious nectar of life!" Jack took a deep sigh of relief as well. He was doing his best to be still and wait though it was very hard to keep his words unsaid. She was content to slowly swing and sip coffee. When Jack could stand the silence no longer he asked, "Did you get all your clients taken care of yesterday?"

"Yep," she replied.

Jack waited a bit then added hopefully, "I went by Norma's and divided hosta. She has lots of plans for her yard." Jack knew Lydia had seen him there but didn't bring it up.

"Did you move her bench?" Lydia wondered.

"I did. It is now in a lovely spot so that her side yard 'looks like a park.'" Jack smiled at Norma's compliment. He really liked her. "We had a nice visit. She has many good things to say about you."

"Yep. I love her." Lydia remarked without hesitation.

Jack tried to keep the conversation going plus he wondered if Lydia had injured herself on the job. "Kurtis said your back was hurting again. How are you feeling this morning?"

"When did you talk with Kurt?" Lydia asked finally looking at Jack. He didn't look good.

"He called to tell me they were on the way to the beach and that I might want to check on you because you were in a lot of pain last night. He said your back hurt so bad that you were crying." Jack looked at her with tears.

She waited a bit then answered as honestly as she could.

"It did. But this nice man I know gave me a heating pad and that helped some." She smiled just enough to encourage Jack to reach for her hand.

"Lydia…" he whispered. "I'm so sorry."

Slowly she slid over next to him and allowed his arm to go around her.

Jack finally broke the silence again when he asked, "Have you had breakfast yet?"

"I have." Lydia answered. She was trying to remember if there was anything left she could cook for him.

"Do I smell bacon?" Jack asked hopefully.

"You do. I fried some for the boys."

"Is there any left?" Jack wondered.

Lydia looked at him and asked, "You've met Shawn and Kurtis haven't you?"

"Good point." Jack sighed.

"C'mon. Let's find you something to eat." Lydia pulled him to his feet and led him inside. Peering into the refrigerator she realized she'd used just about everything getting the boys out the door.

"What did you have for supper last night? Are there any leftovers?" Jack was looking too.

"I had two milkshakes." Lydia laughed. "Made mine a double."

Jack could stand it no longer. He pulled her into his arms and sobbed into her hair. He was a broken man. Lydia stroked his back and cried with him. "It's gonna be okay Jack. I'm here for you. Maybe we should go through this together."

They held each other for a moment then Lydia announced, "Hey! It's a beautiful day! Let's forget this mess and do something fun!" Suddenly she was in charge of comfort. "What sounds good to you? We could rest or take a drive... or rest? I've got nothing Jack. We probably should go grocery shopping."

"I have a present for you," he finally smiled. "Be right back."

Lydia hoped it wasn't florist flowers. She hated wasting money like that when the fields were full of beautiful ones for free. She shook her head when she thought about how weird she was. Jack returned with both hands behind his back.

"These are for you." He handed her a bouquet from a large bush leading into her property. She laughed and said, "These look vaguely familiar. I love hydrangeas!"

"And this is a new dryer element. It should be the right one. I'll install it today in case I ever wet my pants over here again."

Lydia laughed, "My kind of man!" She found a blue Mason jar under the sink and placed the bouquet of color on her kitchen table. "I love it."

She smiled that smile Jack loved so well and asked, "I've got an idea for breakfast. How about waffles?" She'd just noticed her waffle iron in the cabinet with the jars. It wasn't something she used often.

Jack remembered the really bad pancakes she'd made for him the same morning she scorched the syrup. But for loves sake he said, "That sounds great!"

Lydia looked at him and tried to word what she was thinking, then decided not to say it. Jack knew her well enough to know she was holding something back.

"As you say Lydia, just spill it. What are you thinking? Do you need to be alone today to sort things out?" Jack asked.

"No." She put vegetable oil on a rag and wiped down the seldom used waffle iron. "It's just that… you kinda look like crap."

Jack laughed his regular laugh and it made her happy. "I moved out of my motel room so I wouldn't bump into Johnny and…"

"Cassie?" she asked.

"CASSIE! What is WRONG with me? I can't remember that woman's name. Anyway I checked into a place that turned out to be less than five stars." He shuddered as he thought of it. "I couldn't stay there after I saw… let's just say it was disgusting. I ended up sleeping in the truck after about three thirty this morning. So I haven't had a shower. TMI?" He asked.

"Three thirty. That's about the time I was reading your letter wondering if you were praying for me again." She paused then offered. "Why don't you go get a shower? You'll feel better. It takes a bit to make waffles anyway."

Jack looked at her surprised. "Really? Thanks Sweetheart. I'm sorry. Can I call you that?"

"Please do." She smiled. "Grab your stuff and take it to the outside shower. The inside one doesn't have hardly any water pressure. Waffles in thirty."

She began dividing eggs adding the whites to the mixing bowl. Jack circled her waist, kissed her cheek and left the kitchen. Never in his life had a woman told him he looked like crap. He was used to being rewarded well for his good looks. But Lydia's words were music to his ears. For somehow she cared for him in spite of who she'd discovered him to be.

Chapter 30

Jack entered the kitchen a new man. Showered, shaved and wearing jeans and a black t-shirt, Lydia had a hard time taking her eyes off him. He ate the waffles with gusto exclaiming often how good they were. "What kind of syrup is this? It's better than that other stuff."

"You mean you don't like scorched syrup?" She laughed at his polite way of putting things. "I made this out of brown sugar and water. Just stir together two parts sugar to water and bring it up to a boil. I'm glad the waffles turned out okay. After those pancakes I served you it's a wonder you'd want me to cook for you at all." She laughed at the memory.

"I think we were a little distracted that morning." He smiled up at her from his plate of waffles.

She nodded and her face flushed. "Maybe just a little…"

Jack was glad she smiled. "You never did answer me. How's your back feeling today? Is it still your period or have you hurt yourself on the job?"

Lydia looked at him tipping her head sideways. "I think we need to set some groundwork for which topics are acceptable. I do not talk about my…"

"Period?" he smiled a playful smile. "Why not? It's just life. If I know what's going on I can better understand why you get so cranky."

"I DO NOT GET CRANKY!" Lydia laughed in spite of herself. "A tad moody maybe, but we are not going to talk about my… personal stuff out loud in front of God and everybody. Good grief!"

"So answer the question dear. Is your back still hurting for the same reason it hurt last week? I'm trying not to say the forbidden word. But if it's lasting this long we may need to get you to a doctor."

"I've already been to a doctor and it's just a thing. It hardly ever happens so I never know when anymore. Hey! Can we please talk about something else? It's all done so that's not why my back is hurting. Let's talk about the list of unacceptable topics."

"You mean there's more?" Jack swirled the waffle in the hot homemade syrup making sure not to miss a drop. "Man! These are really good! How did you make them? Did I see you beating egg whites?"

"Yep. That's the key. Beat them till they're stiff then fold them into the batter. Of course all that butter doesn't hurt. I'm glad you actually like them and aren't just being pancake polite."

Jack laughed and pushed his plate aside. Retrieving the coffee pot he refilled their cups. "What other topics do we avoid my dear?"

When he sat back down at the table she took his hand. "Jack, I know you have a past. But I don't think I want to hear about it." She paused trying to say the words that she dreaded saying.

"The thought of you being in the bed with other women nearly rips my heart out. But if you promise me that's not who you are any more, I will trust you and try my best not to let it bother me. So just don't bring it up and I'll never ask you about it again."

Jack took both her hands in his and looked her straight in the eye. "I promise Lydia. There will be no more womanizing. I promise to love you and only you."

He said it so freely and quickly that she wondered if he heard the words he'd just spoken. The question lingered in her mind. Surely he knew where she stood. Suddenly she remembered how strong he'd come on to her just a few nights earlier. Jesse's words spoke softly to her soul.

"He must be a one woman man in order for you to rest in his love. A marriage covenant is a beautiful thing designed by God. Do things His way and you'll have no guilt or regret later on."

She decided it must be said.

"And Jack… you need to understand, I don't plan to sleep with anybody I'm not married to. I know it's old fashioned." She stopped and wondered if the blushing would ever end. "But you need to know that about me before we continue. I'm not like the women you've loved and left. I don't think I could survive another broken heart."

He drew her to him and whispered. "I'm sorry about the other night Lydia. Please forgive me. I'll be more careful. I'm just so in love with you."

She hugged him and felt they were making an important commitment to one another.

Jack spoke up determined to set some boundaries as well. "While we're talking about this, I need to ask you to do something similar only the opposite." Lydia laughed at his funny way of putting things. She thought it might be that he didn't want to hear about Blue. She'd learned long ago that when she said his name people around her became uncomfortable.

"What can I keep quiet about for your sake? Spill it honey. I can do it." She held his hand waiting.

"I need you to NOT keep quiet about something. I know you think of Jesse as your counselor but I need to know when you meet with him. It's probably not right, but I'm so jealous that I really want you to be transparent and talk to me the way you talk with him. It feels odd that he seems to know so much about you and I don't." He looked at her with such authority that it surprised her.

She sat there thinking, not realizing that to Jack it felt like hesitation. When she looked back at him his face was clouded with worry and he added. "Maybe I don't have the right to ask that of you, but Lydia the guy worries me."

She started to take up for Jesse and tell Jack that Kenya had left him over twelve years ago. But she knew Jack wasn't ready to hear it.

"I can do that Jack. If a woman called you or asked you to lunch I'd probably hit her in the head with a shovel and bury her in the garden. In fact, that's where I put Cassie!" She laughed then realized she'd already broken rule one.

"Oops. This might be harder than I thought!" She laughed.

Jack laughed too. "I don't think that's the rule I'm going to struggle with." He looked at her then asked, "Anything else? I don't tell you and you DO tell me? This day is shaping up nicely!"

"AND you don't talk about woman stuff to me like regular suppertime conversation. It's just weird."

"Sorry. That's a deal breaker. If I think I can help you, I'm going to say it. Period. Hahahaha... see what I did there?" Lydia was not amused. Actually she was but she tried her best not to show it. She shook her head at him.

Jack couldn't let it go. "In fact, my sister went on birth control and her periods became regular. She has a lot less trouble now."

Lydia looked down and sighed deeply. "Please Jack? You're embarrassing me."

"I'm sorry Sweetheart. I'll behave. Let me make it up to you by repairing your dryer." He lifted her hand to his lips and kissed it. She sighed and thought,

Whatever. Just so you heard the rest of the stuff I told you.

Chapter 31

Lydia began cleaning the kitchen. Jack looked for the breaker box to turn off the power. When he opened the dryer a foul odor filled the room.

"These jeans stink Lydia!"

"Oh no! I forgot to start the dryer again after I got yours out yesterday. Stupid dryer!"

"I have never in my life heard of clothes souring. How does that happen?" Jack started pulling the smelly jeans from the dryer and loading the washer with them.

"It's this terrible heat. We added the laundry closet when we built the sunroom so there's no air conditioner in there. But since you're fixing my dryer it shouldn't be an issue; IF I can remember to move the clothes from the washer to the dryer AND turn the dryer on. I'm not very domestic."

"No kidding!" Jack laughed and Lydia didn't know whether to be glad he was back to being himself or mad that he agreed so wholeheartedly about her lack of homemaking ability.

Jack flipped the breaker back on and started the washer. Lydia continued cleaning the kitchen. Jack joined her and began washing the dishes.

"You don't have to do that," Lydia protested and bumped him out of the way with a hip check. Immediately she was sorry as her back reminded her something was still wrong.

"You okay?" Jack saw the look on her face.

"Yep. Just need to be still a minute." She walked slowly to the sunroom and sank into her daybed. Jack was right behind her lifting her legs onto a pillow. "Where's your heating pad?" He sat on the edge of the daybed and looked down the opposite side for the control. "Is it at the right place on your back?" He asked as he leaned over her to switch it on.

Lydia looked into his eyes and saw the man she'd fallen hard for. Pulling him close she kissed him so tenderly that Jack nearly sank in beside her.

"Wow. That was nice! Did you just pull a fast one to get me into bed?" He smiled that mischievous smile.

"Maybe…" Lydia gazed back at him loving his nearness.

He leaned down for another kiss. "I need to tell you one more thing about the other night, and then I promise not to talk about the past."

Lydia wondered why he'd spoil their beautiful moment. She longed to just rest in his arms and wished she could figure out how to tell him how lonely she was without him taking it wrong. But he was speaking.

"I promise you I did not plan to stay here that night my brother left me high and dry. I know somehow I broke something by staying in your bed, even though you weren't in it."

Lydia was embarrassed again but decided it was best just to go ahead and say it.

"In light of our new agreement on transparency and such, I took the sheets off my bed when Blue died and nobody's been in there since. So yes, it seemed wrong somehow. BUT what's done is done and if you think you can behave you're welcome to stay here til the Parker project is finished. It's only another week. And as you know, I sleep out here anyway. But we'll have to be careful. Like this right here that feels really good? We can't do this! I promise to do better too. I'm just so lonely Jack."

Jack was completely surprised that she offered to let him stay and wondered if she really meant what she said earlier about only sleeping with the man who married her. He lifted her hand to his lips. "Thank you Sweetheart. I love you so much."

She smiled but she couldn't say the words because she was about to cry. Instead she kissed his hand and laughed. "If it's okay, I'm going to take a nap and see if this pain will ease off. Please don't do too much around here. Just get some rest today and think about if you'd like to go to the beach tomorrow."

"That's a good idea, if you feel like it. What time's the early service at church?"

"It starts at 9:15 and we could be on the road by 10:30. It takes about four hours to get there so we could have our toes in the sand by 2:30 or 3 o'clock."

He leaned over and kissed her lightly. Rest well. I'll probably take a nap too. Are you sure you don't mind me being in there?" He brushed the curls from her forehead.

"Nope. Not at all." She smiled and he knew they were good. It was all he could do not to crawl in beside her. He knew he should pray hard before he decided to stay there the next week.

Within three minutes she was sleeping so soundly that she never knew he washed the dishes, fixed the dryer and threw the load of jeans in to dry. Falling face down in the middle of the feather topper he was down for the count sleeping better than he had since the last time he'd crashed there.

Chapter 32

When finally she woke she was surprised at how good she felt. Her back wasn't hurting but best of all her heart didn't have that familiar ache. She whispered,

Thank You Lord. Sorry I stuck You in the drawer.

She stretched and walked carefully making sure she didn't move too fast or undo her back again. Her reflection in the bathroom medicine cabinet revealed a face with no makeup and hair that seemed to have a mind of its own.

It wouldn't hurt to try a little harder for the pretty man, she thought.

With that in mind she pulled her hair up and added mascara. Her clothes were in Jack's room so she'd have to wait to improve that part of her appearance. Even then she wasn't sure there was anything better to choose from. Why did she have to be such a terrible shopper? Once while searching for a swimsuit she commented to the dressing room attendant, "I'd rather take a beating than try on bathing suits." The rather large lady had proclaimed, "That can be arranged!" Apparently it had been a hard morning. With that memory came the realization that she'd have to wear a swimsuit if she and Jack went to the beach.

"Crap!" she whispered. It was one thing to ride down with the boys and just wear cut offs and an old top she'd had since high school. But for Jack? What could she do?

When she left the bathroom and walked through the kitchen toward the laundry closet a man's voice made her jump out of her skin.

"Hello sleepyhead." Jack laughed when she jumped. "I'm sorry. I didn't mean to startle you!" He was still laughing.

Lydia frowned at him. "Don't be sneaking around like that! You scared the life out of me!"

"Are you sure that woman stuff is over because you're still kind of cranky." Jack laughed at her.

She ignored him and headed toward the dryer doubting that he'd moved the wash. The jeans were already dry and smelling nice. "Wow! Thanks Jack! This is awesome! And you cleaned the kitchen too? You're a little bit amazing."

Jack tried out his best Southern imitation. "Aww shucks ma'am. Want to go grocery shopping with me?"

"When're you leaving?" she asked.

"I was going out the door when I thought I heard you get up so I came back to see if you felt like going." He paused and added, "This feels so cowboy-like. Want to ride into town with me little lady?"

She laughed at her funny man. "Be right with you partner." She fetched some money she'd just earned the day before along with her debit card. She might actually turn loose of a few bucks on something besides the necessities. But most likely she'd talk herself out of it.

Once they neared town Lydia asked Jack if he'd mind dropping her off at a clothing store while he picked up groceries.

"Sure," he said, happy she would be shopping for something new to wear. "What are you looking for?"

"That's not a topic for discussion dear." She smiled mischievously and he had to ponder what was going through her brain. For a brief moment he wondered if she were shopping for lingerie on his account.

"Surely not," he thought. But he looked at her quizzically as she left his truck and walked into the shop. As he drove to the grocery store he imagined how nice that would be. She HAD just invited him to stay with her next week. Though he knew better he allowed himself to hope for things he shouldn't.

He quickly finished shopping then parked in front of her store. When she didn't come out after a while he walked inside looking for her. The shop wasn't that big but she was nowhere to be found. Approaching the clerk near the dressing room he asked, "Can you check to see if my friend is back there?" The young lady smiled and asked, "Is she trying on swimsuits?"

"I don't really know, but she has beautiful light red hair about the color of honey and blue eyes that…" Jack realized he was over explaining and stopped as another sales clerk walked from the back.

"She's in the dressing room. Over here is the swimsuit rack. She's having a hard time so maybe you could help her decide.

Lydia could hear it all and was mortified. How did these things happen? She couldn't figure out her size. It had been about a hundred years since she'd bought a bathing suit. Blue didn't like her wearing a two piece but she'd decided they were much more comfortable. And he wasn't there to tell her what to do. But apparently she'd put on a few pounds in the last… how long had it been?

"Ma'am? Your boyfriend asked me to pass these to you. Come out when you have one on and we'll help you decide."

Lydia thought as she reached over the door for the suits.

Yep. You stand there and wait for that to happen Chickie. Hitler will be ice skating in Hell before I walk out in a bathing suit in front of God and Jack and everybody.

She struggled into another one.

Great. The top is too loose and the bottom is waaayyy too small. Now I get to announce that my butt should come with a beeper in case I need to back up like a dump truck. Who wears these teenie-tiny bottoms anyway?

The nice young sales clerk asked, "Need anything? A different color or size? Oh here, your boyfriend handed me this one." Lydia thought she heard the girl laugh. She held up the string bikini and sighed. Tossing it onto the bench she grabbed another.

As she pulled each piece on she stood back trying to look without stepping out of the dressing room. Why did they always put the three-way mirrors in the area exposed to the store? The bottom was still too small. Maybe it was the cut of it. The top actually looked very nice.

The voice of a black woman came to her door. "Honey how's that last one, too small through the bottom? I have the same problem. They make these suits for little girls with no butts. Here. Try this one cut for women who actually have a figure!"

Lydia's neck was glowing but at least someone understood. Pulling the bottoms on she happily discovered they fit perfectly.

"Winner winner chicken dinner!" She informed the search party so they'd quit 'helping.'

Jack called to her, "Come out so I can see." She heard the mischief in his voice. He knew she wasn't coming out.

"Stand right where you are dear and wait for that to happen." She smiled that somehow she'd survived the trauma. Perhaps she'd treat them to milkshakes on the way home. Maybe all those calories of late would start landing in her boobs for a change.

In fact she should probably drink two again just in case.

As she dressed to leave she noticed her neck was still red. It was likely to stay that way as long as she dealt with Jack.

Chapter 33

Jack cooked a wonderful meal while Lydia tried on her new bathing suit in the bathroom. The cute little strapless white top flowed softly with a very feminine ruffle. But it was secure enough to keep Flopsy and Mopsy contained even if she played volleyball. The baby blue and white bottoms fit well and covered her ample rear end. Quickly she moved through the hall to the bedroom to look for something to wear as a cover-up. In the back of her closet she found a white sundress that was too short to wear anywhere but the beach. That would work well over her new suit to ride down in. At least now maybe she wouldn't look like a maintenance man.

As she changed back into normal clothes she prayed.

"This is really nice of you God." She felt better about herself than she had in years. That reminded her to pull her Bible from Blue's drawer. She would keep it near her daybed to help her remember to keep her word to Jesse and now also to the Lord.

After they washed dishes together Jack surprised her by asking, "May I have this dance?"

"What dance?" She asked wondering if she'd missed something.

"The one we're about to have." Jack started his playlist and dropped his cell into an empty glass. Music filled the kitchen as he took her into his arms. She'd always loved to dance as it was one of the best memories of her mama and daddy. They too had danced in the kitchen. Her daddy had taught her as a very young girl how to let a man take the lead. Blue had not approved. His family was dead set against dancing and secular music of any kind as it led to "other questionable practices." She and Blue didn't even go to prom. There was no music at their wedding except for a few hymns. They were fine, but not exactly romantic. Through high school and their entire five years of marriage he hadn't danced with her once.

Now to be held in Jack's arms and pushed around the kitchen floor with ease, Lydia was in heaven. She nearly cried when she realized that yet another gift had been given to her through Jack. He noticed she'd teared up and commented, "That's a good song isn't it? I'm sorry if this reminds you of Blue."

"Oh no. It doesn't remind me of Blue at all. It makes me thankful for you Jack. Blue and I never danced. He didn't believe in it."

Jack stopped and looked at her. "You're kidding right? I thought the man walked on water."

Lydia laughed and said, "He did. He was fine with walking."

Jack shook his head. "Unbelievable. Then how do you know how to dance so well?"

She smiled mischievously as she looked into his eyes. "I said Blue didn't dance with me. I didn't say anything about anybody else." Jack didn't need to know everything about her past.

He pulled her close and whispered, "From now on, all your slow dances are reserved for me."

"Likewise Jack. After all, according to the ladies at the dress shop you ARE my boyfriend."

They danced for a long time. Jack kissed her tenderly, then like a gentleman walked her to the door of the sunroom. "Sleep well darling. I love you." He walked away not waiting on her to say it back. So his heart felt terribly happy as she spoke behind him.

"I love you too honey. Thank you for a beautiful day." He turned to see her smile then made himself walk away.

As each of them settled into bed they realized they'd forgotten to talk about when they'd leave for the beach. Jack started to go ask her then thought better of it. Lydia decided it didn't matter. She'd be up early either way. She dropped her jeans and bra by the daybed. The t-shirt would be fine for sleeping. But if Jack was going to stay there she'd have to get used to gathering clothes before he turned in.

"Lord You know I love having him here. But protect us. The thought of his leaving in a week makes my heart hurt." When she pulled up the sheet her Bible fell out. By lamplight she read the coffee stained pages in 1 Corinthians 13 again. The words reminded her of Jack.

~~~~~~~

It wasn't as good as most nights, especially with that man there. She had even kissed the new man forgetting she was his girl. Plus she had a Bible with her. It made him angry and sick to his stomach. The next time he was in the house he'd get rid of that Bible. He decided to be more diligent. His timetable had been delayed again and he was tired of being disappointed. That man wouldn't be with her all the time. He'd start napping during the day and watch for an opportunity at night if he had to.

Chapter 34

Jack found her on the porch swing before 7 a.m. with her Bible and an empty coffee cup in her lap. Apparently she'd been up a while. "Why is the porch wet?" he wondered out loud.

"I watered my ferns and geraniums this morning before it gets scorching hot." She moved her legs so he could sit.

"Good grief. What time do you get up anyway?" Jack thought he'd risen early but it seemed she'd already done a day's work.

"Around 5:30 if I'm lucky, at least I try to stay in bed that long. I'm kind of crazy. What time do you get up, like on a day when you don't have to be anywhere?" She wondered if this would become an issue like it had with Blue.

"Oh eight or nine. I'm not exactly a morning person."

"Sounds like Blue," she laughed. Then she realized what she'd said. "I'm sorry. I'm sure you get sick of hearing about him."

"Not really. When you talk about him I don't feel so bad about not measuring up. So did that work out for you two, him sleeping in and you getting up early?" Jack was hoping it wouldn't be a problem. He had the tendency to stay up half the night watching old movies. Her reply surprised him.

"No it didn't work out! We fought like stupid kids over it." She shook her head at the memory. "But if I had it to do over again," She wished the truth didn't make her feel so sad.

"What would you do?" Jack slid close to her and put his arm around her. "Would you take an afternoon nap so you could lure him into the wild dangerous world of dancing in the kitchen with his wife late at night? Because if he were smart he'd totally get on board with that."

Lydia looked at him. "I wonder if he's wishing he'd done things differently too? I never thought about that."

"Well yeah! He's standing before the Lord so I'm guessing that he is." Jack shook his head sadly, "But won't we all?"

Jack quickly changed the subject. "Okay! That concludes the sermonette for the Christianettes this morning! Let's get this party started! I actually DO have to set my clock if I ever roll out of bed before eight. So let's head to the beach before it gets any hotter."

"So we're skipping church?" Lydia was surprised.

"Yes darling, we are skipping church! I get the impression you think God keeps a giant score card. But He's happy when we enjoy life and see good days. You can drop your tithe check in next week, and from the looks of things you've already been in His Word a while this morning. So get your pretty self ready and let's go baby!"

Jack thought Lydia's eyes sparkled with happiness he'd not seen before except in the picture when she was pregnant. He marveled as she packed a cooler with a jug of lemonade and plastic cups. Did these beaches not have stores? Sandwiches were quickly made and positioned on top of the ice she broke from trays into a large Ziploc bag. Apparently there were no fast food joints either. After they woofed down milk and cereal, she pulled a gym bag from the top of her closet and placed it on the bed. Gathering an old flat sheet, towels, extra shorts, undies and a tank top she began packing it all in the bag. "Sunscreen!" She said to no one in particular and went to retrieve it.

Jack emerged from the bathroom in navy and white trunks and a baby blue V-neck shirt. She tried not to stare. The man was gorgeous. He held out a pair of shorts and another shirt folded together. "Got room for these?"

"Sure." She reached for them without looking and a pair of underwear fell out. Stacking the items on the bed she rolled them together and slid them into her bag. He noticed her throat was red. He laughed at her blushing.

"C'mere." He gathered her into his arms. "I really don't try to embarrass you. Are we about ready to leave? Are you riding down in that?"

Again she was embarrassed as she stood there in yesterday's clothes. "Nope. I can't quite get the timing down on getting dressed with you in the house. Maybe you can help remind me to gather stuff from your room before you turn in at night." She had pulled away from him and busied herself straightening the things in the bag. He suspected the long string of words were an effort to deflect his attention. So he changed the subject as well.

"Mind if I drive your truck? We can take mine if you want to have air, but I love your old truck." He knew she loved it too. Besides, it had a bench seat and no seatbelts. It reminded him of a country song.

"I'd love that!" She finally smiled that smile again. Jack realized as he looked at her that this was one complicated chick. She added apologetically, "The radio doesn't play though."

"No problem. My phone's charged up. I'll go pack our stuff while you get ready." He kissed her on the cheek and closed the bedroom door behind him trying his best to give her some privacy.

Lydia sighed suddenly unsure of the bathing suit she was about to put on. Maybe she should just wear cut-offs as usual. A glance in the dresser mirror confirmed what she felt about herself. No wonder Jack had women flocking around him. How could he ever be content with just her?

You're such a bumpkin...

She sighed and shook her head sadly.

When she finally emerged from the bedroom Jack was surprised that she wore cut-offs and a t-shirt. Her bathing suit was tossed on the bed. He stood looking at her but she wouldn't look at him.

"What's going on in your brain you crazy chick?" Jack asked but he wasn't smiling.

"I can't talk about it. Are you ready to leave?" She still wouldn't look at him.

"No. I'm going to wait on the most beautiful girl in the world to dress like she's about to ride four hours in a truck with no air. Lydia dear, it's me, Jack. And I'm telling you, I can hardly take my eyes off you." He pulled her into his arms and lowered his head so she had to look at him. "Listen to me. You are so beautiful."

He held her for a while and stroked her back. When finally she relaxed he said, "Now go get ready woman! Like you always say, we're burning daylight!"

She went to the bedroom and dressed in the bathing suit that yesterday had seemed so right. Without a full length mirror to confirm or deny her insecurities she added the white sundress. Stepping into flip flops, she pulled her hair into a ponytail and sighed a deep sigh.

She stood in the hall adjusting the thermostat to eighty. Jack watched and wondered at the method of her madness, but was very glad at how cute and comfortable she looked. She tried to smile but hoped Jack wouldn't comment on her appearance. She knew what she was.

"Did you happen to pack Advil?" He asked out of the blue.

"Good idea." She answered as she grabbed the whole bottle. "Did I already give you a headache?" She smiled at her own stupidity.

"No, just trying to prepare in case Ms. Cranky Pants rides along." She wasn't laughing so he added, "You look lovely by the way."

"Whatever." Lydia finally smiled again.

Once they were in the truck Lydia relaxed and of course ditched the flip flops. Off they went and it was remarkably only 7:37 am. Jack rolled slowly up the drive so as not to stir too much dust since their windows were down. "Why did you turn the air conditioner off in the house? Is that like making sure the iron is unplugged?"

She shook her head. "No need in the air running all day when we're not even home. The house is so tiny that it will be cool within ten minutes once we get back." She was glad they weren't talking about her appearance.

"Oh. Just trying to keep up with how you do things down here."

She appreciated that and was about to tell him so when he started a song on his phone. "I have a very tender love song to play for you. It fits us perfectly."

"…I love big butts and I cannot lie… when a girl walks in with an itty bitty waist…"

Lydia didn't recognize it. In fact it was strange, unlike the songs they'd danced to the night before. When finally she was able to pick up on the words she smacked his arm. "JACK STEPHENS! That is NOT nice!"

He was laughing so hard but reached to turn the song off lest she hear the rest.

Thankfully she was laughing too.

"I cannot believe you played that song for me. How dare you?!" She would definitely leave her sundress on for the day. And her neck would probably still be glowing when they got to the beach in four hours.

Jack pulled over, stopped the truck and got out.

She rolled her eyes and sighed.

Now what?

Pushing the bench seat forward he brought two pillows out for her. "Here. Lean against the door with one behind your back, and use the other under your knees on the seat. Maybe you won't hurt as much."

The man made her crazy.

"And lock your door so you don't fall out if I take a curve too fast." He reached across and locked it for her.

She obeyed swinging her legs onto the bench seat as she informed him, "No need to worry about curves. There's not a single one between here and the coast."

Jack refrained from saying what he wanted to about her curves. Instead he pulled her feet onto his lap rubbing them while he drove as if it were the most natural thing in the world. Lydia was glad that her feet were not nearly as rough as her hands.

His eyes were finally on the road as they pulled out of the gravel drive. But she couldn't take her eyes off him. Perhaps she could get used to being loved after all.

162

Chapter 35

They found a park on the beach in North Myrtle somewhere around Cherry Grove. Together they spread the sheet placing the bag and cooler to hold it down in the stiff breeze. Jack liked the idea of having more area out of the sand than just a beach towel. Lying close to Lydia was definitely a perk as well. Remembering how shy she was he decided not to suggest she remove her sundress. He pulled his shirt off and stretched face down enjoying the warmth of the sun. He nearly jumped out of his skin when cold lotion hit his back.

"Would it kill you to warn a guy?" he asked laughing.

On her knees beside him she rubbed the sunscreen in with a thorough massage. "Sorry my hands are so rough." She apologized as she smoothed in the lotion.

"It's okay. That's the sign of a working girl," Jack replied absentmindedly. Once he heard what he'd said he sat up abruptly. "Umm… what I MEANT was… here baby. Let me rub some of that on your back."

Lydia looked at him shaking her head. She laughed and said, "Shut up and lay back down." Jack obeyed. When she finished he asked, "Need me to…" He was trying to be careful how the words sounded that were about to come out of his mouth. Lydia helped by informing him that she'd greased down before leaving the house. Lying beside him she wondered why she'd declined his touch.

They rested near each other for a while in the wonderful breeze, Jack shirtless and Lydia in a dress. She was beginning to feel silly for not removing it when Jack asked if she'd like to take a swim. She surprised him by taking that stupid dress off and allowing him to pull her to her feet. Hand in hand they walked to the ocean's edge where they discovered the water was perfect. Jack pulled her in with him as they waded farther out into the breakers. They floated easily in the surf over wave after wave. Lydia loved having him right there with her. Usually the boys took off leaving her to swim by herself as they body surfed or enjoyed some other rough play. She was content to float lazily in the salty water. Just when they thought the surf was harmless a large wave knocked them both off their feet slamming them to the ocean floor with fury. Jack came up looking for her and found her laughing.

"I think I need a raft!" He shook the water from his head. "Want to go with me to find one?"

"Nah… I'm happy. You go ahead." She pushed herself easily onto the top of the water which was suddenly calm again. Back stoking away from him he realized she could swim well and left her there. He wondered why she did things like that, choosing to be alone rather than walk with him.

He found a rental shack a few strides up the beach and secured a canvas raft. Instead of taking it straight out to meet Lydia he sat on the sheet resting in the sun. He wondered if his plan would work. It sure wouldn't hurt to try. So he sat and waited while she swam. Apparently the woman loved the water.

Finally she came from the surf walking toward him. His plan had worked. All he wanted was to look at this beautiful girl that he loved with all his heart.

She has no idea does she Lord?

He pulled out his cell and took several pictures while she looked down the beach. He put his phone away before she caught him.

"So… is the waft for widing da waves?" Lydia smiled as she reached for a towel.

"Want to rest a minute first?" Jack offered wondering if her back still hurt.

"Probably wise," she agreed. Resting face down she sighed deeply. "This feels so good. Thanks for coming today."

"Oh believe me baby. It's my pleasure." Jack hit her back with sunscreen. He laughed when she jumped. "Payback is hard isn't it?" On his knees he tried to duplicate her wonderful massage.

"Not too hard," she hated to tell him. "I don't think you know your own strength there Hercules."

"Sorry. Didn't mean to hurt you." Jack took a lighter touch and gently worked in the sunscreen.

"At least your hands aren't rough." She smiled.

She realized it had been a very long time since anyone had so lovingly cared for her. He finished and part of her was relieved and part of her was sad. He stretched out beside her and took her hand. She turned to look at him allowing her gaze to meet his own. For a long tender moment they stayed that way saying nothing. She wondered if he could hear her heart pounding. Pulling her again to her feet he invited, "We'd better go use this raft. I only rented it for an hour."

As they walked toward the water she made him laugh when she spoke.

"Kinda like a working girl."

~~~~~~~

Their day was full of many firsts. Lydia became more comfortable with his care while Jack began to understand her insecurity. Jack learned to appreciate all the lemonade and food he wanted without dropping big bucks on touristy type snacks. Lydia quit fretting about her hair and let it dry in the ocean breeze. They both reclaimed their youth in a pickup volleyball game where Jack loved watching her set the ball for him and she loved watching him spike it soundly to college guys who couldn't return it. She wasn't aware he was so athletic. He was pretty impressed with her as well.

When finally they gathered their things and headed to the truck they shook the sand from the sheet and spread it across the tattered seat. "What kind of food do you want for dinner?" Jack asked. He gazed at this woman with the mass of copper curls highlighted by the sun and a sprinkle of new freckles across her nose.

"I feel too icky to go anywhere nice. How about pizza? Basil's makes hand tossed any way you like it!"

"Sounds good baby." He leaned over and kissed her lightly. She loved his new pet name for her. The day felt completely magical.

The restaurant owner came out and talked with them for a bit. He asked if they were going to the street dance and informed them that they would not be disappointed.

When he walked away Jack asked Lydia, "What do you think? It would be a lot of fun. I could get us a hotel room and we could drive back tomorrow."

"Ain't no way baby!" Lydia shook her head at him. "Though I'd love to stay for the dance, we cannot put that kind of temptation in front of us." Her blushing instantly gave her away.

"You're right. I'm sorry Lydia." Jack took her hand and kissed it. "How about this? What if we stayed for an hour or so then I drive us back tonight? I'm a night owl anyway."

Lydia thought on it. "As long as you can drive while I snore. I give up the ghost about nine o'clock on a normal day. And I'll for sure be passed out after everything we've packed in. Do you think you can stay awake?"

"Absolutely! Let's do it!" Jack was excited at the thought. "By the way, you look really pretty so please don't worry about what you're wearing."

"Thanks. Me and the boys come often. You'll see everything from shorts to bathing suits to khakis and loafers." She smiled that he'd even think about that. "But which do you prefer, sundress or shorts?"

"For me or for you?" Jack had that playful look again then he answered. "I like what you have on. That cute little sundress shows off your long legs."

She tried to deflect his attention. "I have long legs? So that's why my work jeans keep getting shorter. I love wearing high waters with my Brogans. It's a really good look."

Jack shook his head and wondered why she said things like that.

Chapter 36

Jack was thoroughly impressed with the shag moves he saw the seasoned dancers making. For a fleeting moment he noticed all the women there wishing someone would ask them to dance. He found himself making a mental note for future reference. Quickly he reminded himself,

You're an idiot Jack. Do not go there!

An older gentleman named Dennis obviously knew his way around the dance floor. Lydia informed Jack that he and his cute wife Melanie danced competitively. She led Jack over to meet them and he was surprised when Dennis and Lydia shared a dance. Even though the guy was old enough to be her father Jack realized he was jealous. He would definitely have to take lessons or else he and Lydia would come so often he'd learn to make the same moves.

Lydia however, savored the slow dances when Jack easily glided with her tenderly like no one before. He sang "My Girl" to her as they danced and her heart pounded when he looked at her with those eyes. She wondered if she could fall any harder.

They danced longer than they'd planned and ended up leaving after ten. As they walked hand in hand toward the truck she asked him, "Are you okay to drive? We can figure out a way to stay if you feel too tired."

"I'm fine Sweetheart. You're right about going back tonight." He looked at her as she got comfortable in the truck.

"Jack if you feel the least bit sleepy then please, let's stay. If anything ever happened to you I don't think I could recover." She looked at him solemnly and he appreciated her words. He couldn't remember anyone besides his father being that concerned with his well-being.

"Don't worry. I drank enough lemonade that my bladder will keep me awake." He laughed and she felt better. "On that happy note, let me pull into this station and we can fill up with gas and make use of their awesomely clean restrooms."

She was glad. Why had she not told him she needed to go? Surely she could speak freely with him by now. He sure did with her.

Once they headed down the road she settled into the pillows feeling like a queen. With her brown legs stretched toward him and her bare feet in his lap he sang with the songs that played from his phone. She was out before they got on the main highway.

Jack picked up his phone and got his dad's voice mail. "Hey Pop. Just wanted to say thanks for praying. Lydia and I are doing well. I've never been so happy in all of my life. I hope you can meet her soon. Do what you can to prepare mother for me. She and Lydia are basically polar opposites. But I love the girl. If Mom knows that maybe it will help. Love you Pop."

Lydia woke enough to hear the words and felt very loved and happy, except for the idea of meeting his mother.

Chapter 37

She didn't wake again til they hit the gravel drive to her house. "Hello Sleepyhead." Jack changed gears then rubbed her foot. "You should've stayed asleep and I would have carried you in."

"Lord have mercy," she mumbled and didn't know why. "What time is it?"

Jack laughed and answered, "About 2:30. I can totally carry you in if you'd like." He parked the truck by the back deck and wished they'd left some lights on. Jack walked around to her side. "C'mere darling. I've got you!" He pulled her playfully from the truck and flipped her over his shoulder.

"Jack stop! You're going to hurt yourself and then what will we tell the paramedics?" She laughed as he stepped inside barely clearing the door frame without banging her head.

"Hold on mama! Papa got a brand new bag!" He flipped her over onto the daybed. "Okay. You can go back to sleep now. Hope I didn't wake you." Still laughing they jumped up from the daybed simultaneously and headed for the bathroom.

"I'm not kidding Jack. You can pee outside. I've got to go!" She slammed the door in his face and called back to him, "Don't stand there listening. Go outside or something."

"You'd better hurry. I'm coming in there." Jack warned.

She finished then slowly opened the door. "La la la la la… what's the rush honey?"

Jack pushed past her and she closed the door behind him laughing.

Finally! she thought. *A guy who's bladder doesn't hold a gallon. The man is absolutely perfect!*

She laughed at the thought and began unloading the truck.

A distinct snapping of branches in the nearby woods made her heart nearly stop. She froze waiting to see if there would be more. When her legs would finally move, she frantically stumbled inside not daring to turn her back on the woods. Her heart pounded in fear.

Jack came from the bathroom and she whispered. "Jack honey, I'm not playing around. I heard someone in the woods." She found it hard to breathe.

He went straight to the daybed and retrieved the gun from the holster next to the wall. He checked to see if it was loaded and joined her as she looked toward the dark woods from behind the sunroom door.

"Do you have flood lights?" Jack asked.

She stepped toward the switch and flipped them on. The light helped but didn't reach into the woods. "Maybe it was just a deer," she spoke trying to calm her pounding heart. She looked at Jack. He was still looking toward the woods. She was glad to see he seemed to know his way around a pistol.

"Did it sound like a deer?" He turned to ask her.

She shook her head no. "I think if it was a deer it would've bounded off. It sounded heavy, like a man's footsteps." She'd heard animals in the woods plenty of times.

This was different.

"What's left in the truck? Anything we need tonight?" Jack asked still looking out the door.

"No. Let's lock up the house and get the rest of it tomorrow. Oh my goodness I'm so glad you're here."

"Where's your phone Lydia?" Jack had just realized his was still in the truck on the seat.

"It's in the bag in the truck."

"Okay, wait right here and I'll go get them." Jack started out the door.

"No Jack no! Don't go out there. Please honey just stay in here!" she begged him.

Checking the gun again he told Lydia, "Go get dressed for bed in the bathroom. Lock the door and close the shower curtain so no one can see in the window. Don't come out until I tell you. I promise I'll be careful. I'm just going to grab our phones and the extra keys from the shower."

When she thought about the extra keys she had to agree but it still scared the life out of her. "I'm gonna watch you from here so I know what's happening. I'll change after you get back." Her eyes begged him.

Quickly he was out the door and going through the truck grabbing phones and bags. He tossed them in through the door to her as she waited then disappeared into the shower for the spare keys. Back inside he locked the door.

"Okay. Go change. I'll check all the doors and windows. We'll look around to see if it looks like anyone has been in here, then we'll decide if we need to call the police."

Completely creeped out, she grabbed clothes as Jack stayed near. Retreating to the bathroom she realized she couldn't shower and wash her hair.

"Yuk," she thought.

Then she also realized she couldn't very well sleep in the daybed surrounded by windows if someone was lurking outside. Jack adjusted the thermostat in the hall wondering about their sleeping arrangements and whether to call the cops just because Lydia heard a noise. She wasn't easily frightened and he didn't doubt her, but what would they tell them if they called?

When Lydia exited the bathroom dressed in thick flannel pajamas Jack tipped his head sideways to look at her. "Are you cold?" To him it felt like it was about a thousand degrees in the house, not to mention all the sun still radiating off their skin.

"Nooo… I just can't stand the thought of someone outside looking at me." She made a pouty face and he pulled her into his arms, still holding the gun. "I don't blame you Sweetheart. Me neither. Good grief you're hot!" He let go of her, handed her the gun and retrieved clean shorts to sleep in. "Be right out and then we'll think of what we're doing next. If anyone comes through that door you shoot to kill. Do you hear me?" He tipped her chin up. She shook her head yes, once again glad that they were on the same page in the oft debated area of weaponry.

When he emerged she took one look at his shirtless body and thought to herself,

This is not good.

"Here you take the gun. I need to change again. I'm dyin' hot in these pajamas." Grabbing shorts and a tank top she entered the bathroom for the third time since they'd returned home. Changing quickly into sleeping shorts and tank top she came out and asked Jack, "Okay. What's the plan?"

He took one look at her and thought,

Wow. Much better!

Lydia spoke before Jack had a chance to say it. "I don't really want to call the police. I know what I heard, but I hate having people all over town knowing you're staying with me. I hope that doesn't hurt your feelings Jack, but folks love to talk."

"I agree. Everything is locked up tight. I checked windows, closets, under the beds. Can you think of anywhere else we should check?"

She stepped tentatively into the sunroom and opened the laundry closet. Someone could fit in there if they sat on the deep freeze.

"Clear." She called like a chick on a cop show.

"Lydia you have no curtains in this house. Why is that?" He'd always liked that before; now not so much.

"I don't need curtains. There's never been anyone out there looking in." She explained innocently.

"Not that you know of." Jack looked at her worried. "Did we leave the gate open this morning?" He tried to remember.

"I think so." She couldn't remember either. "We must've. I think you stopped and got the pillows out but I don't think we shut the gate." She'd begun to hate that stupid thing.

"Alright. Let's go to bed. C'mon." He took her hand and moved toward the bed. She stayed in the hall not knowing what to do.

"Baby, I'll behave. You can't sleep out there in the sunroom. It's way too exposed." He was tired.

She had an idea. "Here. Help me hang the sheet over the double window in the den. I'll sleep on the couch." She grabbed the beach sheet he'd tossed in the door moments ago. Once they got it hung over the window which looked onto the front porch she felt better. "Let me just get another sheet for the couch and a pillow off the daybed and I'm set."

When she had it situated Jack pulled her into the hall outside the bathroom. He had the feeling someone was watching them. "I do not like this. I don't care what time you get up in the morning don't go outside, not even to the swing. And whatever you do, don't take a shower outside even with the latch on. Please Lydia. Are you listening?"

"Okay." She nodded yes. He was really freaking her out.

"Now don't argue with me. I know you've got issues with that bed in there, but I can't sleep back here with you out on the couch alone by the front door. So please, take the bedroom so I can hear if anyone tries to get in."

"Yes dear." She tried to lighten the mood. She turned and started toward the bedroom and he pulled her back.

"Sorry. Didn't mean to get all manly with the ordering you about like the little woman. I just love you. C'mere." He kissed her wishing their day had ended on a happier note. "If you need anything call me." He kissed her again but longer. Her heart pounded.

"Mercy Jack." She pulled away and closed the bedroom door behind her.

We'll never make it like this Lord. But the thought of his leaving nearly kills me. Please do something, okay?

She left the fan off so she could hear if anyone tried to break in. Switching off the lamp she looked out the window into the dark. She recognized all the shadows including the huge oak, the woodpile, the well house, and some smaller things. Nothing was moving so she thanked God for that. Blue had told her many times that as long as it was as dark inside as out then no one could see in. They had actually walked outside to make sure before she agreed to leave the windows bare. Then it occurred to her that she usually left the lamp on in the sunroom while she undressed.

A shiver went through her soul.

Standing by the bed that had been hers and Blue's she knew she couldn't sleep there, at least not yet. She picked up her phone and a pillow and walked toward the den in the pitch dark house.

"Jack it's me."

Jack sat up on the sofa he'd just made ready for sleeping. Lighting the way for her with his phone he waited til she sat beside him. They both wondered what to do.

"I'll take the recliner, you take the couch." Jack suddenly had a solution. He moved to the nearby chair as Lydia warned, "Don't lean back too far or it will tip over."

He pulled it close to her and tossed his phone on the end table. "Wake me if you need me." Jack offered as he settled in trying not to think of the killer lurking outside or the beautiful woman beside him or the chair that could dump him on his head if he dared to relax.

About the time he dosed off the light on Lydia's phone lit up with a text. He picked it up thinking it was his and discovered she'd received a message from Jesse.

"Something doesn't feel right. I'm praying for you. Please be careful."

Jack was tired and he was mad. He sat up and called the jerk.

174

Jesse answered, "Lydia, are you okay? I have a gut feeling something's wrong."

"I'll tell you what's wrong!" Jack's voice came over Lydia's phone. "It's wrong for YOU to be texting MY girl in the middle of the night. Don't let it happen again. I'm sitting here with a loaded gun. Do you understand me?"

"Jack! Is she with you? Please make sure she's okay!" Jesse tried to talk but Jack wasn't having it.

"I will take care of Lydia. You leave her alone. Surely I've made myself clear." Jack hung up.

He lay back in the recliner steaming mad. Lydia heard the whole conversation and didn't blame Jack. If whatshername had texted Jack in the middle of the night she'd feel the same way.

But her heart hurt at the misunderstanding. Jesse only wanted what was best for her and obviously sensed something was wrong.

Chapter 38

Lydia was proud of herself for sleeping all the way til 7:27 a.m. She rose quietly remembering Jack's plea that she not go outside. Sitting at the kitchen table with her Bible and a hot cup of coffee she wished she knew the words to pray. The thing with Jesse was worrying her worse than the thought of someone creeping around the house. She wondered what he'd texted her. It was very unusual for him to send something in the middle of the night.

She tried to pray and even asked God for the words. Glancing at the beach bag still by the back door she smiled. "Thank You Lord." Her heart was suddenly overwhelmed with joy at the memory of the day before. "Thank You so much. I loved it."

Her Bible fell easily open to 1 Corinthians 13 since the day she spilled coffee there. Verse seven was her go-to verse. *"Love never gives up, never loses faith, is always hopeful, and endures through every circumstance."*

She closed her eyes and pondered the words. She could use them like a prayer. *"Lord we need that. Help us so much with this love."* She thought of Jack and how strongly she desired to be in his arms. *"I don't know how to keep these things apart Lord."* She whispered. *"I already love him so much."*

She heard Jack coming and smiled.

One good thing about an old house and creaky floors. It's hard for anyone to sneak up on you.

She loved his sleepy face and hair. He looked like he hadn't shaved in a week when she knew he shaved every day. His tanned shirtless body didn't have an ounce of fat except for just a little above his belly button.

Lord have mercy! You must do something about these feelings of mine. It's been a very long time… She stopped her prayer and felt her face flush as Jack came toward her. He must've been really tired as he didn't speak but walked past her to the bathroom.

Give him some space. He told you he's not a morning person.

She poured him a cup of coffee and refilled her own.

He didn't look much better when he came back to the kitchen. Though his coffee waited in front of his place at the table he walked past her again and into the den. Returning slowly he sat down placing their phones on the table between them.

"Good morning." She smiled tentatively at him. He had yet to look at her.

"We need to talk," he spoke wearily. She knew those words didn't usually end well. Her heart sank.

"I need more information on your close friend Jesse." He looked at her with eyes that were full of suspicion.

She swallowed hard and asked God for help. "Sure. I heard your end of the conversation with him. Why did he call?"

Jack's tone was accusatory and sounded harsh. "He didn't call. He texted you at 3:30 in the morning! Is that a normal thing you two do with one another?"

Lydia refrained from speaking as she looked at her phone. She pulled up the texts between her and Jesse hoping nothing sounded bad, then handed it to Jack.

Jack looked at the thread between them. "So yes, he just out of the blue sends you a message asking how you're doing in the middle of the night?!!"

"It's all right there Jack. Read it and decide if I've messed up." Her heart was pounding.

"This is all of it?"

Quietly she spoke. "I don't delete texts if that's what you're asking. I don't get that many and the ones I do are generic... except for yours." She looked at him with such sad eyes that he suddenly realized how he sounded.

"I'm sorry Lydia. Let's start over." His tone was softer.

She asked, "What would you like to know? I promised I'd be transparent about Jesse. Ask anything you want."

Jack was glad for the opportunity. He'd thought about it all night and actually had a mental list.

"Tell me about the counseling. Where does it happen, your place or his?"

Lydia was stunned at the things Jack had apparently considered. She tried to answer without getting upset. "Here, but on my front porch. He never comes inside not even in cold weather. I've never been inside his house but I have sat with him on his swing. I do his yard and I plant stuff over there to thank him for my counseling." She tried to think if there was anything else. "I took him a cracked birdbath I found on the side of the road and planted a flower in it because it reminded me of something he told me."

"What was that?" Jack was curious.

"He said that God uses brokenness and that God has a plan for me too." Lydia teared up at the memory.

Jack reached over and took her hand. "Okay. If he's a real counselor then he should have a degree from somewhere. Do you know anything about his credentials?"

"He got his Master's from Southeastern Seminary at Wake Forest three years ago. I baked him a batch of oatmeal crème filled cookies."

Jack was starting to feel like a real jerk but had to ask the hard one. "Has there ever been any physical stuff between you? Like for instance, does he hold you when you're upset or…"

Lydia's neck turned red. "He hugs my shoulders from the side, and kisses the top of my head. He's very tall. I have taken his hand a couple times. Jesse's been through some things too."

Jack thought that might be key. If the guy had her sympathy Lydia might be naïve enough to be drawn to him.

"What kind of things?" he asked.

She swallowed hard and wondered if she should continue. Jesse had been her friend for a long time and they'd shared many confidences. She wasn't about to divulge Jesse's heartache.

"Things he told me privately." She paused trying to think of what she could say without breaking that trust. "Jack, I can give up my friendship with him if you want. You are very important to me. But you need to know, I have very few friends in this world and even fewer people that I trust. Remember the picture with 'Death Wish' on the back? Jesse took that. I was determined to be done living. He hunted me down and hauled my butt home, or I am sure I wouldn't be here today."

She thought a minute then added, "So far as what he's going through? The gist of it is that his wife left him and he loves her so much that he prays continually that she'll return. He took his wedding vows very seriously. That's all I can say because he truly hopes God will bring her home to him. I do too."

She felt the tears coming and tried to swipe them away without being obvious. She looked at Jack and added. "What's weird is that I wouldn't be talking to you at all except that Jesse convinced me to give you another chance."

She left the kitchen retrieving the things she needed. "I'm going outside for a shower. I've GOT to wash the saltwater out of my hair. When I'm through I'll call Jesse and tell him anything you want. Look through my phone so you'll know what's gone on between us. I'll tell you how we met if you want, but not til you're in a better mood. It's hard for me to talk about. I'm not real proud of who I am."

She walked out the back door not worried about the suspected man in the woods. The shower door had a latch and she was too sad to think about some lurking danger that probably was all in her head.

At least the shower would be soothing to her soul.

Chapter 39

Jack didn't like the idea of her showering outside not one little bit. He picked up their phones and plunked his tired self into a plastic chair on the deck near the shower. Facing the woods now that it was light he could see clearly there was no one there. He thought about the night before and how close he'd come to pulling Lydia into the bed with him. He shook his head at how quickly things could come undone.

Stepping back inside he grabbed her Bible and went back to the deck where he could hear if she needed him. He scrolled through her phone feeling like a heel but wanting to see for himself. There was nothing suggestive or out of the way, only comforting words about praying for her or asking if she had firewood and such. The last text she'd sent him simply said, "I promise." He wondered what she'd promised.

The Bible fell open naturally to 1 Corinthians 13 where he read the familiar words he'd tried so hard to put into his life since he too had made a promise. "Love is patient, kind, not jealous, or boastful or proud or rude. Love doesn't demand its own way is not irritable… keeps no record of wrongs…"

The list of things that love is NOT seemed to describe everything he tended to be. What had come over him? And after the wonderful day they'd had together at the beach. He turned and watched her feet as she took a shower.

"Lydia?"

"Yep."

"You aren't moving."

"Is that alright with you?" She sounded a wee bit miffed.

"Are you okay?"

"Peachy."

"Don't use up all the hot water. Some other people in this house might need to take a shower you know." He tried to sound like fun Jack but he didn't think she was buying it until she laughed an evil laugh.

"Muwahahaha!"

A few minutes later she passed him on the deck washed, dried, and dressed with her hair in a towel. Her tone was clear as she walked by.

"All yours. And when you come out of there I expect you to have a shirt on."

~~~~~~~~

The shower soothed Jack's weary soul as well. He pondered the details about Jesse and prayed while the warm water pounded his body. When he recalled her words about Jesse encouraging her to give him a second chance, he was humbled at his own failures. No telling what Cassie had told her. What an awful thing for Lydia to hear when she had just begun to trust. Now here he was accusing her of things she hadn't done. He shook his head in wonder at her forgiveness. He knew he should leave it up to her regarding the friendship she had with Jesse as well as the counseling. But what if once he left Jesse decided to give up on his wife and lean on Lydia for support? The thought nearly made him sick.

His phone lit up with a text from his brother. He hadn't even thought to let him know he wasn't coming in for a while that Monday morning. It was then he realized that he didn't have a towel, much less a shirt. And Lydia's phone was with him. He shook the water off like a dog, which was exactly what he felt like.

Looking at Johnny's text apparently there had been an issue where he needed to access the bank account to see where they stood financially on the Parker project. He appreciated Johnny taking the initiative for a change and decided to encourage him when he texted the information back. Maybe they had enough left to do something extra for Denise. He wondered if Lydia would want to go with him there to walk through the house to check details and finishing touches.

What are you thinking man? Cathy will be there! He paused to think. *Cathy?*

Lydia had threatened to whack the woman in the head with a shovel. He had visions of Lydia snatching her blonde hair out by the dark roots. Maybe he should take Lydia after all! That would definitely be worth the price of admission.

Her voice startled him.

"Thought you might need these." She flipped a towel and clothes over the dry end of the shower. "Hurry up Jack Rabbit. You're burning daylight."

"Yes dear." He replied in fake submission. He was relieved at the sound of her cheerful voice.

While he waited for the steam to clear, he decided to check one more thing before he returned her phone. Maybe Lydia had a picture of Jesse. Typically a person only takes pictures of people they care about. He knew how glad he was the day before when finally he got a great shot of her coming out of the ocean, all tanned in her swimsuit, looking like a perfect ten. Scanning through her photos there was a similar picture in her phone as well. A man walked toward her on the beach. Jack laughed that she'd taken a picture of him too. He looked at his image and thought, "At least I've lost my beer belly since last year."

When he entered the kitchen he smelled bacon and realized how hungry he was. He was surprised to find that she was dressed very nicely in white jeans he'd never seen and a pretty peach colored sleeveless blouse. He smiled and decided she really WAS peachy. It buttoned down the middle and fell nicely showing off her "itty bitty waist."

Careful Jack… he warned himself. *She might knock you into next week if you bring that song up again.*

"Wow! You look really pretty. Where are we going?" Jack asked wondering.

She looked up at him and spoke with determination. "I don't know where you're going, but I plan to go by the Parker project." She turned back to the eggs she was scrambling. Jack wondered if eggs were the only thing that would be beaten that day.

"Dressed like that?" he asked. She looked at him wondering what he meant. He fumbled a bit. "I mean… you look really good. Are you working… or just visiting?"

"Are you asking if I'm taking my shovel?" She served the eggs and bacon without an explanation. She followed up by adding "Maybe…"

Jack took her hand and bowed his head. She bowed hers too. "Lord, thank You for showing us what love is supposed to look like in Your Word. Help me to have strength. Thank you for yesterday, but most of all thank You for Lydia. She means the world to me. So help her not get arrested today. Amen."

"Amen." She added without looking at him. When finally she did Jack kissed her hand and smiled at her.

They ate their breakfast in silence, mostly because Jack was starving and Lydia had nothing to say. She didn't want to bring up the subject of Jesse lest she get Jack started again. She hated revisiting those horrible days. Maybe Jack would just drop it.

"So tell me about Jesse saving your life." Jack finished his eggs and got up to make toast.

Lydia sighed a deep sigh.

"It's so depressing. I was over medicating after Blue died. Jesse's cows pushed through the fence and he found me flaked out under a tree near the ridge. Can we please just drop it?" She teared up so quickly that Jack immediately regretted bringing it up.

"In fact, I've got a better idea." She picked up Jack's phone, punched in Jesse's number and saved it in his contacts. "Call him yourself. He's got a much better handle on things than I do." She tossed his phone back onto the table.

"I'm sorry Lydia. Here's what we'll do. Obviously I don't trust the man. I'm glad he's helped you through the years but now that's my job. I'll be leaving soon and I don't like the idea of him being over here. But I guess that's your call." He turned to butter his toast and was surprised with her answer.

"It IS my call! And I choose you Jack. I understand. Because if I go over to the house today and Cassie's all over you like white on rice I'm going to jerk her arm off and beat her to death with it!"

Jack laughed at the imagery. "Well then let's get this show on the road! Are you going to dry your hair before we leave?"

Apparently the man had never noticed she didn't use a blow dryer. For some reason it aggravated her. "I can hang my head out the window on the way if you'd like."

"No really, why are you going by the house all dressed up? Have I missed picture day or something?" Jack finished his toast and wiped up the crumbs.

"I'm dressed nice because I'm trying to impress the handsomest man I've ever met, and I'm going by the house to let Cassie see that I'm still in your life in spite of her best efforts. And maybe to see how she acts around you… and you around her."

"SEE! You're doing the same thing I am with Jesse! I knew it!" Jack seemed relieved that he wasn't the only one jealous.

"There's only one little difference Jack." She looked at him without smiling. "Surely I don't have to say what it is."

She washed the dishes while he made himself busy. As he folded the sleeping items in the den he thought.

Just that one little minor detail about sleeping with a woman that I don't remember. But Jesse did hug her shoulders and kiss her head. I still don't like the guy.

184

Chapter 40

He heard her speaking to someone on the phone and to his shame stopped and listened.

"Hey Jesse. Yep. Made it through the night. I know… that's strange because we actually think there might have been someone in the woods when we got home. Yep. I took your advice and took Jack to the beach Sunday. It was a lot of fun! Hey, I need you to know that he's staying here for a week, but I'm keeping my promise. I heard his conversation with you last night. He was pretty tired. Yeah… well it was weird hearing from you in the middle of the night like that."

Jack thought, *Damn right it was weird!*

Lydia continued with Jesse. "I think in the interest of the ones we love we should call off our counseling. I'm doing alright. Yep… I will. I'm actually trying to spend time every morning with God. He doesn't seem to hate me quite as much as He used to. I know… that's what I keep hearing. I know you do… and I appreciate all you've done to help me. I'll keep praying for you too. Thanks Jesse. Bye now."

She tossed her phone to Jack and walked back through the kitchen.

He heard the back door open and close and watched as she took an old towel from the clothesline and walked down the hill toward the pond. The wind picked up her hair and twirled it behind her. He could tell she was brushing tears away as she continued to walk up the next hill toward the barn. He lost sight of her as she continued toward the ridge.

While he waited on her to return he called to check on Johnny but got his voice mail. He called to talk to his dad and got his voice mail too. He wanted to call Lydia but she had left her phone with him, probably because she didn't want him to call.

Something inside whispered,

Or maybe she doesn't want you to think she was walking away so she could call Jesse back and apologize for you being a complete idiot.

When she still didn't return for a while, he suddenly remembered the suspect in the woods the night before. Terror washed over his soul. What if the guy was hiding in the barn waiting to catch Lydia alone?

He ran to her truck with keys in hand and drove toward the ridge to find her. On a hillside by a funky shaped plot of wildflowers she kneeled on a towel sobbing like a baby.

Walking over to where she kneeled he pulled her to her feet and gathered her into his arms wiping her tears. "I'm so sorry Sweetheart. I didn't mean to hurt you." He stroked her back hoping she could let it go. "Please forgive me." He held her and was surprised that she continued to cry. Stroking her back gently he was glad when the sobs turned to deep breaths and she finally relaxed.

"We can go now. My hair is dry." She laughed as she tried to stop the tears and be happy. "Did you remember the shovel?"

Jack looked at her sadly and shook his head wondering about her past and her relationship with God. He wondered if this was a normal practice for her in the little sanctuary on the hill. He couldn't think of a better place. The words he heard her say to Jesse came to mind and he wondered how she could ever think that God didn't like her. In fact she'd used the word hate.

They stopped by the house and locked the doors. Lydia told him she wasn't worried about it anymore and asked if he had put the gun away. Jack asked if they could take her truck as he really liked driving it. He pulled her close to him on the bench seat and sang a song to her with the one playing from his phone.

Lydia did her best to recover as she turned her friendship with Jesse over to God. He had put Jesse into her life anyway. Surely He'd know what to do. The thought of the sadness in Jesse's voice nearly started the tears again so she pretended to be interested in the rows of corn they passed on their way into town. Fields of white tassels waved from the tops of dried out stalks as if to say the rain had come too late. Remembering Jesse's advice she breathed again a prayer for wisdom.

Jack noticed her very quiet sadness and kissed her hand as he drove stealing a glance when he could. He prayed she'd let go of her friendship with the man he was so jealous of. Reluctantly he prayed for wisdom too.

By the time they arrived at Denise's, Lydia was nearly her old self smiling at Jack's jokes. Pulling into the drive she loved the way the place looked. The recent wind which followed the good soaking rain had dried up the muddy places. All the plants were nestled in nicely and the landscape appeared to have been that way for years. She was actually very proud of their accomplishment.

"I want to add ferns to the porch and pots of pink geraniums to the steps. But other than that do you see anything I've missed?" She asked Jack as they walked toward the front door on the new brick pathway.

"Baby, I absolutely love it. You're amazing! And the amount of money you spent is so minimal compared to what we're used to paying. Want to hit the road with me? We make a great team!" Jack surprised even himself when he suddenly could wait no longer to ask.

Lydia surprised him too when she replied, "Actually I'm thinking about getting out of the business. It may be why my back hurts so much." She saw the disappointment on his face and added, "But I could still hit the road with you and be part of your team. Talk to me about that sometime. Maybe I can take Cassie's place." She purposely added that last little barb as she was still stinging from his trust issues earlier that same morning.

She surprised him again when Johnny greeted her with a big hug and she elbowed him away. "Don't hug me Johnny. I am not in the mood."

He was genuinely hurt and looked at Jack. "What did I do?"

Lydia had her mind made up and decided to just say it out loud. "Where's Cassie?" Her voice was firm and full of determination.

When no one answered she walked toward the back of the house. Returning empty handed she looked at Johnny. "Well?"

"I sent her home. You tried to warn me Jack but I didn't listen. I had no idea you…" He stopped and looked at Lydia. Obviously she knew. Her throat was red and her hands were on her hips.

"I'm sorry Lydia. When I decided to break up with Gina I went a bit crazy. But I didn't know about Cassie and Jack until last night when she compared us."

Lydia held her hand up to silence the man who made her want to throw up. "No more details. I am SICK of it!"

She charged outside to get some air with her wild hair flying behind her. She walked toward the road exasperated. How did people live like that? Sleeping around and never being satisfied to love one person? She actually thought she might be sick at the thought of Jack in that woman's bed. Had she really hoped to see Cassie and tell her what she thought of her nasty lifestyle? Her blood was boiling so she just kept walking.

She thought about Jesse's suggestion to call fire down from heaven. Her smile at his words quickly turned to sadness when she thought of what she'd soon be missing. AND Jack was leaving too.

"It's not fair God." She spoke it and she meant it. "Why do You always do stuff like this to me?"

She walked clear down to the corner and back. Her flip flops smacked out the rhythm of her anger. She noticed that her strides got longer as the anger subsided. Entering the house again she asked the men who were on stepladders trying to hang a large light fixture what she could do to help.

They looked at each other and Jack finally spoke. "Whatever you do, stay AWAY from the breaker box." He could tell his attempt at humor was not well received.

She turned her head sideways and informed him she was leaving.

"Keys." She held her hand out for Jack to toss them down. He switched hands on the heavy fixture knowing better than to keep her waiting. He decided she was much like the ocean they'd enjoyed only yesterday. Warm and relaxing one minute, then bam! A man could find himself knocked on his rear end wondering what hit him. This time however, he knew was his fault.

~~~~~~~

188

She drove to the barbecue joint she'd taken them to the first day on the job. Happy memories flooded her soul as she noticed the empty corner booth where they'd shared so many laughs. What would she do without them? She loved Johnny like she loved Shawn and Kurtis, only he was grosser. But she loved him. And Jack. She doubted she'd want to join his crew and travel with him. But she could do a long distance relationship if that's what it boiled down to for a while. Maybe someday they'd…

"Yes ma'am. I need two barbecue plates and one barbecue sandwich without slaw… two large Cheerwines and one ice water… yes, to go. Thanks."

She sighed deeply and pulled money from her back pocket.

"Let me get that for you." A deep familiar voice spoke behind her. "Tell Jack it's on me." Jesse placed money on the counter, kissed her head and walked out the door.

She started to charge out behind him, but didn't.

Why did Jack have to be such a butt?

~~~~~~~

Walking into Denise's house with the food the guys were surprised again. She placed their lunches on the kitchen countertop which she still hated, and unwrapped her sandwich. "Try not to choke on it Jack. Jesse paid for it and said to tell you it was on him. I'm going out to the porch to eat."

She stopped.

"And before you ask, I did not plan to meet him there." She thought about it a second more and added, "In fact, I'm going home." She wrapped her sandwich, grabbed her water and headed for the door.

"Wow. I thought that was last week." Johnny mumbled to no one in particular. Jack was glad Lydia didn't hear it lest she do a fly-by on her broom.

189

The brothers were thankful for the time to talk without anyone around. They worked hard to finish the details and made a list of touch ups to do before Friday. Jack told Johnny about their day at the beach, how over the top in love he was, and also about Jesse. When he recounted the facts to Johnny he heard again how he'd sounded to Lydia. Even Johnny had to say, "No wonder she's so ticked off at you Jack. You gave her the third degree and obviously she's not the type to sleep around. Why would you do that?"

Jack wondered too. His phone lit up with a text. It was Jesse. "She's in love with you Jack. I won't call or text her except through you. Please be good to her."

Chapter 41

For the first time ever Lydia was afraid to enter her house. She walked
in anyway trying not to be a baby. She checked under the beds and in
the closets happy to be alone in a locked house. She checked the gun
making sure Jack had put it where she could find it in a hurry, all
because she thought she heard something in the woods. If she were
honest she'd also admit that the events stemming from that fear had
probably caused a lot of unexplained grouchiness on the part of a
normally very patient man. She must make sure he got ample sleep
from now on. Maybe that's all they both needed.

She looked at the daybed and knew she wouldn't be able to rest well
even if she were to lie down. She was still so wigged out by the
unknown intruder who never actually intruded. She sighed wearily.

Her Bible lay on top of the soft summer quilt nearly calling her name
out loud. She'd heard somewhere that the Psalms were good about
calming fears so she opened the Book down the middle like Norma had
shown her so many years ago. Lying back on the daybed with a pillow
on her tummy the words from Psalm 51 spoke to her from the
makeshift podium.

"Oh give me back my joy again;
You have broken me- now let me rejoice.
Don't keep looking at my sins.
Remove the stain of my guilt.
Create in me a clean heart O God.
Renew a loyal spirit within me…
Restore to me the joy of Your salvation
and make me willing to obey You."

Salvation. It had been so long ago that she'd understood. Norma had
helped her as a little girl to know she could trust Jesus to make her His
child. How had she drifted so far?

Maybe it was her own brokenness, the weight of the guilt she felt for
losing her baby. The drugs she'd taken after Blue's death had knocked
the edge off. The doctor said they were safe, but in her heart of hearts
she knew she should've been strong enough to deal with her pain

without the prescription. Now her baby girl was lost too. She would never forgive herself or God either for that matter.

"Remove the stain of my guilt." Oh how she wished it could happen. Like a call from Jesse who often reminded her that God loved her, the words that followed invited her to pray.

"Create in me a clean heart O God. Renew a loyal spirit within me… Restore to me the joy of Your salvation and make me willing to obey You."

Allowing the tears to flow freely again she closed her Bible and her eyes. She tried to pray but the words were stuck in her throat. She whispered the only thing that would come.

"I need help God. Please just help me."

Scanning down the page hoping for a Word that would let her know God was listening she noticed comfort she'd never seen before.

"The sacrifice You desire is a broken spirit. You will not reject a broken and repentant heart, O God."

A deep sigh escaped with the tears that seemed to flow without stopping. She wondered if she might be going crazy. That was probably her greatest fear.

"Well Lord, I am definitely broken. Please God… don't reject me anymore. I need You so much."

Peace washed over her and she melted into the covers. Maybe she'd be able to nap after all. She placed the Bible on the floor by her bed and stood to drop her jeans and bra as was her custom when no one was around. She'd be under the covers anyway.

~~~~~~~

He watched from his hiding place as she began to undress, for him no doubt. He loved when she did that. Maybe his time table would be moved up today. That new man had interfered but she was alone now. Perhaps he and Lydia could steal a few moments without him. He laughed at how she'd checked every closet when she came home. It was a private game they played and he liked it. One day soon she'd do that and find him waiting, maybe after her nap.

~~~~~~~~

Before she could undress her phone buzzed in her back pocket. Jack's voice greeted her.

"I'm sorry Sweetheart, but I just realized that both trucks are at your house. Can you please come get me and Johnny so he can have the work truck?"

She buttoned and zipped her jeans and walked toward the truck. A nap would've been nice, but really she was glad for an excuse to return to the guys. She needed to give Johnny a hug and Jack the benefit of the doubt. He probably wasn't as big a butt as she'd labeled him earlier.

Chapter 42

She found Jack and Johnny standing in Denise's back yard taking measurements. "C'mere Lydia and tell us what you think." Jack invited.

Johnny stood to the side not daring to look up. He was so ashamed of his behavior before the woman. He loved her like the sister he hoped she'd be one day. And she was coming straight for him.

Oh well. It won't be the first time I've had my face slapped.

"I'm sorry Johnny." She hugged him with all her might. Johnny rested his head on hers and returned her hug. Jack was glad to see his brother actually tear up. Though he'd tried to talk to him since his own about-face seven months earlier, Johnny shut him out. Apparently Lydia's tenderness had touched his heart.

"Thanks Lydia. I love you," Johnny smiled.

"Yeah… whatever." She smiled back at him.

Jack broke the awkwardness by asking, "Baby what do you think about adding a cover to the patio? You saved us so much money in the front and we're ahead of schedule so we thought about doing this area too."

Lydia studied for a bit trying to visualize. "What did you have in mind?"

Jack took his notepad and started sketching. "We'd add a pergola and bring it out to here… put some thick columns on the corners, maybe a nice table and chairs for outdoor meals… she's got a decent grill but we could build a prep area… there."

"How would she get back here in her wheelchair?" Lydia wondered.

"Through here… she could exit the side door instead of the patio sliders. The ramp takes her to the carport, but here's where your crew would come in. Do you think you could do those same brick pavers from the carport to the patio? And then maybe fill in some nice plants between the house and the pavers? There might even be room enough for a small tree."

Jack looked at Lydia and wondered if she liked the idea or just wanted to be done. He'd really made a mess that morning. She may just wash her hands of the whole thing, including him. As usual her silence worried him.

"I love it." She spoke simply and pointed to the sketch. "What if I fill in this area with plants as well? I can even come back this fall and plant bulbs so she can have blooms right outside her glass doors as early as February. That sure helps lighten the wintertime blues."

Jack smiled and kissed her cheek.

Lydia wasn't even embarrassed until Johnny went "Mmm hum…" under his breath and grinned like a mule eating briars.

She tried to change the subject. "We've only got three days left though. Isn't she coming home Friday?"

"Friday at lunch." Jack knew they'd be pushing it but wanted to remind that they had part of Friday to work too if they needed it.

"Let's do it!" Johnny added suddenly excited to see Jack and Lydia happy again. "Okay big brother, you're the boss! How do you recommend we proceed?"

"If you'll get the materials this afternoon after we go to Lydia's to get the work truck, then she and I can load plants from the farm onto her truck and be ready to roll in the morning. When you finish gathering supplies, if it's okay with my girlfriend," he smiled at Lydia, "then come back to the farm around seven for supper. I'll treat us to steaks."

"Sounds good to me!" Johnny was glad to be back in the fold. "In fact, I need to do one more thing here before we take off. Why don't you go get the steaks now while I finish up?"

Lydia tossed the keys to Jack. Surprisingly she liked having him drive, even if he did obey the speed limit. "Do you mind if we ask Shawn and Kurtis to supper? I want to run all this by them too. I hope they'll have time to help. I lined them up with my other customers this week since I thought we were through here."

Jack started her truck. "Sure! I thought we'd ask Jesse over too." He said it as if it were the usual thing to do. Lydia looked at him and teared up.

"Thank you Jack." She slid across the bench seat and kissed him.

"Call him and see if he can come." Jack was pulling out of the drive when he heard her say

"Nope."

He looked at her as he shifted the truck into third. Trying to save a fight he handed her his phone, "You're right. You dial but I'll invite him."

She did and he did. It made her heart happy to hear Jack say to her friend Jesse, "Hey man. Want to come over to Lydia's tonight for a steak? No, I'm cooking." She didn't hear what Jesse said but it made Jack laugh. It was the happiest sound she'd heard since he sang "My Girl" to her on their beach trip.

Thank You Lord, she prayed from an overflowing heart.

By the time they shopped for groceries Johnny was ready to ride back to the farm with them. For a brief moment Lydia wondered how it would be to join the brothers' crew. She liked sitting between them hearing them laugh as friends. It was much like riding with Shawn and Kurtis. But when she thought of her boys and Blue Meadow she knew she'd never leave.

Chapter 43

Johnny left the farm quickly to gather supplies so they could get an early start on Tuesday. Lydia changed into work clothes and was happy to have Jack's help when they gathered things for the new project. A Japanese maple would be just right in the small space. Liriope with purple plumes were dug and divided for a nice border. Three of her signature watermelon red crepe myrtles would make a nice backdrop for the far corner of the yard. She called Johnny to see if he could get the same split rail fencing for along the property line. If they didn't get the fencing done by Friday she could always go back later and put it in.

Jack had never seen the entire farm so he was amazed at all the things she had growing. She had taken the wheel once they reached the farm and scared the life out of him barreling down the dirt road. He wondered if she'd taken driver's education in Hazzard County with the good ol' boys Luke and Bo Duke. She noticed him clutching the door handle with a death grip and asked, "Am I scaring you darlin'?" She laughed and slowed down. "Sorry. I'm just excited about those steaks you've got marinating. We need to get this show on the road!"

They finished gathering a variety of hosta as Shawn and Kurtis came down the gravel road in Shawn's truck to meet them. The boys hugged Lydia and started telling her about their beach trip and the girls they'd met. They had plans to see them again soon and might even go back Saturday. Jack loved their interaction with her like two little brothers anxious to please. She laughed so freely and it gave him comfort that he could count on them to be there for her when he left next week. The thought of leaving made his heart sad. He silently asked God to intervene and wondered again if she'd consider traveling with him.

His thoughts were interrupted by her laughter. Kurtis was imitating Shawn trying to dance. She comforted her overgrown boy by offering. "Don't worry Shawn. I'll teach you to dance. We'll work on it next week every night til you're ready to go back and show those chicks what they've been missing."

She still laughed as Kurtis kept flailing his arms and making fun of his buddy. "Don't forget to bite your lip for the white boy moves. That's always a great look." Shawn wasn't laughing but everyone else was. Kurtis had his imitation down!

Lydia finally quit laughing long enough to warn, "Okay stop it Kurtis. Or we'll show Jack how you walk when you catch poison oak on your man parts."

Now Shawn was laughing and couldn't wait to walk like he'd ridden a horse to Texas and back. Jack shook his head. No wonder Lydia loved having those two around her all the time.

When they returned to the house Shawn and Kurtis sat on the side of the deck and removed their work boots without being told. Lydia sat on the bench and pulled hers off too. They washed their hands in the little sink on the outside of the shower. Johnny pulled up followed by a large silver Toyota Tundra work truck.

A tall man stepped from the cab. He looked to be about 240 pounds of lean muscle. His frame was at least three inches taller than Jack's which was saying a lot since Jack was over six feet tall. The man removed his sunglasses and tossed them back into the truck. Steel gray eyes greeted them as he smiled a broad smile. Jack thought to himself that if the guy's long hair had been dark instead of blond he would've been a great person to play Jesus in an Easter drama; or even more accurately a superhero in a Marvel comic book. The man was chiseled. He walked toward them with giant strides.

"You must be Jack." He shook Jack's hand firmly. "I'm Jesse and this is for you." He presented him with a large loaf of bread. "Made it myself!" He laughed and Jack thought,

Well of course you did. Then he saw it was in a Panera bag.

Calm down Jackass. The man can't help he looks like Thor.

Lydia introduced Johnny while Kurt and Shawn started talking Panther football with Jesse and led him inside. Jack noticed that Jesse made no attempt to hug Lydia. And she made no effort to hug him even though she'd hugged Johnny and the boys as usual. She was really doing her best to put Jack at ease and so was Jesse.

198

"Oh, these are for you Lydia." Jesse reached into a back pocket. "I thought they'd give a boost to your Claudia Garden." He smiled as he handed her a large envelope of wildflower seeds.

"Thanks!" She smiled her beautiful smile. "How do you take your steak?" She quickly tried to change the subject.

Jesse looked at Jack. "I take steak any way I can get it! Thanks for inviting me Jack."

Jack asked, "Medium as in pink, or less done?"

"Medium sounds perfect. As long as it's not mooing, I'm good." He glanced back through the kitchen archway and said to Lydia, "I like your sunroom. Blue built that?"

Lydia smiled happily. "Yep. Not bad for a boy who never owned a tool belt, huh!"

Jesse nodded in approval and noticed the mussed daybed with her Bible on it. "It's really nice. I love the view out back toward the pond." He turned toward Jack. "Hey, what can I do to help? I'm not good in the kitchen but I can put ice in the glasses or something."

"Sounds good," Jack answered. He was starting to see how Lydia warmed up to Jesse. He seemed like a nice guy. But why did he have to be so good-looking?

Jack checked the potatoes baking in the oven. Lydia took corn on the cob from boiling water and moved the pot out of the way so Jack could use the two working burners. Her two cast iron skillets made quick work of the steaks. Johnny sliced the bread and Kurtis made a big salad.

Shawn came from the den. "Liddy you have to get a television. It's almost football season for crying out loud. If you expect us to come over and eat your food all the time you're gonna have to do better."

"I know," Lydia answered. "The dinosaur died. But really the only thing I watch on TV is football so a television is on the bottom of the list. We'll live. We can always watch you dance."

That set Kurtis to laughing until she followed with, "Or Kurtis walk."

She set the table as everyone gathered around. Jesse asked, "Does it matter where I sit? I know Miss Lydia likes to have her back against the wall."

Jack didn't know that, but three out of five of the men in her presence did for Shawn and Kurtis pulled the table out a bit as if she always sat in the back. Jack sat to one side of her and Johnny quickly took the other side lest Jesse end up there by default. Jack informed them that all the steaks were medium as he did not serve anything gray or dry. Jesse said with authority, "AMEN brother! That'll preach!" Jack laughed in spite of himself.

They enjoyed the meal together and filled the boys in on the latest development at Denise's. Thankfully Kurt and Shawn were on board. Jesse spoke up and asked, "Can I help? I'll be leaving Friday for a while, so I purposely didn't line up any work this week."

Lydia continued to cut her steak while Johnny spoke up, "Sure. We'll be lucky to get all this done in three and a half days! Come on over!"

Jesse looked at Jack and waited. Jack finally replied, "Absolutely. We can use all the help we can get! What time do you want to start in the morning Lydia?"

She looked up surprised that suddenly she was in charge. "Hey, I'm a slave driver. Just ask my crew. I'll defer to your wisdom Dearheart. You've done way more of these things than I have."

Jack was obviously pleased with her reply and kissed her cheek right there in front of Johnny, Kurt, Shawn, Jesse, God and everybody. She didn't even blush.

After they cleaned the kitchen and Jesse started to leave, he spoke directly to Jack. "Thanks for everything man. Hey can you pray with me about my trip next week? I'm meeting my wife for a get-away." He paused and swallowed hard. "Pray that God helps her to love me again."

Jack suddenly felt honored that Jesse would speak to him about such a personal issue. "I'll be happy to. And Jesse, thank you for all you've done for Lydia. She said you've saved her life several times. Thank you." He extended his hand toward Jesse who took it and hugged him with a slap on the back. Though it caught Jack by surprise he felt good to be in the company of someone so kind.

Lydia didn't witness any of it however as she had just returned from the den where her boys were explaining to Johnny the rules of Rook. Jack nodded toward her to Jesse as if giving permission. Jesse smiled, kissed Lydia on the head and squeezed her shoulders from the side. "Bye girl. Take care of Jack. You need a good cook!"

Lydia laughed at him and replied, "I'm not keeping him for his culinary skills."

It made Jack happier than he could imagine.

Chapter 44

The work was hard and they were exhausted. Johnny had plenty to finish inside so having Jesse on the crew turned out to be a Godsend. He and Jack quickly formed a good friendship as they did the construction portion of the project. Lydia and her guys planted and watered and carefully formed level pathways with brick pavers. The weather co-operated nicely and the plants were holding up well with a slight break in the heat. An occasional breeze reminded them that July was ending and fall would arrive in another month or so. Jack commented with relief one day that he was really thankful for the few days of lower temperatures. Jesse laughed and mentioned that Autumn was God's reward to Southerners just for surviving Summer.

Jack wished he would be in North Carolina to enjoy the coming season. He questioned Lydia's thinking. He wondered if she'd purposely asked the boys over for dance lessons in order to keep her distance from him. If so it was definitely working. Because by the time they worked all day as hard as they could, returned to the farm, got showers and ate supper she and Jack both were nearly passing out tired. She took up her regular practice of sleeping in the sunroom with Bible in hand. Catching a few verses by the light of her cell each night gave her good things to think on as she fell asleep. Jack stayed up a while after she went to bed. He listened to music and wondered if he could spend another day there without a television. Before turning in he'd look through the sunroom to where she slept. She usually was on her side facing the outdoors with her nighttime ponytail spilling over the pillow. He longed for the day she would allow him to join her there.

Their morning routine was established quickly. She'd be up and out of the bathroom an hour before his clock went off. He'd find her on the porch swing, sometimes with a light throw over her legs as she stayed in her sleeping shorts until ready to go. He started setting his clock a half an hour earlier just to drink coffee with her feet in his lap.

He wanted to ask if he could move in with her. But even as easy as a plan normally formed for Jack, it just wasn't clear. In his head he knew he was ready to take a very big next step but doubted that she was. If only he could pull out a sketch pad and draw something up for their future. Was he ready to live that far from home and continue to run the company, or perhaps ask her to move in with him? Neither option seemed right. He thought of the debt he still owed his father that would take quite a while to settle. Though his dad had forgiven it, Jack was determined to pay him back. Plus he'd just completed his loft apartment and truthfully he missed it. But Lydia would be miserable there.

But Lydia…

How could he bear to leave her? Looking at her one morning before work as she twisted her hair up on top of her head, he pulled her into his arms and kissed her as if he'd never let her go.

"Merciful heavens Jack!" She caught her breath and rested in his arms for a moment. She patted his chest then whispered, "We'd better get going or somebody's gonna have some splainin' to do!"

"Baby, what are you thinking? Talk to me." He pulled her back into his arms and his eyes pleaded with her. He was surprised when she teared up.

"I can't imagine life without you Jack. I don't know what to do." She hugged him then took his hand. "C'mon. Right now we've got to get our rears in gear!" They hurried out the door and on to Denise's. Friday was fast approaching.

~~~~~~~

Soon! The new man would leave and they would be together again. He had waited long enough. Nobody could argue with that. His favorite part was her fear. But she'd gotten brave again lately and quit checking the closets. She'd even returned the keys to the shower. He'd drop her a few more little clues just to see if she remembered how to play their private game.

~~~~~~~

Jack prepared a special supper for Lydia and her boys on Thursday night. Duplicating the Alfredo sauce from Olive Garden he made pasta with shrimp. Shawn and Kurtis woofed it down as if it were their last meal. Lydia loved this beautiful time with her make-shift family around the table. Just like a real mother she reminded the boys later as they practiced the proper way to hold a girl. Her daddy had been a stickler about that as he'd danced with her so many years ago. She could picture his dark curly hair and hear his deep stern voice.

Don't let some guy mash himself up against you like you're married. If it feels wrong then it probably is. Keep your distance so he doesn't get the wrong idea.

It had embarrassed her to death for her daddy to speak of such things. It ended up being wasted instructions as Blue refused to dance or even have a radio in their home. Thankfully Jack didn't feel the same way and always had a good playlist ready. She liked the stuff he found for them as it was all new to her. She hadn't listened to the radio in years and realized what she'd been missing; except for that song about big butts. She could certainly do without that.

She danced with Shawn and commented on how smooth he was getting. "Now we don't have anything to make fun of. Keep taking the lead. That's your job and I promise she'll like it. If she doesn't then she's not your type." She smiled up at him and could tell he was proud of himself. Satisfied that her work was done she informed them that the dance party was over.

"Oh, don't forget your cookies." She handed Kurtis a box of Gingersnaps. The guys looked at each other and shrugged as they left. Lydia shook her head and laughed.

Goobers.

They stood on the porch in the cool evening air as wind chimes softly confirmed that better weather was on the way. Kurtis, as usual informed her of their plans so she wouldn't worry. "We're gonna sleep in Saturday morning so we won't have to stay here Friday night. We figure that might be yours and Jack's last night together for a while and you don't need us around. We're gonna stay late Saturday night at the beach and catch up with those girls then drive home. We'll keep each other awake so don't worry Liddy." He hugged her then so did Shawn who added, "You know I'm the good one so I'll make sure Kurt behaves himself."

Kurtis rolled his eyes. "See y'all in the morning for the big reveal. Denise is gonna love it!"

Jack shook his hand, "I sure hope so. You guys did an outstanding job. I'd hire you again any day!" He reached over to shake Shawn's hand as well.

With a final word of instruction Lydia's mama heart had to remind them one more time. "Guys please don't let your raging hormones short circuit your brains. And don't let some chick bat her eyelashes at you and cause you do something you'll regret. I'm telling you, women are crazy."

"Yes Mommy Dearest!" They replied in unison like they always did when she became advisory. If she'd been wearing shoes she would've thrown one at them.

"Please be careful," she added as they left. She and Jack watched til they were out of sight.

Once inside they locked the front door then Jack pulled up another playlist. He hoped that she was ready to move their relationship to the next level. He'd never waited on any woman so long.

"C'mere woman and bat those eyelashes at me." He began a slow dance that was so smooth that she quickly forgot how tired she was and melted into his arms. She wished she'd dressed better for him as this WAS one of their last nights together. But there she was in worn out jeans and a white t-shirt AGAIN. At least she was clean having washed the dirt of the day off before the guys had arrived. He didn't seem to mind and whispered as they danced, "May I have the honor of your company tomorrow night? I thought we'd go on a real date."

"I'm sorry sir. I do not date." She tipped her head back to look into his eyes… those eyes.

"Then would you go with me to the funeral home? That way you'll have to wear that black dress I saw hanging in your closet. We may get sidetracked on the way as I'm not sure if anyone will die that we need to pay our respects to."

She laughed at his obviously rehearsed approach to asking her out. "I suppose I could. And we may need to stop somewhere to eat." She added trying to help the man out.

205

"EXACTLY! And if they happen to have music it would be a shame not to dance." He twirled her then pulled her into his arms kissing her passionately.

Reaching up to where her hair was twisted he removed the clasp that held it. She wasn't sure why it embarrassed her when her hair came tumbling down. Tucking the clasp into her back jean pocket his hand lingered there and she felt her face flush. Finding her voice she finally said, "I think it's sufficiently put away dear." She shifted his hand back to her waist and laughed a nervous laugh. The song he had playing was not very nice and she was about to tell him so when his hand moved up and unfastened her bra through her t-shirt. The romance ended quickly as she pulled away and spoke without affection, "Good night Jack."

She went to the bathroom and closed the door leaving him standing in the kitchen. Her heart pounded like crazy and she stopped just short of locking the door. She changed quickly into sleeping shorts and hung her jeans on the back of the door. She stayed in her t-shirt and fastened her bra back even though she wasn't used to sleeping in one. Usually she said goodnight to him and went straight to the daybed without more hugs or whatever. Tonight she had a feeling he'd be waiting for her. Trying to calm down she reprimanded herself. She had allowed him to stay there longing for as much time as possible with him before he left. What was the man supposed to think?

Pulling her hair back up she washed her face, and hoped he didn't try to talk about it when she came out. She was too tired. Sometimes she got the impression that he thought a multitude of words would cure anything.

Sure enough, he sat in a kitchen chair waiting for her as she exited the bathroom. Looking at her with those puppy dog eyes he said in his most remorseful tone, "Lydia darling, I just love you so much."

"Thanks." It was the best she could do. She walked past him on the way to the sunroom. Taking her hand as she walked by he pulled her to his lap.

"Can we please talk? I love you more than I can say and I miss you already. I can't stand the thought of doing life without you. Please let me hold you."

She couldn't look at him and she sure couldn't stay in his arms. Her heart hurt too at the thought of his leaving, but also at the thought of his advances knowing how hard she was trying to keep things right between them. When she didn't reply Jack made one last ditch effort to get her to stay up with him a bit longer.

"Can we please make up before we go to bed? The Bible warns us not to let the sun go down on our anger. "

She pulled away then turned with blue eyes flashing, "Then perhaps people shouldn't do stupid stuff so close to bedtime." She left him sitting there and headed to the daybed.

~~~~~~~

Breakfast was not pleasant. He'd set the clock early so he'd have time to prepare the sour cream pancakes she loved so much. But she was already making quick work of a bowl of cereal. He made things worse when he asked, "Is Jesse going to be there today?"

"I'm sure I don't know. I don't talk to the man without you present." She put her bowl in the sink and went to the bedroom to get ready for the reveal. Standing in front of her open closet she noticed the black dress and hoped they'd still go out. Surely the day could only get better. Pulling on the blue dress he loved so well, she wanted to look as nice as she could, even if she was still mad at him. In her heart of hearts she knew she loved him. If it weren't for the passion she felt, she'd just tell him to stay, making her house his new home base. But obviously that couldn't happen now since he'd gone and messed things up last night. She may not always be that strong.

Her cowboy boots weren't an option since they were on the deck caked in mud. Stepping into the chunky summer heels she'd just have to try not to fall.

Hold your head up woman and act like you've got some sense! Everything turned out beautiful because YOU are a Landscape Artist!

She smiled at the memory of the fear she'd struggled with the day she'd gone to meet Jack for the first time. Fear had almost robbed her of a beautiful new beginning.

Lord… thank You. You've been so good to me, she whispered.

Tipping her head over she shook her hair loose from the ever present clasp and remembered her embarrassment from the night before. Why did she have to be so awkward? Her own insecurities were definitely part of the problem. Maybe she and Jack could talk on the way into work.

Taking her Bible from the daybed she found Jack on the porch swing. Sitting down carefully, so as not to spill their coffee, she turned sideways and put her bare feet in his lap.

"Thank you," he said looking at her remorsefully. "You look really pretty today. In fact you always do. That's my problem." He laughed an uneasy laugh.

"So it's my fault?" She asked wondering if that's what he was getting at. She knew better than to actually believe he thought she was pretty all the time.

"NOOO, nooo… that's NOT what I meant at all." Jack laughed and she found herself laughing too.

He tried to fix things. "I guess I shouldn't have let my raging hormones short circuit my brain." She laughed at his quoting the warning she'd given the boys.

"Maybe it was that sexy song. Or maybe I think about you way too much." He was trying but she wasn't ready to let him off the hook.

"Why DID you play that song? It was dirty, Jack!" She looked at him waiting for an answer. "When he said 'Strip it down,' I don't think he was speaking of cars or furniture."

Jack really wanted to make up so he tried. "It's not dirty for people who are married and madly in love."

"Key word being…?" Lydia turned her head sideways and looked at him.

"Married… I know. But that's how I feel about you Lydia. It's just too soon to be saying the M-word. I don't want you to go running away like a deer bounding through the forest or I would've already brought the subject up. Maybe it's time we moved in together for good and started acting like adults. I don't know how you feel about the future and I'm about to leave. I wish you'd talk to me."

Through the years he'd learned to infer that he was the marrying kind without really asking. He was surprised that he was actually considering it this time.

Lydia's tone suddenly softened. "I had no idea you felt that way already." She looked at him thoughtfully but wondered what he meant by 'acting like adults.' Surely he knew where she stood so far as their physical relationship.

He added hopefully, "Let's talk about it tonight over dinner okay?"

"Sounds good." She nodded and tried to read his expression.

He put his coffee cup down and rubbed her feet.

"Wow Jack. That's a sure fire way to get out of the doghouse."

"I'll remember that. I'm sure this won't be the last time I need that information." He smiled that smile she found so hard to resist.

Chapter 45

Though they rode to work together they decided to talk about the future later instead of starting a conversation they'd find hard to finish before they arrived at Denise's. Lydia was startled to see a local news crew there. She'd have to work hard to stay out of the way of that nonsense. Jack informed her it would be great PR for her business and that he planned to introduce her as the one responsible for the gorgeous landscaping. She was mortified at the thought making him laugh and shake his head at her fear.

"Please don't Jack," she begged. "Look at me! I'm such a bumpkin in this dress and these stupid shoes. Introduce the boys if you want but please leave me out of it." She seemed desperate and it surprised him how urgently she pleaded. She saw the look in his eye and knew he didn't understand. She decided then that she would leave before it had time to happen. At times he made her so mad.

When Denise returned to her beautiful new home the joy on her face was worth all the work. Lovely brick pathways made navigating the yard smooth and pleasant. The split rail fence appeared to have been there forever. They'd even been able to finish the fence in the back. Pink Seven Sister roses spilled over at every turn. The ramp flowed seamlessly from the porch down to the carport. Now she could load her wheelchair into her car out of the rain.

Inside halls and doorways were nice and wide and much easier to access. The new bathroom was spacious and equipped with bars she could use to lift herself into the tub. A handheld shower and lowered mirrors made the space very user friendly. New hardwood floors throughout the house provided Denise with smooth sailing.

She loved the kitchen best of all. Johnny apparently had been inside her head to pull off such an impressive design. Cabinets were lowered and everything was within easy reach. Her favorite part came when he hugged her from behind and kissed her cheek. She wondered how long he'd be staying in town and decided to get brave and ask him later.

Pictures were taken for Pop's gallery wall. He would be very proud. Jack made a speech to all the workers thanking them for their outstanding labor of love. Checks were handed out for all those hired including Blue Meadow Farm. He remembered Lydia's first day on the job and how he had doubted her. Looks were certainly deceiving. He gave bonus checks to Shawn and Kurtis besides what Lydia would pay them. Those guys had worked very hard and he was glad to call them friends.

As everyone began leaving the Parker project Lydia started to get teary. Quickly she headed to her old pick-up, feeling like she might come undone and not really sure why. The local news crew was interviewing Jack so she didn't feel like staying. A pretty young woman in a white summer suit held a microphone near Jack's face and smiled adoringly at him. She was stunning with silky black hair neatly falling over her shoulders. Jack obviously enjoyed her attention. Lydia hurried home as fast as she could go. Even her comfortable blue dress could not restore her confidence at that point. She was and always would be a bumpkin.

~~~~~~~~

That stupid gate was left open again. She was sure she had closed it, but all the days had run together lately. Kicking up a cloud of dust behind her, she had no idea why she was in such a hurry to get home. Oh how she would miss Jack, and Johnny too.

But Jack…

He deserved someone like the nice reporter who would look good on his arm up North where they have dinner parties and cocktails and such. Lydia knew she would never fit in such a place. Not that he had asked, but a girl could dream couldn't she? Actually that was more like a nightmare. She hated the thoughts of flying and of meeting his mother. She hated new things, and she hated hobnobbing. Why even think of it?

But Jack….

She loved his good natured humor… the sparkle when he looked at her… with those eyes. Not to mention the pounding of her heart when he held her in his strong arms. In those moments she knew she could do anything with him as her man.

Tears slipped down her face as she thought of his leaving. Why had she dared to hope? Hope she knew, was a dangerous thing.

~~~~~~~

She'd left in quite a hurry that morning. Her back door was unlocked again. And apparently the trash needed to be taken out. Something smelled really bad. She decided to check the closets just to be sure. She'd certainly relax better once she declared the house all clear. She headed through the kitchen and gave the garbage can a quick sniff. It didn't smell and the compost bowl was empty. From there she stepped into the little hallway in front of the bathroom. Taking a quick left into the boy's room she suspected one of them had left food or fish bait there to spoil. As usual nothing jumped from their closet and no one hid under the bed. In fact there wasn't room under there. Evidently that was their hidey hole for all things beachy. Two canvas rafts, a wadded up beach towel and a small cooler lurked beneath. Thankfully the cooler was empty so she still wondered.

What was that awful smell?

Into the bathroom she went with a quick look behind the shower curtain. That revealed nothing so through her bedroom she checked. That bed would be empty again soon as Jack would be leaving after church Sunday. Peeking under the bed she found it empty of course but smiled as she noticed the sunscreen had fallen from the bag and landed there at some point. The thought of their beach trip and his wonderful massage, his care for her and their funny words with one another made her heart happy. If Jack asked her to marry him that night she would gladly say yes. She paused at the thought of it and for a brief moment imagined a wedding, maybe even there on Blue Meadow.

July 31st, she thought.

Today marks the end of our time together at Denise's but our first real date. Maybe it's the beginning of something very special.

She smiled again as she dared to hope.

As she rose from her knees after checking under the bed, the noise of a floorboard creaking brought the hope to a halt. The sound came from inside her closet. For half a breath she stood frozen in her tracks with heart pounding. Chills ran down her spine as she willed her legs to move. Stumbling backward into the hall she broke into a run. She dared not turn to look but was jerked hard backward as the stranger grabbed her hair and spun her around.

"Hello Gingersnap. I been waitin' for ya."

Her heart nearly stopped as she recognized the man as the same one she'd seen on her porch months ago. He smelled so bad she nearly gagged. She pulled hard against his grasp and stumbled backward into the kitchen. He jerked her upright by the front of her dress. With one hand on his massive chest trying to keep him away, she swung wildly with the other striking the tall vessel on the counter. Instinctively she fumbled franticly through the ceramic pot which held her kitchen utensils. Feeling the wooden handle of a butcher knife, she drew it in front of her with a trembling hand.

"Get out of here right now mister!" She spoke in her bravest voice.

He let go for a moment but laughed and taunted her by stroking her face. "Aw Sweetie… you're nice to errybody but me."

His meaty hands grabbed her arms with such force that she couldn't break free. She surprised him by jabbing the knife upward right when he lunged. Blood sprayed them both as he stumbled forward knocking her backwards out of her shoes. His eyes had a terrible surprised look and his breath was heavy on her face. With her hand still clutching the knife she felt the weight of him falling. Striking her head hard on the edge of the countertop she was out cold. Blood oozed from a nasty gash at the base of her skull. The intruder stretched face down on top of her, a freshly sharpened butcher knife buried deep in his chest.

~~~~~~~

Jack was kicking himself. Why hadn't he planned better? The media had arrived early and caught him off guard. Plus he'd gotten so caught up in the attention of the beautiful young reporter that he never noticed Lydia leaving. Apparently she'd taken off because of the news crew. She'd warned him that she would but he hadn't really believed her. At least he had a date with her that night. Surely it would end better than the night before. It still hurt that she'd pushed him away. Maybe she just needed a more romantic setting.

He rehearsed the speech in his head that he would give about their relationship. Hopefully she could get on board. Maybe she could see the logic in having him move in permanently. He'd promised to love only her so surely it was time. Why wasn't she answering her phone?

Johnny was enjoying talking to Denise. Jack hoped he would follow through with his break-up plans with Gina. That woman was a piece of work. In one short conversation Lydia had helped Johnny realize what he needed to do without even trying. Their own father had warned Johnny that he was like the hard ground in the parable of the sower that often had good words given to him, but just as often allowed Satan to snatch them away. Jack had given up that fight a few years back. It was like beating his head against a wall trying to talk sense into his brother.

Jack wondered if Lydia was mad at him for talking so long with the reporter. He felt a little guilty but really that wasn't like Lydia. She was by far the most understanding woman he'd ever met. Maybe she had left her phone at home. But he was sure he had seen her taking pictures with it earlier. Perhaps he'd ride over to her house to talk to her about his plans. Or maybe he should just wait til dinner. He wondered if she had gone straight home. He might ride by Norma's to see if her truck was there.

He noticed Johnny and Denise still sitting on the new porch swing chatting happily. Perhaps it would be good to give them some time alone since everyone else had left. From the look on Johnny's face he probably wouldn't mind Jack taking the work truck for a while.

Chapter 46

Her gate was open and he wondered why she even bothered with it. As he approached her house he noticed her truck was parked as usual by the back door. He had loved his days with her out in the country with no neighbors in sight. But if they were to be a couple she'd need to spend time in New York with him as well. He smiled at the thought of her there in her threadbare clothes and worn out boots. Eventually he'd lay down the law and make her go shopping. He laughed again at her craziness. Every other woman he'd known had loved letting him buy them things.

He waited on the front porch but there was no answer.

Maybe she had taken the Four Wheeler to the back of the property and left her phone at the house. He walked around the side and tried the back door. It was locked. Though he'd never done so before, something prompted him to get the spare keys and go inside anyway. It would probably make her mad but he was kind of worried since he couldn't reach her. When the keys weren't in their usual place, he remembered the night they'd come home from the beach. Had he put the keys back or were they still rattling around in a pocket somewhere? After thinking a bit he was sure she'd put them back in case one of the boys needed to get in. Recalling the footsteps she'd heard in the woods his heart dropped to his stomach. Though he hadn't spoken to the Lord in a while he prayed.

I've got a really bad feeling about this God. Show me what to do.

He tried not to panic. Where could she be?

He knocked loudly calling her name. He took out his phone and called her again. He could hear her phone buzzing somewhere inside the house. Cupping his hands on the window over the table he could see through. His heart nearly stopped as he was greeted by a bloody mess.

His beloved Lydia lay buried under the weight of a massive man.

He cried out to God and ran to the back door. He kicked it in splintering the doorframe and fell to his knees beside her. "Lydia!

Sweetheart!" He checked for a pulse and couldn't find one. His heart beat wildly as he dialed 911.

He pushed with all his strength to roll the stranger off her. Holding her in his arms he waited the longest seven minutes of his life. She was completely unresponsive. Paramedics loaded her into the ambulance as he climbed in beside her. They scratched out of the gravel drive and down the road, sirens blaring.

Jack looked at the paramedic but couldn't speak.

The young man took her blood pressure and spoke to Jack trying to offer hope. "She's barely alive and has lost a lot of blood. But her vitals are decent considering. Heartrate is weak but I know the girl and she's strong, bless her heart. The stuff she has been through! Now, who are you?"

"I'm her fiancé. She just doesn't know it yet." Jack mumbled without thinking.

The paramedic looked at him skeptically and smiled.

"Good luck with that buddy."

~~~~~~~

A day later Jack still waited by her side in Critical Care. He noticed her eyes flutter awake.

"Hello Sweetheart." He spoke softly looking into her bloodshot eyes. "How's my girl?"

She did her best to speak. "Could I have some water? Oh… my head."

He spooned ice chips into her parched lips then lifted her hand. He kissed it trying hard to hold back the tears.

"Thanks for sharpening my knives." She mumbled and was out again. When he was sure she wasn't watching he let the tears flow freely.

~~~~~~~

He stayed at the hospital with her night and day through the whole ordeal. When finally they moved her to a regular room, a nurse rolled a recliner in with a pillow and blanket for Jack. Lydia was heavily sedated and seldom stirred but he didn't want to risk her waking up alone. Hopefully he would take her home soon where she could start recovering. The hospital routine provided very little rest for either of them. Her pastor visited almost daily encouraging Jack with very few words. His presence was comfort enough.

Shawn and Kurtis were in and out almost too much for Jack's preference. But they promised to clean the blood from the kitchen floor once the police had everything they needed. The cops tried to piece together the events but would need to talk with her when she began to feel better. They seemed to be in no rush as the evidence was cut and dry. The man had stalked women for years. They'd been to the farm and discovered his hidden lair. From the looks of things he'd been there quite a while holed up in an old van. Jack wondered if Lydia needed to know she'd been watched for so long. He thanked God that apparently the intruder's plan had been interrupted by Jack's stay at the house. He shuddered at the thought of what could've happened but still wondered if Lydia would ever be the same.

Norma Rae came as often as she could and loved sharing with Jack. She broke the monotony with her cheerful disposition and chatter. He liked hearing all the tales about Lydia growing up even if it was from her husband's mother. He got the feeling however that there were many missing pieces to the story of her childhood. Norma mentioned Lydia's mother had died young and briefly spoke of her father. "He was a good man as long as he wasn't drinking." Jack decided that was a polite Southern way of saying he was a mean drunk. And apparently there had been bad blood between him and Blue. Norma teared up and changed the subject so Jack decided not to ask any other family questions. After that he stuck to generic conversations about how hot it still was for early August.

So many well-wishers and construction guys came by that Jack finally asked the nurses to limit her visitors to the list he gave them. She was getting very little rest and Jack wasn't sure if all those people were friends or just curious. He thought about texting Jesse, but knew he'd be there in a heartbeat if he did. Jack excused himself for not letting him know by rationalizing that Jesse was on a much needed getaway with his estranged wife. He could always tell him once they got home.

Johnny came by the hospital every day for a quick visit. Jack finally convinced him to get back to work and keep the business on task. Lydia opened her eyes for a bit when Johnny kissed her forehead. He teared up and whispered "I love you Lydia. Wake up and get well. My brother needs you." She smiled weakly then drifted back to sleep.

~~~~~~~

A few days later she seemed strong enough to process the question he needed to ask.

"Lydia, I need to talk to you about something."

She looked at him with swollen eyes and expected the worst. He'd been by her side for days. Surely he needed to be on his way. She dreaded the thought but understood. About that time a nurse came in to check her blood pressure.

"You're doing good honey! 110 over 80. Let me get you some fresh ice water."

He tried to begin again when an orderly began emptying the trash and pushing a dust mop across the shiny linoleum floors.

He stood and moved his chair out of the way then resumed his post and tried again.

"I've been thinking about…"

The nurse returned with the ice water. "Thanks" he said on Lydia's behalf. Then a patient advocate stopped by with a clip board and fifty questions. At least it seemed like that to Jack. He was exasperated.

The room cleared and he was about to try again when the doctor popped in. "Hello Mrs. Miller, Mr. Miller. You've been through quite the adventure haven't you! Gave that SOB what was coming to him though! Good girl! He's stalked women all over Rowan County and has somehow always gotten off with a slap on the wrist. But by god, he won't be bothering anyone anymore. So how're you feeling today?

218

Headaches getting better? Any anxious thoughts? Fears? Sleeping okay? Keep taking the prescribed medication in order to stay ahead of the pain. We'll probably send you home in the morning barring some disaster. Do you have someone who can help you out for a few days? If not we can give you the numbers of caregivers for hire."

"No need." Jack finally found his voice. "I'll be staying with her."

"Which is til death do us part right Mr. Miller?" The hip young doctor laughed at his own joke then added. "But do you have someone who will stay during the day? She's going to need help for a while until the dizziness subsides. She's earned herself quite the concussion!"

Jack looked into her eyes which had suddenly filled with tears. "Don't worry. I'll be with her night and day."

"I hear you man though it'll be a while til she's up to anything frisky. I'll be back in the morning to sign your get out of jail free card. Well… not FREE."

"Yuk yuk yuk." he laughed. The doctor was totally in love with himself and Jack hoped they never had to see him again… except of course for that get out of jail but not for free card.

When he finally left, Jack took Lydia's hand and asked quickly and quietly, "May I stay with you for a while? After all, I am Mr. Miller. I promise to cook and smash all the spiders in the shower with the flip flop."

She smiled weakly and whispered, "Thank you."

~~~~~~~

The ride home was bumpy and made her head hurt. Jack was driving her old truck slowly and had both windows down trying to keep her cool. She thought she might hurl. As they pulled into her drive she wondered why the gate was locked. It hadn't worked before so why bother now? As soon as she was able she would bring her tractor around and rip that worthless piece of crap out of the way.

Jack pulled up to the front of the house then came around and helped her from the truck. She stood still, trying to stop the spinning. She would need to water those hanging ferns soon or they would be toast. Finally up the steps onto the porch she decided to sit on a rocker for a moment. A cool breeze was just what she needed and spurred her to try moving again. Jack held the door open with one hand and wrapped his other arm around her waist. "Where would you like to rest?" he asked.

"Sunroom," was all she could muster.

As he helped her through the kitchen she suddenly stopped and looked at the floor.

"Bucket… back deck." She gripped a kitchen chair tightly.

He hated to let go of her but recognized the urgency. Retrieving the mop bucket just in time she hurled right there in front of God and Jack and everybody. The thoughts of the nasty man's hands grabbing her made her retch until she had no more strength.

Poor Jack. Never in all his life had he carried a mop bucket full of vomit for the sake of love.

Suddenly it hit him hard.

He'd just been assigned as caregiver for a woman he wasn't even sure he could take home to his mother.

Chapter 47   Mid-August

He wondered if he should call the doctor again. She had said less than ten words since he'd brought her home. He helped her to the bathroom each morning where she had to sit just to brush her teeth. This woman who had pushed wheel barrows of dirt a very short time ago barely had the strength to move from the sunroom daybed where she had set up camp. Once again he had taken the room with the double bed. He just wished she were in it. Every morning he would put out a clean shirt and shorts in the bathroom where she would sit and sponge off at the sink.

Thankfully Kurtis and Shawn stopped by often helping him with the grocery shopping and mowing. Because of them he had not needed to leave the house. They were even able to keep her business running somewhat. But Lydia barely spoke to them.

Pastor Dale called to ask if he could come by. Jack was glad to hear from him and hoped he might get her to open up. He had such kindness about him and used to make her laugh. The visit went well enough. Before he left he prayed a good strong prayer not only for Lydia, but also for Jack. Jack realized how tired he was and how quickly he was drifting. As soon as her pastor was gone she became withdrawn again. Jack knew it was time.

"Call me ASAP." Jack sent the text to Jesse he should've sent two weeks earlier. His phone rang immediately. He spoke quietly to Jesse.

"I'm sorry to bother you, but I knew you'd want to know about Lydia." Jack began. He was surprised at how quickly he got choked up. The thought of nearly losing her made it hard to speak the terrible words.

Jesse spoke with alarm. "What's wrong Jack?" Jesse held his breath knowing how often Lydia had asked God to take her life.

Jack tried to speak as he walked to the bedroom and closed the door. Though Lydia was sleeping he still didn't want to risk her overhearing lest she relive the horrible attack.

"She walked in on an intruder." Jack's heart hurt as he said the words. "But according to the doctor she'll recover."

Jesse could hardly speak. "Oh dear Lord." Jack could tell Jesse was grief stricken.

"She's home from the hospital. She has a nasty concussion and lost a good bit of blood, but I'm concerned about her mental state more than anything. She's hasn't spoken much at all since we got home. And she's so weak. I'm really worried about her. Are you still away with your wife?"

"I'm on my way home now. Can I come by around seven this evening?" Jesse asked hopefully.

"Yes. She needs your visit. It will be good for her." Jack said the words he knew to be true but still resented having to admit. "How did it go with your wife?" Jack wanted very much to hear that they had reconciled.

"Not good." Jesse swallowed hard. "I'm going to be honest with you Jack. I'm really struggling."

He stopped short of revealing that his wife had delivered divorce papers a year earlier. His trip to meet her as a last ditch effort to save their marriage had only served to completely sever ties. When she introduced a former friend of Jesse's as her fiancé Jesse spent two weeks at the retreat by himself begging God for help. Now he was wishing he'd returned home sooner. His best friend lay dying and he wasn't even there.

He could hardly speak. "I'll be there as soon as I can. Thanks for calling Jack."

As each man thought on the events of the summer they had similar questions. Why had God allowed them to hope? How could He possibly work their circumstances out for good?

Jack picked up his Bible for the first time in a while and moved to the front porch. He was so tired. The words of his faithful father gently spoke to him and he searched for the passage.

Beside Luke 8:4-15 he found written in his Pop's distinctive handwriting,

"Stay Strong Son!"

The familiar story Jesus told about a farmer who sowed seeds on different ground came to Jack like a sober warning. How many times had his dad read the words and reminded him not to let the things of the Lord be choked out by his own desires. With conviction he realized that though he'd begun to grow he'd easily been sucked back into an old mindset often pushing Lydia to follow his lead.

On the other hand her soul was much like the rich soil of Blue Meadow. With only a small amount of prompting her heart had begun to grow in Christ. Tender sprouts of faith had quickly grown, but rather than nourish and cherish her, he'd begun to push his own selfish agenda. Often he'd dropped words to indicate he planned a future with her when truthfully he still longed for his old lifestyle. He was not as ready as he thought to leave the past behind.

Plus he knew his mother would not approve of her. Lydia's lack of sophistication would never measure up in her circle of friends. But he had hoped to school her in those things. He had prayed so diligently for God to warm her heart toward him and to give them more time together. Now that He had, Jack felt trapped. For how could he leave her in her current condition?

He moved back inside and walked wearily to the sunroom. Two cheap ceiling fans whirred and rocked above while songbirds chirped happily outside the open windows. The curls around her face moved in the gentle breeze but she never stirred. Jack pulled an ottoman toward her bed and sat near.

Silently he prayed.

Lord, could You give us another chance? I don't know why I get so concerned about my mother's approval. And I don't know how I can even consider returning to the places I've been. But You hear my thoughts. There are times when I feel like I can't live without Lydia, and other times like today when I think I can't take another minute here. Please help us through this. Give me an answer God. I've asked You so many times to help her trust me. Now that she does, I feel like running. Lord God! What is wrong with me?

She turned on her side with her back to him as if shutting him out.

He started to stay beside her and stroke her back. But he was so tired. Instead he put the ottoman where it belonged and walked outside to the deck. A storm brewed and dark clouds hung heavy above him. Birds scattered to find shelter as the wind picked up. Jack remembered sitting with her there not so long ago. She had taken her hair down, shook it loose in the breeze and smiled that beautiful smile. He'd longed for her. But the beautiful girl with the sparkling eyes was gone. She had descended into a deep dark place with no windows or doors and wouldn't let him in.

Perhaps it was time to give up the hope he once had of settling down with her.

Or maybe they just needed more time.

~~~~~~~

Lydia purposely turned her back to the man with unfeeling hands who sighed often at her lack of strength. Though she couldn't form the words, she'd gladly tell the pretty boy as soon as she was able.

You're free to leave whenever you please. I'd rather die than have you stay here out of pity.

She heard him walk away and the dark cloud nearly swallowed her whole. She was too weak to fight and no longer cared. Blue Meadow meant nothing and held only sad memories and terrible fears. Her thoughts were foggy but she made one request clear to the God who held her life in His hands.

Lord… if You love me at all, please… I'm begging You. Take me home.

For some unknown reason she remembered the dogwood tree she still wanted to plant for Jesse before she joined her beloved Blue and their baby girl.

~~~~~~~

Jesse prayed for Lydia as he drove through the pouring rain with windshield wipers beating frantically. Something inside warned him that Lydia was still in grave danger. For years he'd protected her.

224

When Kenya served him with divorce papers a year earlier he'd dared to hope. He'd thought that perhaps after being separated from her for twelve long years God would allow him to finally pursue Lydia. He prayed night and day about it and begged the Lord to help her love again. But God had asked him to wait. Seeing her with Jack had been hard but he'd done his best to put her happiness ahead of his own.

Assuming that he'd misunderstood God's plan, he tried again to reconcile with his wife. But that door had been slammed shut with unmistakable finality. Once again he heard the voice of God gently advising him to wait. In obedient submission and surrender he prayed,

Your will, not mine Lord. But I ask with all that is in me that Lydia find happiness and be deeply cherished. Please protect her. You know how long I've loved her.

Chapter 48

A gentle knock came at the front door. Jack answered it and was surprised at Jesse's big hug. He thought they might both cry. Jesse sat down in the recliner wearily.

"Is she sleeping?"

Jack answered honestly. "I can't tell. It's as if she's asleep but she seldom stirs. I have to force her up if she moves at all. She's not eating and drinks very little. I'm so worried about her."

Jesse looked at Jack. "Did they catch the guy?"

"I found them both on the kitchen floor in a pool of blood. She was unconscious with a huge man…" Jack had to stop talking. "I could hardly get her out from under him. Apparently she grabbed a knife when he attacked her and stuck it in his chest. He was dead. She hit her head going down." Jack felt a wave of nausea as he recalled her blood soaked dress and how covered they both were by the time the ambulance got there. "They had to shave the base of her head. It's a nasty gash."

Jesse looked sadly at his friend. "I'm so sorry Jack. Of all the times for me to be out of town…" His voice trailed off and he quit speaking.

"Did you make any progress with your wife?" Jack asked hopefully.

"Nah… it was pretty bad!" Jesse laughed a hollow laugh.

Jack wondered at Jesse's obvious pain over his wife. He found himself relating and swiping at tears again.

"C'mon. Let's go see Lydia. I'll cook steaks while you visit." Jack rose and headed for the sunroom with Jesse close behind.

Jack moved the ottoman near her bed and Jesse sat down taking her hand. "Wake up girl. You've got company." Lydia barely stirred. When her eyes finally fluttered open, she smiled weakly. "Jesse!" she whispered. "Did Jack leave?" She closed her eyes again. Jack sat on the bed beside her. "I'm right here Sweetheart. I'm not leaving." A pang of guilt stabbed at his heart.

Jesse passed her hand to Jack. She opened her eyes and looked at Jack. "Thank you." She was out again.

Jesse asked, "What kind of drugs do they have her on?"

Jack retrieved the bottles as Jesse looked at his friend. Her eyes were surrounded by dark circles and her dirty hair was wadded on top of her head. Dry cracked lips seemed to silently beg for liquid. Her skin was terribly pale and she looked almost gaunt.

Jesse teared up and checked the prescription bottles. "Is she on anything else?"

"The doctor said to give her these in the morning and evening for anxiety. She seemed so drugged that I cut back to just the evenings hoping she could sleep at night. What are you thinking? Still too much?"

Jesse took her hand again. "Lydia look at me." He spoke firmly. She hardly noticed. He rose and called someone he knew. As he read the bottle giving the dosage Jack heard him say as he walked into the kitchen, "I know it shouldn't be too much, but she's barely responding. It's been two weeks. She seems drugged to me. Remember how she reacted to that stuff when her husband died? Yeah… okay. What do you recommend? No… I'm sure she'd rather be at home unless she's in danger. Okay… yeah. Alright. Thanks man. I appreciate it."

Jesse filled Jack in. "She tends to react very strongly to drugs. Normally it takes only half a dose to knock her out. The doctor I called said to start weaning her off. I'll write it down for you. I think she'll be fine in a day or so. But then comes the hard part. You're going to have to keep an eye on her for a while. This type medication dropkicks her into a deep depression. They actually do the opposite of what they're designed to do. She is one different chick." Jesse laughed a little.

Jack suddenly felt relieved. It wasn't him she was shutting out. It was life in general. He could deal with that.

"Thanks so much Jesse. I tried calling her doctor but didn't get anywhere. He kept saying to give her a few more days bed rest. This makes sense though. Thanks so much." He said it again.

Jesse looked at Lydia as he told Jack, "I'll be here if you think of anything I can do to help either one of you." He motioned Jack into the kitchen and spoke quietly. "I bought her a gun quite a few years back and she told me she kept it by her bed in case she ever needed it. If it's still there, I'd definitely secure it if I were you."

Jack couldn't retrieve it fast enough. Lydia never moved. He unloaded it and placed it on the top shelf in the closet. Returning to the kitchen he prepared the best steak Jesse had ever had. They sat as friends at the table and prayed together that Lydia would soon be on the path to recovery.

Chapter 49

She needed a shower. Her scalp was still caked with blood and her body hurt. But how could she do it without keeling over? Jack had helped her so much for so many days. She hated to ask him to do one more thing. Plus she tried to process how she could stay modest.

He guided her to the front porch one evening but she couldn't stand the motion of the swing. They sat in rockers beside each other in silence. Lydia worked hard for the words.

"Hey Jack?"

He seemed almost startled by her voice. Looking at her with sad eyes he took her hand. "Yes dear?" He smiled a sad smile she hadn't seen before, something akin to relief as he waited. "What can I do for you Sweetheart?" He nearly whispered.

She looked away from those eyes and felt his hand grip hers as though he longed for her to speak. She tried again. "I need… help."

He swallowed hard and offered. "Is it something I can do for you or do you need Jesse?" He could hardly keep the tears back. But he would gladly call Jesse if it would somehow pull her out of the terrible despair.

She surprised him with a soft laugh.

"No… you please." She leaned back in the rocker resting her head against the slats as though she'd exerted too much energy already. "Can you please make me a shower?"

It was the most words he'd heard her use in a very long time.

"That is music to my ears darling!" Jack swiped at a tear.

"Do I stink?" Turning her head slowly toward him she actually smiled.

Jack rose from his seat and knelt in front of her with his head on her lap. The tears wouldn't stop. Lydia stroked his head and noticed his hair had grown out.

"I like your hair. When did it get to be… so much?" She asked with wonder. It was as if she were waking from a very long dream.

Jack looked up into her eyes which seemed to recognize him. She smiled and tried to lean her head forward but the dizziness started again.

"Whew. I get so fainty-fied."

Jack laughed. "Rest a bit then we'll see about that shower. I'll put a chair in there so you don't have to worry about passing out. We can make it happen!" He was so thankful for something he could do to help.

"Should we wait til tomorrow since it's so late?" She asked not moving her head.

Jack laughed again, "Sweetie it's only ten in the morning. I think you might have your days and nights mixed up." He noticed her face cloud over. He could tell she was trying to speak so he waited.

"That nasty man called me Sweetie… and Gingersnap…" She gasped then put her hand over her mouth. "Those cookies the boys…"

She looked at Jack with fear. "Oh dear Lord…" She shivered and Jack pulled her slowly up from the rocker into his arms.

"I'm here Lydia. You're safe. I've got you darling." Jack held her tightly trying to keep her head still against his shoulder. "Let's go inside where we can sit together. Careful… turn slowly." He guided her to the sofa in the den but felt her legs give way just before they sank into it. Cradling her in his arms he felt completely helpless as to what he should do next.

Silently he prayed for strength. At least she'd recognized him and even smiled. The tiny bit of humor she offered gave him hope that eventually she'd snap out of it. But with the memory of who they were together would also return the reality of the attack. This was the first indication of that. He wondered if they should talk about it or if it would be better handled by a professional.

Like Jesse.

His phone dinged. Shifting her carefully he pulled his cell from his pocket. There was Jesse right on cue as usual.

"How's our patient?" he asked.

"She's here with me." Jack answered in order to indicate to Jesse that he couldn't speak freely. Lydia looked up and smiled.

"Hey Jesse." She tried but sounded very weak. It was still a breakthrough of sorts.

"What's up girl? How's your noggin?" Jesse spoke to her as Jack held the phone.

"It's spinnin' and spinnin' but Jack's gonna take me a shower." She answered with a smile.

"Sounds good. Maybe he will put a chair in there so you can relax." Jesse was thankful that she seemed to be coming around.

"He knew of it." Lydia was proud of Jack's care and wanted Jesse to know that, but she still couldn't seem to say the words she meant.

Jesse understood. "Give Jack a big hug. He's working really hard to get you better."

She squeezed around Jack's neck. "His hair grew big. I like it."

Jack nearly cried he was so happy. "Thanks Jesse. I'll call you later." That was also his code phrase to let their friend know there was more to tell.

Moving a pillow he gently situated her on the sofa trying to make her comfortable. "I'm going to get things ready for your shower. Will you be okay here for a minute?"

She looked fearful and took his hand. Trying to form the thought she asked, "Are the doors… tight?"

Jack sat back down beside her and looked into her eyes. "They are tight. Locked and safe! But why don't you go with me? That way you'll see for yourself." Somehow he understood that she didn't want him out of her sight and it felt very good.

Slowly they walked toward the bedroom. "Let me grab a chair and you can show me what you want to wear." He leaned her against the bed where she held to the cast iron footboard. Once he retrieved a kitchen chair she sat and pointed to a lower drawer. There he found an old bathing suit top and cut-offs.

Jack put them on the bed near her chair. "Can you dress in that while I wait right outside the door?"

"Yep." She smiled and reached for the pieces. "I got it." She began to pull her shirt over her head as Jack left and closed the door behind him. He stood praying as she did her best to dress. Knowing how private she would normally be, Jack waited a bit then called to her through the door, "Are you decent?"

She laughed and called back, "Are YOU decent?"

Jack sighed. "Lydia? Are you dressed?" He waited. Maybe this had been a mistake. In the mornings when he put her clothes in the bathroom she'd emerge dressed as if that were the norm. But she seemed pretty loopy and he wasn't sure how to proceed.

"Lydia? Can I come in?" He waited. When finally he opened the door a crack he found her in the old bathing suit top but still in the gym shorts she'd put on that morning. The cut-offs were on the floor.

She sat in the chair leaning face first over the bed. When Jack walked in she tried to lift her head. "I couldn't tip far enough to do the bottoms. Can I please wear this?"

"Yes Sweetheart. Wait right there and I'll put my trunks on so I can help you. You're going to feel much better after this." He sure hoped so anyway. Grabbing his bathing suit from a drawer he changed quickly in the bathroom. With towels in hand he tried to think of what else she might need.

Dry clothes.

He gathered those as well and gently helped her from the chair. They made their way slowly through the kitchen and sunroom out the back door to the shower. Situating her on the bench beside towels and clothes he steadied her. A plastic chair from the deck was placed near the middle of the little shower room for her to sit so he could wash her hair.

When the water temperature felt right he helped her into the chair. As the warm shower hit her body she began to feel a speck normal for the first time since the attack. Taking his time he slowly untangled her hair. Shampoo bubbles turned pink and washed the blood away from her scalp. The wound at the base of her skull was still painful but at least the scar would be hidden when her hair was down. When Jack was satisfied that her hair was thoroughly rinsed he lathered himself taking advantage of the opportunity to do so. She watched as he turned off the water and shook his head like a shaggy dog.

"You are… delicious." She smiled at him.

Jack laughed and used his best cowboy voice. "Why thank you ma'am. You're rather delicious yourself." Grabbing a towel he stood her up slowly and wrapped it around tucking it under an arm. With another towel around himself he offered. "I have dry clothes there on the bench for you if you think you can get…"

She sat down wearily in the wet chair.

Jack reached around to her back unfastening her top. Recalling their last fight he said softly, "Hold onto the towel and keep it around you. I'm just trying to help, okay?"

She gazed at him with eyes that seemed more aware than he'd seen in quite some time. She held to the towel. "I got it." She nodded slightly. "I can." She smiled.

He stepped from the shower and wondered if she could get her shorts off especially since they were wet. About that time they came sailing over the shower door and hit him in the head.

"Woohoo…" she called out weakly.

"Hold to the chair as you dress Sweetheart. I'm right here if you need me." Jack dried himself as he waited. He felt better than he had in days. If only he could get somewhere for a haircut. But at least she had approved even if it was in her drugged condition.

"You okay in there?" Jack spoke from just outside the shower door.

"Don't go."

"No problem. I'm hoping I get to rescue you while you're butt nekkid." As soon as he said it he was sorry. What if she didn't get his stupid humor?

She laughed and almost sounded normal. By the time she finished and dressed she was as weak as a kitten. Stepping from the shower she found him waiting. The warm deck felt good so Jack led her to another plastic chair and set about combing her wet hair. Her head began to hurt again, but his care was too wonderful to stop. A storm was brewing from the west. The wind kicked up a bit and the breeze felt good. He slid his chair close and kissed her gently. For a long tender moment he held her in his arms. For the first time in quite a while he thought they might make it.

~~~~~~~

While she sat on the deck enjoying the outdoors Jack wondered again how the heat didn't seem to bother her like it did him. He gathered their wet things and hung them on the line like a true Southerner. They'd be dry soon with the little breeze that was stirring. Stepping into the shower he changed into dry shorts and a shirt. Glancing into the small mirror which Blue had apparently used for shaving he wished again for a haircut. Maybe they'd get into town soon where he could find a barber. He'd ask Shawn about that later. With trunks in hand he headed back to the clothesline to toss them on the line.

Though her back was to him Jack received quite the shock. There stood Lydia on the deck dressed only in a pair of panties which she seemed also about to shuck.

"Whoa Lydia! Stop baby! Don't turn around." Jack called to her as he pulled the towel from the line and wrapped it around her. "You can't do that Sweetheart. Hold onto the towel."

He gathered her clothes and tried to lead her inside.

"What's wrong with you Blue? I always do this." She seemed annoyed and turned to look at him.

With sudden recognition she caught her breath. She hurried into the bathroom and closed the door.

Jack opened it a crack and dropped her dry clothes behind her on the floor. Walking slowly away he wondered if she'd thought he was Blue in the shower as she looked at him so lovingly. And he'd kissed her for the first time in weeks so thankful to have her back. As he thought about it he consoled himself that she'd stayed modest in the shower. Maybe she realized who he was then.

Lord… I am so tired. I cannot win this game. I want her so bad… You know how I feel. Please intervene for us. Clear her head and help me NOT emerge the bad guy.

He stood in the kitchen trying to think of something for lunch. She'd loved the chicken salad the night they'd made it together. It seemed an eternity ago that he'd finally found himself alone with her. Tossing a couple chicken parts into a pot to boil he knew it wouldn't be as good as when he stewed a whole chicken. But it would be fine for lunch. Searching the cabinets he remembered that she stored the walnuts in the refrigerator for some unknown reason. There were no grapes but there were raisins in the fridge as well. That would do. Why wasn't the chicken starting to…

Stupid stove.

He moved the pot to a different burner and began again. Realizing it had been a while since he'd pushed Lydia into the bathroom he panicked. Though he'd cleared all the medication that she might overdose on he wondered if somehow he'd missed something.

"LYDIA!" He knocked on the door loudly. He listened and heard nothing. Opening the door a crack he found her sitting on a closed toilet with her head on the sink sobbing her heart out. At least she was dressed.

"C'mere." He pulled her up and into his arms very thankful that she didn't push him away. Her shoulders shook as she cried until she was snubbing like a child.

"It's okay baby. I've got you." Jack felt his tears coming as well. He heard the pot boiling over as it splashed onto the hot burner warning that he might burn the house down. At that point he didn't care.

Jack hoped that somehow she could get past the embarrassment. She'd made such strides that morning. Oh how he hoped they wouldn't go backward. But he'd learned in the few months they'd known each other that Lydia was hands down the most private person he'd ever met.

"Lydia, look at me darling. It's okay. Don't feel bad. It's those stupid drugs that are keeping you foggy, but they'll all be gone soon and we'll get back to normal."

She looked up at him with a tearstained face. "Oh Jack… I'm so sorry I called you Blue. After all you've done for me. I'm so sorry."

He held her for a while trying not to let her see his tears. "Thank you baby," he whispered.

She pulled back and looked at him. "What's that smell? It's not me. I've had a shower!" She smiled and seemed more lucid than she had in days.

Jack steadied her then moved to the kitchen pulling the pot from the burner. "Just making lunch." Lowering the heat he returned the chicken to the burner so it could finish stewing. He really hated that stupid old stove.

She walked slowly to where he sopped up broth with a rag. Circling his waist from behind she rested her head on his back.

"I love you Jack."

He turned to meet her. Kissing her tenderly he decided this might be the best moment of his life. She still loved him, and she called him by name.

Chapter 50

As Jack worked on lunch she sat at the table watching. Taking a sip of the lemonade he'd poured for her she commented, "Wow! Tangy!"

He turned to look at her.

"Well you won't give me your recipe so I don't know how to make it like you do!" He was smiling and hoping beyond hope that their regular bantering back and forth would return.

She cocked her head sideways setting the glass down. "Since when did you ask for my recipe?" When she looked up at him with a playful smile he realized they were almost back to normal. Crazy, but normal. He'd gladly take it. He decided to test the waters a bit.

"You seem a lot better today. How do you feel?" Continuing to mix the salad he didn't look at her. She always took a while to process things while he knew that he tended to move on every part of his life much quicker. He'd found it hard to wait for her in more than one area of their relationship.

She remained silent so long that he wondered if she'd fallen asleep. Turning to look he saw her pushing back tears again. She sighed heavily.

"I… think I might be going crazy." She couldn't look at him. "Or maybe I already am." Her heart ached with the realization that she'd revealed her greatest fear to the very one she loved best.

Jack wiped his hands on the dishtowel and sat beside her. Holding her close he whispered, "Darling, crazy people have no idea they're crazy. So this is a very good sign!" He kissed her head and stroked her back. "Do you think it would help to have Jesse over? You could talk things out with someone who knows more about these kinds of things than I do. You've been through a lot Sweetheart."

He continued to hold her but was surprised she didn't immediately warm up to the idea of talking with Jesse. He felt her relax against him but she didn't say anything about his suggestion. Finally she looked at him sorrowfully. "If it weren't for you Jack… I would be done this time. So if God answers my prayer and takes me home… just know that I love you."

Her words shocked him and he responded sternly.

"NO Lydia! I will not agree to that." Jack's tone surprised her. "I won't know that you love me unless you stay strong enough to keep telling me yourself." He tipped her chin up and looked into her eyes. "You're all I've got Lydia. You can't give up now! After all we've been through? Things will surely get better!" He hugged her tight and prayed it was true.

"Promise me darling, please promise me." He held her close and whispered. "Please love me enough to keep trying. We'll conquer this together, one step at a time."

She couldn't speak and the tears wouldn't stop. Her head pounded and she just wanted to be done. "I love you Jack." She pulled away but saw the hurt in his eyes so she stopped. "I need to lie down and see if my head will ease off. Would you please try to find some Advil? There wasn't any in the bathroom. I was sure I had an extra bottle in there."

Jack helped her to the daybed where she turned on her side toward the window. He covered her with the sheet and left to retrieve his hidden stash and a small glass of milk. He knew she hadn't eaten anything that day and wondered how her stomach would react. Sitting on the edge of her bed he spoke softly. "Here you go baby. I hope this helps." She surprised him by saying, "Wake me in about an hour or so. I don't need to sleep the day away. Then I can enjoy some of that chicken salad I love so much." She smiled a weak smile.

He kissed her head gently. "Thanks darling. I'll call Jesse and we'll have a late dinner together."

She turned on her back and looked at him. He could tell she was trying to pull up the words so he waited.

"I don't want him over here just yet."

Her words surprised and worried him all at the same time. She must've seen the fear on his face for she added, "Not tonight dear. I have a headache." She smiled hoping that her attempt at humor made sense.

Jack smiled. That was enough to help her relax. Turning toward the window she was relieved to feel him rubbing her back. So she turned on her tummy. "That feels so good. Thank you honey." Tossing her pillow on the floor she closed her eyes and hoped her head would stop pounding and her heart would quit aching. A tiny part of her wanted desperately to live and enjoy the man God had brought into her life. If only the terrible cloud would lift.

~~~~~~~~

When Jack could tell she was asleep he walked to the front porch. Sitting on the swing at his end he wished she could bear the motion of it again. He treasured their moments there with her feet in his lap.

He picked up his phone and called his friend.

"Are you in the middle of something?" he asked Jesse. Jack could tell there was a lot of commotion going on as apparently he was on a job somewhere. Like Jack, Jesse also worked construction and had his own company.

"Always!" Jesse laughed. "Is she starting to come around yet? It should be about time."

"She is…" Jack suddenly remembered Jesse's warning that coming off the drugs would drop her into a deep depression. "She's in a bad frame of mind though and I'm scared half to death."

"Want me to come over after work? Do you think she's ready to talk?" Jesse asked.

"I don't want to hurt your feelings," Jack thought about how that sounded and tried to be funny. "I know how sensitive you can be."

Jesse laughed. "She must've made it clear she didn't want me there. Believe me it's not the first time I've heard that!"

Jack tried again. Even if Lydia didn't want him there, Jack knew he needed him. "Let's try tomorrow. Plan to come for dinner unless you hear otherwise."

"I'll be looking forward to it!" Jesse added as he went back to work.

Jack was looking forward to it even more and hoped that he wasn't making a mistake by postponing the meeting a day.

As he returned to the house through the front door he realized there was a rifle hanging above the mantle. How did he miss that when he'd safety proofed the house. Pulling it down he unloaded it then returned it to its place. Something warned him to check the vase on the mantle. Sure enough there were more bullets.

Thank You Lord. What else should I do that I'm not thinking of?

Walking through the kitchen he realized he'd sharpened all the knives and couldn't very well get rid of them without her noticing.

God please help. I don't have a clue how to take care of her. I can't do this without You. Somehow work a miracle on our behalf.

He found himself kneeling by the bed crying out to God in tearful silence. It felt really good to speak to the Lord like he used to. But his heart ached and his stomach growled reminding him that he needed food.

He rose from his knees, tossed the bullets in the back of his underwear drawer and looked up to find Lydia waiting. She walked into his arms and sobbed into his chest. Finally she was able to speak.

"I couldn't sleep for thinking about that yummy chicken salad." She smiled and his heart once again thanked the Lord for a quick answer to prayer.

~~~~~~~

Lunch was especially good that day. Though Jack had never added raisins to chicken salad it turned out to be a really tasty option. Now if he could just get that lemonade recipe.

Lydia was enjoying food for the first time in a very long time. "I've never had chicken salad like this. It's so good."

"Has your head eased off?" He realized she wasn't looking at him but instead had busied herself with freeing crackers from their wrapper. Finally she answered.

"I think this food will help. I'm so foggy." She still didn't look up. Jack had to press.

"Does it hurt down your neck into your back?"

She looked up with wonder. "How did you know that? Yes! It goes all the way down between my shoulder blades."

Jack offered tentatively. "Would you like me to give you a back rub later? Did that help at all a while ago?"

He knew things could get dicey, but he also longed to help her if there were any way possible to ease her pain.

"I would love it. Between that and this delicious lunch maybe I can live to tell about it." She seemed almost chipper. Then she stopped eating and looked up. "Did I call you delicious in the shower? Oh my goodness. I am such a cupcake." She laughed at herself. "Oh well. At least I didn't cuss."

She stopped again. "Did I cuss? That's my normal M.O."

Jack was laughing too at that point. He was so glad to hear her laugh that he decided not to tease her about cussing. She'd actually let a few choice words fly at the doctor while she was in the hospital. But it wasn't anything the guy didn't deserve. Of course she'd also asked the nurse for whiskey and warned her not to water it down. But that would be a conversation for another day.

"Sweetheart… I don't know how to ask you this… but are you sure on the massage? I mean… you know who I am and that I'm really trying to help but…" Jack hadn't stammered that much since his sophomore year in high school when a pretty senior girl had asked him to the prom. He was about to renege on his offer when Lydia moved slowly toward the bedroom. "Let me get ready. There's baby oil in the bathroom."

Jack sat stunned at the kitchen table. What was going on in her head? Before she wouldn't even dance with him to a particular song and had nearly slapped his face for getting fresh. Now she was headed to the bedroom and telling him where to find baby oil. He realized he hadn't seen her blush since bringing her home from the hospital.

I need you Lord. I'm not kidding. Do You see what's happening down here and how my head is about to explode? Please help.

He busied himself cleaning the kitchen waiting for her call. Thinking of Shawn and Kurtis he made sure the doors were locked and rested in the fact that the driveway alarm still worked.

"Ready Jack… whenever you are." A muffled invitation came from the bedroom.

He'd been ready since the first day he laid eyes on her. But was she lucid enough to get what she was doing? He opened the bedroom door tentatively finding her face down on the bed on top of the comforter. Though she was dressed only in shorts she was covered with a pillow under her midriff. Her hair was pulled up so her back and shoulders were exposed but that was all.

It was plenty.

As he sat on the side of the bed he warned, "This might be cold so don't let it make you jump."

She didn't look up but answered, "Thanks."

He started with her neck and worked the oil in thoroughly down her spine especially between her shoulder blades. "Try to relax Sweetheart. I can feel the tension gripping your muscles."

He continued to work on her back and he began to relax as well. She turned her head to look at him. "Could you work on that place in my lower back that I hurt on the job? Just use a lighter touch. It's still really tender." She pushed the waist of her shorts down a bit.

Lord… help me finish here without hurting her feelings. She's on the edge anyway. I sure don't want to make things worse. I'm serious Lord.

Jack softened the pressure but she winced in pain.

"Maybe we should just leave well enough alone there."

"Sorry baby. I'm so sorry you're hurting." Jack worked more on the place between her shoulders, then again on her neck.

"Your hair is filling in and has almost covered the scar. Is it still sore?"

"Yep." She answered opening her eyes. "That was wonderful Jack. Thank you so much." She smiled at him again.

"Do you need anything? I mean… will you be okay getting up by yourself and all?" Jack still fumbled.

"I'm good. If you don't mind put that baby oil back in the bathroom. Is the chair still there?" she asked.

"No but I can get it if you need it." Jack wondered what she was up to.

"I thought I'd try shaving my legs. I haven't been this scruffy in a long time." She laughed.

"Me neither." Jack finally laughed too.

"If my head's not too swimmy tomorrow I'll cut your hair for you."

He looked at his beautiful girl lying on the bed making conversation as if they did this sort of thing every day. "Okay…" he answered absentmindedly. "I'll go put a chair in the bathroom."

"Thanks honey." Lydia waited til he left and got dressed. The pain was finally less thanks to his massage.

Sliding the chair up next to the deep tub, she applied oil to her legs which she'd placed over the side. Reaching for her razor she found it missing.

I always leave my razor right there, she thought. *Oh well. It's time for a new one anyway.*

Leaning backward she checked the cabinet under the sink but there were none there either.

"Jack honey… have you seen my razor?"

Crap, he thought, then laughed at how quickly he had picked up the southern expression of displeasure.

Retrieving a new one from his hiding place he brought it in to her still not sure what he'd find when he opened the door.

"Here's one of mine."

She looked at him curiously. "You use pink razors?"

He tried to cover the fact that he'd stashed away everything he could think of that she might harm herself with except the kitchen knives. "No… that's yours… I was going to use it… I knew you wouldn't mind." He walked out shutting the door behind him. He heard the water in the tub start and stood close hoping she wouldn't pass out when she tipped her head.

Good grief. Can we just get back to normal? Whatever that means in her crazy world!

Chapter 51

Shawn and Kurtis came by to check on Lydia and were so glad that she could halfway carry on a conversation that they stayed longer than Jack liked. He was exhausted. They gave her the lowdown on all the clients, her little ladies who were missing the cookies she usually baked, plus the new classes they'd be starting soon. Jack noticed that she smiled off and on but didn't interact with them as much as normal. She gave no instructions, no warnings about floosy women, and had no interest when they mentioned church. When they told her about a group of kind people who were praying diligently for her around the clock she hardly acknowledged it.

As they left Kurtis tried to cheer her up by saying, "Alright Liddy, you have to get back to baking cookies soon. Grandmaw made it clear that she's losing her niceness without your treats. And Norma Rae said she's been having men all over town hittin' on her since she's getting her girlish figure back. I don't think we want either one of those things happening! It all depends on you!"

Lydia never even smiled. Instead she replied with a hint of sarcasm, "Tell them they can always buy *Little Debbie's.*"

Kurtis shot a nervous look toward Jack. Shawn was already headed toward his truck but turned and walked back up the porch steps and gave her a long hug. Leaning down and looking into her eyes he said quietly, "I don't want no stinkin' Little Debbie." He glanced at Jack as worried as he'd ever been. He too had picked up on the difference in her demeanor.

Once the boys left she asked, "May I have some Advil please? I don't know where we keep it anymore." Jack detected a hint of anger.

"Sure honey. I put it away til you came off all the hospital drugs so you wouldn't accidently take too much." He retrieved it and met her at her daybed. "Let's put a couple more here by the bed so when you wake up around two or three in the morning you'll have another dose. Maybe we can keep your pain from getting any worse."

She looked at the weary man and knew he was trying desperately to help. She gazed at him kindly. "You're amazing Jack. Thank you for all you've done. I love you so much."

Jack sat on the daybed beside her holding her close. The words he'd waited so long to hear from her now frightened him. It seemed to be her way of saying goodbye. He would put the knives somewhere secure before he went to bed.

He stroked her back trying again not to tear up. "Lydia… Sweetheart… please stay strong. If for no other reason… I can't live without you."

She laughed an empty laugh.

"Sure you can! AND you wouldn't find yourself in this continual crapstorm of mine."

Jack had had enough. He spoke sharper than he meant to.

"Stop it Lydia. In fact, I'm calling Jesse right now. We're going to get you past this tonight."

She sighed deeply. "No Jack please… I can't. Please just let me go to sleep. I'm so tired."

Jack understood. He was tired too. But the signals she was giving were scaring him. He tried again. "If you can't talk to Jesse tonight then at least talk to me. I'm not letting you rest until you do."

She couldn't speak. But she could tell that Jack wasn't going to let her go until she allowed him in. Finally with much effort she whispered.

"I'm so afraid Jack. That man watched me sleep right here… and undress…" She tried to catch her breath. "I can't stay here. I'm trying to be brave but… I just don't care anymore." She gagged. "Oh Lord… get me to the bathroom."

Jack snatched her up and ran with her making it just in time to watch her hurl into the tub. He had to walk out but at least this time he wouldn't have to wash out a mop bucket. When finally she'd lost everything she'd dared to consume, she shut the door and rinsed the tub. Sitting on the closed toilet she waited, finally brushing her teeth. Jack sat in the kitchen processing the things she'd said.

Of course she was afraid. He just hadn't realized how much she'd put together. They'd never spoken of what happened before she killed the guy. Did she even know he was dead? It was then that it occurred to him that Lydia was dealing with more internally than physically. He knocked softly on the bathroom door.

"Honey, when you can… I have an idea that might help us both." Jack waited.

She opened the door and walked wearily out.

"C'mere. Let's just hold each other and rest for a bit." As he led her to the sofa he realized again that every place in the house had an uncovered window nearby. It had to be unsettling for her.

They sat on the sofa together and she leaned heavily on him. He wished he'd brought a blanket but at least there were pillows there. "Here, let's just lie down together and sleep. I've got you."

She didn't put up a fight at all. In fact she rose and reached across to a quilt rack pulling a summer quilt to them. Flipping it over their legs she relaxed beside him as they lay on their sides like two spoons in a drawer. The terrible headache stretched downward again into her shoulders. And the place in her lower back felt as though she'd been stabbed with a butcher knife.

How appropriate, she thought. A deep shiver went through her soul.

But with his arm about her waist and his body next to hers she relaxed feeling safe and loved. Before she knew it, the rhythm of Jack's breathing matched her own as together they rested better than they had in nearly a month.

Chapter 52

When she woke she was surprised that Jack was already awake. But he was still on his side pushed against the back of the couch. Apparently the man hadn't moved all night. When he realized she was awake he seemed to have permission to move and stretched sleepily. She turned on her back to look at him.

"Good morning honey. Do I need to move so you can get up?" she asked.

Without reply he pulled her close kissing her forehead. Resting a while longer he finally asked, "How'd you sleep?"

She stroked his scruffy beard. "My head is not even hurting. My back's definitely worse for wear but hey, it's a start!" She smiled looking at him. "How about you? Are you dying on this lumpy couch?"

He sighed a long sigh then answered. "I'm a little bit dying on this lumpy couch." He smiled and looked at her with sleepy eyes. "I think we need something. I dreamed about it last night."

"What's that dear man of mine?" she asked wondering. She felt so safe in his arms and hoped he'd just be still with her there for a while.

"We need curtains, like on every window." Jack seemed happy at the thought of making that happen.

"You dreamed about curtains? Wow. You are domestic." She laughed and realized she felt kind of happy.

"C'mon. Let's get up and see how you're doing today. If you feel like it we'll take a trip to Ikea." Jack began moving toward a sitting position. Lydia stretched and stayed where she was. He stopped.

"C'mon woman. It's all I can do not to radish your body. Move it or I won't take you shopping with me." She laughed and pulled him down again whispering, "I like radishes." He looked into her eyes. "Lydia… behave yourself. I'm not kidding. I am not coming out of this as the bad guy. I love you too much."

He rolled over the top of her and made his way up. "Jesse's coming for supper tonight so let's get a move on."

She pulled the covers up and settled back into the couch. "I don't want Jesse over here."

Jack laughed. "Sorry Sweetheart. He's coming. I've already asked him. Why don't you want him here?"

She didn't answer so Jack walked into the kitchen. Remembering the knives he found a box on a shelf above the dryer and emptied the knife drawer into it as quietly as he could. But where could he put it? Peeking through the doorway into the den he noticed she'd either gone back to sleep or was pretending. Walking to the sunroom he opened the utility room door and placed the knives in the deep freeze. Just as he began stacking frozen packs of meat and vegetables on top she startled him.

"Whatcha doin'?" She stood right behind him.

"Oh… trying to think of something good for supper." Jack lied.

"Jesse likes hotdogs. I've got weenies in the little freezer. Want me to put them out to thaw?" Lydia offered.

"That sounds great." Jack closed the chest freezer though the knives weren't completely hidden. He'd come back later for that.

"I might have some barbecue slaw left too…" She gazed into the refrigerator. "Oops." She held the handle of the door and slipped to the floor. "I think I moved too fast." She laughed as she slid down on her rear in slow motion. Jack helped her stand and walked her slowly to the bathroom.

So much for shopping at Ikea for curtains.

He called to her through the bathroom door. "Lydia… did you do that on purpose because I threatened to take you shopping?"

"Muwahahahah!" She laughed her craziest laugh. Jack made his way back to the deep freeze to finish covering the knives. Spotting a couple packs of steaks he pulled those out and put the wieners back. He had a feeling Jesse was about to earn more than a hot dog. Hopefully he wouldn't mind reruns.

~~~~~~~

They took a drive around the farm that day enjoying the break in the weather. For late August in North Carolina, the heat was not too bad. As Jack drove slowly down her dirt road she showed him a large plot of wildflowers. "Can we get out here for a minute?"

Jack stopped the truck and helped her walk toward the garden.

"Blue planted that for me in memory of my mama. I'd always teased him about lining flowers up in a row like soldiers. So he ordered a ton of seeds, plowed up that hill into the shape of a heart and scattered the seeds all willy-nilly just to show me he could. Every year the flowers bloom there in her honor. There's a handmade sign in the middle somewhere which says, 'Claudia's Garden.' He really loved my mama."

Jack recognized it as the same place he'd found her kneeling on a towel that day he'd hurt her feelings with his stupid jealousy over Jesse. He gazed at Lydia again so thankful she'd survived the horrible ordeal.

"So your mother's name was Claudia? That's pretty."

"I think so too. She would've liked you. Lord have mercy she was feisty!" Lydia smiled at her memory.

"When did you lose her?"

"She was sick a long time, but she died when I was seventeen."

She changed the subject. "Up on that ridge is where me and Blue had thought we'd build the house. Isn't this a pretty view?"

"Beautiful." He smiled at her thanking God that she was getting back to normal. "Let's go back before you get too tired. How're you feeling?"

"Better." Her one word reply said it all.

Chapter 53

Jesse came as planned for supper. Though the steaks were fantastic, again, Lydia wouldn't look at him and had even shrunk away when he tried to hug her with his usual greeting. Jack couldn't figure it out and glanced at his friend who was obviously hurt. Lydia stared at her plate pushing the food around with her fork. Jack tried to carry the dinner conversation by himself.

"So Jesse, are you a football fan?" he asked.

Jesse answered, "I am. In fact I'm partial to the Panthers even though I didn't grow up in North Carolina."

Jack knew the boys had often remarked how much Lydia enjoyed watching football. Now if he could just think of a way to involve her in the conversation. The room was silent. Jack tried again.

"Do you think they have a chance this season?"

Jesse smiled and wiped his mouth with the cloth napkin. "I think their chances are very good now that they've finally got a decent wide receiver! Plus Cam is maturing nicely and there's nobody better than Luke Kuechly." He glanced at Lydia hoping she'd pick up on their long standing joke about her crush on Kuechly. But she wouldn't look at him.

A light went on somewhere in Jack's brain. He wondered how he'd missed it.

"Wait a minute. Are you Jesse Mills, wide receiver for the Carolina Panthers?" Jack asked.

He smiled. "Yep, one and the same. Except make that former wide receiver. Currently I am Jesse Mills the Home Improvement Specialist."

Suddenly the guy's size made sense. "So how did you end up living here?" Jack thought he was from Texas if he remembered correctly.

"My agent knew I planned to be a Panther my entire career or retire trying. So when he saw a hundred acre farm come up for auction, he knew I'd be interested. I planned to buy the whole thing but a cute young couple talked the owners into splitting the main farm into two plots so they could afford the part with the house on it. I kept watching them at the auction. They were so full of hope and excitement. Their bid won them this thirty seven acres and mine the other sixty three."

Lydia finally looked up at him. "How many years ago was that?" She felt ancient and for a moment couldn't remember. "Has it been twelve years?"

"Yep, twelve years." Jesse looked at her fondly then back toward Jack. "Although Blue and I met on several momentous occasions, Lydia and I didn't get to know each other for a while."

Lydia finally spoke up. "You can say it. Jack knows part. I had been through some things before we were married so Blue was very protective. He and Jesse had more than one stupid fight. I used to imagine Jesse as this jerk who wouldn't leave my husband alone, when actually they were just too much alike. A couple of hard headed country boys who couldn't play nice." She smiled a tiny smile and Jack sighed deeply with understanding.

Jesse laughed out loud. "I'm not going to say that it was all his fault… but it was." He winked at Jack.

Lydia looked at him with mock anger. "Do I need to slap your jaws?" She laughed quietly. "That's what I asked Jesse on the phone one day when I was exasperated at both of them. I should've just delivered the cookies I'd baked whether Blue liked it or not. It probably would've cured a world of hurt."

"Yep. Cookies make everything better." Jesse laughed again glad that Lydia was acting like her old self at least for a minute. He knew the worst was about to come.

"Alright little lady. How do you want to do this? Should we move to the porch and rock while we talk or do you need to lie on the couch and make me feel like a real therapist for a change? I've got to do something in the counseling department or your boyfriend is going to kill me with kindness." He pushed his plate back and patted his stomach. "The man knows how to cook a steak!" He smiled at Jack knowing he was praying for the next step for Lydia to be a successful one.

Lydia surprised them both when she said with determination, "Well I'm not doing this without Jack. It was his big stinkin' idea so let's move to the den where we can at least be more comfortable. We can do dishes later." She rose tentatively and held to the table til the room quit spinning. Jack took her arm and led her to the sofa.

"I'm sorry I need to lie down. My head is not right. But you knew that already didn't you Jack?" She didn't look at him when she said the words.

"I'm not touching that." Jack tried to make light of the fact that she was miffed at him for calling Jesse.

Sorry... he thought. *I love you too much to leave you where you are.*

Jack situated her on the couch with a pillow under her head. He took a seat at the other end and put her feet in his lap. Jesse moved the coffee table out of the way and pushed the recliner toward the middle facing Lydia.

Perfect he thought. Couldn't have planned this better myself. Now Jack can get the gist of her fears.

"Okay Jack, since Lydia insists on your being here, I need you to help by not saying a word. And Lydia, you need to forget about Jack for the moment. As usual be as honest as you possibly can. Deal?"

She didn't answer but closed her eyes instead letting a tear escape down her face.

Jesse softened his tone. "Lydia?" He waited. Her eyes were closed and the tears were already spilling freely. He looked at Jack and motioned him to wait.

"Take a couple deep breaths and relax as best you can." He waited glad that she complied. "Okay a couple more but not too quick. I don't want you to get fainty-fied as you and Norma say."

She laughed and took a few more breaths wiping her face as she relaxed.

"The first thing we're going to get out of the way will help you most of all. If you can tell what happened the day you were attacked I will record it and you won't have to give another statement to the police. It's a new policy they've implemented. Just be as accurate as you can remember. We can add more later if necessary, but this case is not pending an investigation. So relax as long as you need to then we'll get the worst part out of the way. Just begin when you're ready." He hit record on his phone and placed it near her head on the end table.

Jack recalled a similar incident when he had told Jesse off and tossed their phones on the same end table the night they'd returned from the beach. Suddenly he realized for the first time that Lydia's attacker was in the woods that same night. Apparently Jack being there had postponed his plan. He prayed a prayer of thanks as they waited on Lydia to begin. He just hoped she would talk. He knew from past fights that her former husband was not the only hard headed person in the family.

She began slowly.

"I came tearing down the road mad that we'd left the gate open again… which we may not have now that I think about it. I was angry at Jack for the night before… we'd had a fight… AND for trying to get me on camera at the Parker project. So I left the job site early. I was really sad that he'd be leaving soon and we hadn't talked about what we were doing. The back door into the sunroom was unlocked AGAIN. I figured we'd forgotten it that morning because of our stupid fight. I went inside and locked it behind me."

She sighed deeply and slowly continued.

"When I walked into the kitchen I smelled a terrible odor and thought we needed to empty the trash. I was already afraid because the door was unlocked so I headed toward the bedroom to check the closet. But I checked under the bed first. That's when I heard the floor boards creak. I KNEW there was someone in the closet but my legs would hardly move. I stumbled backward trying to get to the gun you bought me. But that man…"

254

She sat up and gagged. Jack jumped up and retrieved the mop bucket putting it near her head. When he placed a bag of frozen peas on the back of her neck it made her smile. She looked at him and uttered the Southern blessing he'd so aptly earned. He sat down beside her and stroked her back, then slid to the end trying to do as Jesse had asked.

Wearily she continued. "I don't even know how or when I grabbed the knife. I just reached backward as I stumbled and took it from the bucket on the counter. It shouldn't have been there. I have a knife drawer but that didn't occur to me. It happened so fast. I pointed the knife at him and told him to get out. But he touched my face…"

She retched again but nothing came up. Jack went for a wet cloth.

"Sorry. This is so gross. I'm sorry." She apologized.

Jesse put a hand on her shoulder. "You're doing really good girl. Almost there. Go ahead and finish."

She sighed heavily. "He grabbed my arms and kinda snatched me like… toward him. That knife went right into his overalls… right by the bib pocket."

She shook her head slowly as she spoke. "He smelled so bad… and blood went everywhere. When he fell forward he knocked me so hard backward that I felt like a ragdoll. Next thing I remember I was in the hospital and my head has been pounding ever since."

She sighed deeply. "Sorry. I need a potty break. Just give me a minute and I'll be back." She rose tentatively. Jack started to help her but she said, "I got it," and walked away.

Jesse stopped recording and looked at Jack as he whispered. "Actually I'm somewhat relieved. It could've been so much worse. She'll get through this Jack. You're doing good. Let's see what we can get finished tonight. I'll be out of here as soon as possible. Before she comes back, what changes have you seen in her?"

Jack hated to be so honest about their personal business but felt it surely had something to do with her current state of mind.

"She doesn't seem to care about much of anything and has thrown out little hints that we'd all be fine without her. That's the main reason I called you. But also, her personality has changed. Things that used to be so important don't matter anymore. You know how private she usually is. I think she's given up."

Lydia walked back to the couch and sat close to Jack shivering. He grabbed the quilt and covered her as she leaned on him. Looking at Jesse she spoke with determination. "Alright. Let's finish up. I'm really tired and I know Jack is." She pushed Jesse. He looked at her and smiled.

She spoke again with resolve. "Chop chop man. What else do you need to know?" She almost dared him to care. She was so sick of it all.

Jesse went straight to the heart of the matter. "Has anyone told you that the man is dead?" He looked at her with those steel gray eyes that always pierced her soul. She waited and processed the new information.

"No… I did not know that." She spoke quietly. Looking up with relief on her face she sighed heavily. "I had this image of him lurking in the woods waiting on Jack to leave. Oh my goodness." She looked down for a while then back at Jesse. "Are you sure? Because he was huge and that knife was not that big." She shivered at the memory. "I figured they stitched him up and turned him loose."

"I'm sure Lydia. He will never bother you or anyone else again. He's stalked women for years but the police have never been able to catch him. Now I'm going to tell you something else that you need to hear that's going to be hard. But you need to know it for two reasons. First of all, so that you don't hear it randomly from someone in passing and be caught off guard. And second, so that you understand God's protection on your life."

He sighed heavily then continued with great effort. "The man's name was Willie James. He was a sexual predator and has assaulted many women. But you were spared that by God's great grace. Lydia honey, so many people love you and pray for you that you'll never know them all on this side of heaven. I am one of those and certainly Jack is as well. Do you have any idea how loved you are?"

She shook her head. "No Jesse. I do not know that. Can we please be done? My head hurts so bad." Jack couldn't believe she felt that way.

Jesse wasn't budging.

"Lydia, I know we've covered a lot of ground previously regarding your upbringing and lack of self-worth. But you have to admit that Blue loved you. The man worshiped the ground you walked on. Don't you think it's possible that others could love you just as much if they were given the chance?"

She waited again trying to outlast him. The horrible dream she kept having was so real she'd begun to believe it.

"Blue does not love me. He's mad at me because of Jack so he took his ring. I used to kiss it every day and think of him, but it's gone. So it wasn't just a dream like I thought at first. I know how crazy that sounds but..."

She held her hand up to show him. A deep white indention where the ring used to be confirmed what she thought to be true.

Jack rose and left. His heart ached as he thought of her needless pain. Returning he handed it to her nestled inside her husband's wedding band. He could stand it no longer. He had to speak.

"Baby, they removed it at the hospital. I put it in the little vase on your dresser with Blue's wedding band. It was just a bad dream. Do you remember when we talked about standing before the Lord there will be things we wished we'd have done differently? Well one thing's for sure. Blue is thanking God continually for bringing you into his life and for the time you had together."

She looked at the ring with such surprise. Turning it in her hand she read the inscription inside. It was indeed her ring. Placing it back on her finger she kissed it and whispered with wonder. "I can't believe it. Thank you Jack. Thank you so much."

"OKAY! On that happy note, I have a homework assignment and a gift. Then I'm outta here." Jesse smiled at them both then spoke.

"Homework assignment: Remember what you do when you get in a funk and those ol' demons mess with your head?"

Lydia smiled weakly and replied like a school child. "I find someone to take care of besides myself."

Jesse added, "Yes! But this time we're going to throw some music in the mix. I brought you a radio. It will fit under the cabinet in the kitchen. It's set to the Christian station and I want you to play it as much as possible."

She immediately protested. "Nooo… Jesse you know how I hate that mess. All that stupid four part harmony and milking the crowd and kicking off their shoes and shouting. I'm not having it!"

He laughed at her tenacity. "It's not like that you crazy chick. I promise that you are going to love this music. It will lift your spirit and restore your joy. Speaking of which, where's your Bible? I haven't heard you speak of being in the Word at all since the attack. If you're blaming God, you've definitely got the wrong guy. He is your Protector, Defender, Deliverer and He can be trusted! He's the One who gave you the strength to defend against the enemy. He's the One who brought Jack into your life and into your home at just the right time. Willie James stalked you for a month or more but his plans kept getting delayed because of God Almighty! It's time to praise His holy Name for keeping you alive. He's got a plan and a purpose girl and don't you EVER forget it!"

"AMEN!" Jack shouted making Lydia jump.

She sat thinking on the things Jesse said.

"Can I ask one more thing?" She looked at Jesse as though she had used up all three wishes.

He laughed again. "Well… I suppose just one more… But only because that steak was fantastic!" He smiled at Jack.

Lydia looked down then finally at Jesse. "What if I don't feel bad for killing him? I guess I really am a horrible person with a terrible cold heart."

Jesse motioned to Jack. "Hug the girl and tell her it was God Who gave her strength. It was between her and Mr. Nastybreath and God chose her."

Jack did as he was told and gathered her into his arms holding back the tears.

Jesse spoke to her again with great kindness. "Now the question is girl, what do you plan to do with this fresh start God has given you?"

He smiled and circled Lydia and Jack into his big arms squeezing them with more joy than any catch he'd ever made as a wide receiver. Though his heart was heavy with his own personal struggles, God had been able to use him for His glory.

Chapter 54

They waved goodbye to Jesse from the porch. Lydia was ready to collapse she was so tired. Going to the bedroom she gathered clothes to sleep in as Jack walked in from the bathroom.

"Sorry Sweetheart. I'll come back when you're finished." Jack turned to leave.

"Hey Jack?" she called behind him.

He turned to look at her, glad for how far they'd come. "Yes dear?" He smiled tenderly and waited by the door.

"I'm putting the wedding bands back in the dish in case anything comes up and I forget." She pulled hers off, kissed it and nestled it inside of Blue's. "Thank you for being so good to me... and just for..."

She stammered and Jack knew she was back. She even blushed which gave away her frame of mind. Pulling her close he held her and stroked her soft clean hair. She smelled so good but still seemed rather frail. "Are you going to be okay sleeping in the sunroom or would you like to take the sofa and I'll be near you in the recliner?" He didn't want to offer the choice she'd taken the night before.

She sighed deeply. "We should've shopped for curtains today." She tried to smile at him. "I don't know. Let me try the daybed. Good grief. I am such a wimp."

Jack shook his head and spoke tenderly. "No you're not. This is a big step baby. You're doing great. Maybe tomorrow we can at least get blinds for the sunroom windows. You can pull them to the top during the day and close them at night until you get used to resting well again. Or whatever you want. It's your house." He smiled but somehow the words reminded her again of the conversation they'd never had. Again she wondered if he'd be leaving soon.

She tried to be brave. "That's a good idea. But for tonight I think I'll try the recliner from Hell. That thing is a death trap but at least it's more comfortable than the lumpy couch. Good grief!" She laughed weakly knowing she'd worry about someone coming up on the porch looking in the windows. But what else could she do? Her heavy sigh gave her away.

"Would you rather sleep in here? This bed is so comfortable and I know your back is still hurting." Jack offered. Until they hung curtains there really were no good options for her.

She answered quickly, "No Jack. I'm sorry for coming on to you so strong on the couch this morning. What's wrong with me?! You're such a good guy. But I don't trust myself in here with you." She blushed and pulled away.

Jack realized she'd misunderstood. Under no circumstances could he trust himself in there with her either. "You're right. But you could have the bed and I'll go somewhere else."

"Oh. No that's okay. Let's hang a sheet over the window in the den. That'll help. Then I won't be thinking about someone standing on the porch looking in."

"Good plan. Then tomorrow we'll figure out something with blinds or curtains. Believe me I'll be glad for something to do. I've never had so much time off in my life!" He watched absentmindedly as she opened the cedar chest.

She found the sheet they'd used at the beach. As she pulled it out all manner of items tumbled forth clattering onto the hardwood floors: Pink razors, bottles of Advil, prescription drugs, rifle bullets and a roll of trash bags. She looked up at Jack and asked, "Trash bags?" She laughed then gathered him into her arms. "Bless your heart. I've put you through so much. Please forgive me honey." They both teared up then laughed.

She scooped the things from the floor, stood up slowly then began putting them where she was used to storing them. "Now at least I won't be thinking I'm going crazy because I can't find anything. Here. You're in charge of the bullets." She laughed and pointed a finger at him. "Now if I can just find a knife sharp enough to cut the butter we'll be back on track!"

~~~~~~~

261

As Jesse drove home he prayed for Jack and Lydia. Again he asked God for wisdom and strength to be the friend that they needed. He considered what he knew of Jack's past and pleaded for Lydia's protection.

Lord, You know how I feel about her. Jack seems to have made a commitment to You and to her. But only You know his heart. Protect her dear God. She is very vulnerable right now and weaker than she's been in years. Guard her heart and strengthen Jack to do well. And Father...

He struggled as he prayed the words of submission again.

I have no idea where this will eventually leave me. But You do. I love You Lord and I trust You. Take good care of her for me, not only now, but in days ahead. You alone know how much I love her. May Your will, not mine be done.

Epilogue

In the months that followed the hearts of the men in Lydia's life were revealed by their actions. Each of them made decisions that affected her deeply. She struggled to recover physically and emotionally but found the greatest struggle to be within her soul. Her dog-eared Bible with the coffee stained pages had disappeared. So she used an orange New Testament she had tucked away in Blue's drawer. The little Gideon Bible received in fifth grade provided great comfort. Within it was a note she'd saved there a year earlier.

Jesse's handwriting stretched long and deliberate across the inside of the card much like everything else he did. She smiled at the thought of her unhurried friend as she read his words again.

"Time heals and time reveals Chickadee. Be still and know that the Lord is God. Waiting is never easy, but it's often the way He unfolds His plan. Trust Him and He will direct your path. Never doubt that He has a purpose for your life Darlin'. He loves you very much and so do I."

The porch swing swayed slightly as she considered Jesse's words. Windchimes played a gentle song and the early morning breeze made her glad she'd brought a blanket. She held the card to her chest and dared to hope that God had a plan for her future. Softly she whispered words of surrender realizing she'd never prayed them before.

"Lord, I love You. I trust You'll do what is best."

Though her life was upside down and her head and back still ached, unexplainable peace washed over her soul.

Brilliant color splashed across the eastern sky as the morning sun warmed the grassy hills of Blue Meadow Farm. A gorgeous sunrise seemed to promise that the most creative Artist of all had a beautiful design sketched out for her future.

Instead of fear, she smiled with anticipation for what God had planned.

~~~ o ~~~

Made in the USA
Monee, IL
08 February 2020